# Tusks, Tails & Teacakes

## A SLICE-OF-LIFE COZY ROMANTIC FANTASY

T.L. STONE

*For everyone who's looking for their place in the world. There are more people like you than you know.*

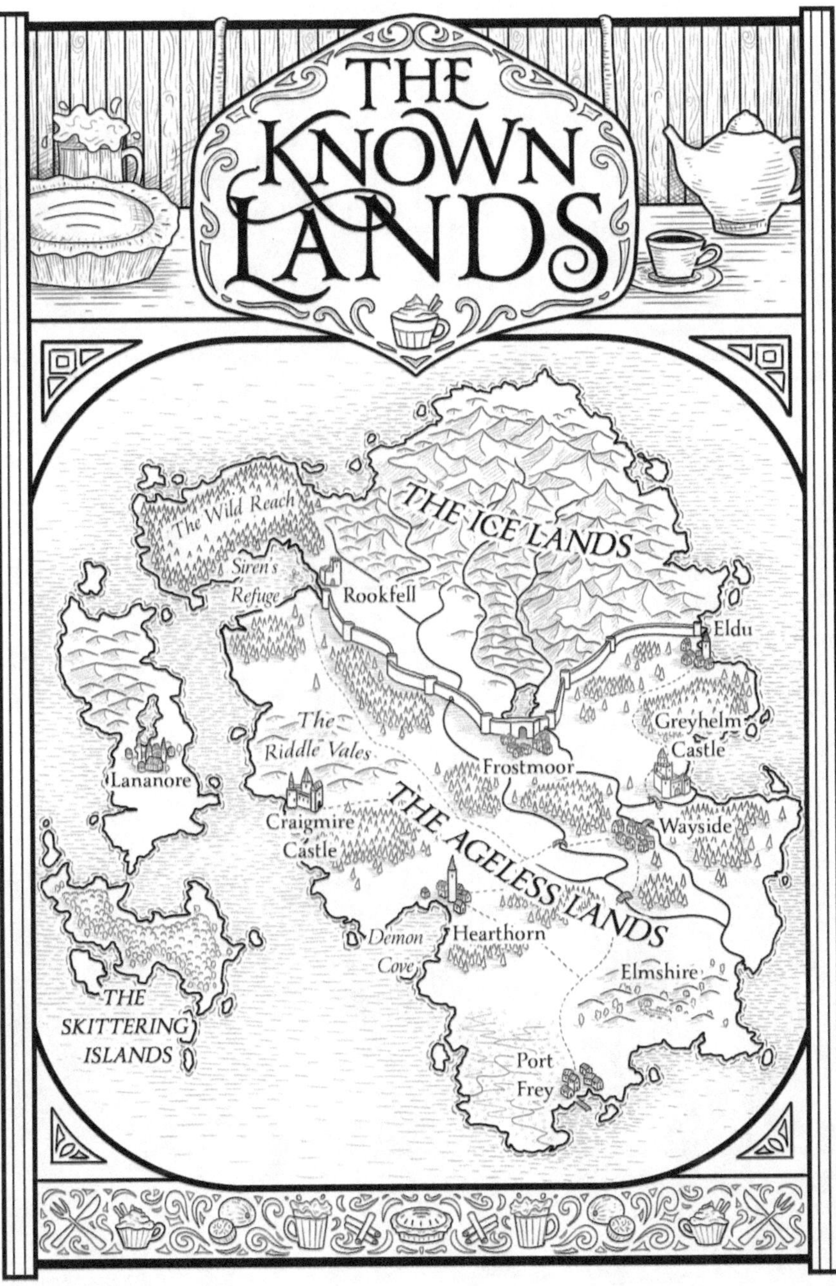

THE KNOWN LANDS
The Wild Reach
THE ICE LANDS
Siren's Refuge
Rookfell
Eldu
The Riddle Vales
Greyhelm Castle
Frostmoor
Lananore
Craigmire Castle
THE AGELESS LANDS
Wayside
Demon Cove
Hearthorn
Elmshire
THE SKITTERING ISLANDS
Port Frey

LIRA HAD NEVER EXPECTED to be running from a horde of wraiths. Running from guardsmen? Certainly. That was part of the job. But wraiths?

The spike sang as it whizzed past Lira's head. She dove, tucking into a roll before springing up again. An embittered moan followed her as she ran along the ramparts, her feet deftly balancing where the stone wall narrowed and leaping over the parts that had crumbled away. The storm seethed around her, wind lashing at her pale cheeks and snatching her long, auburn hair from its tight bun. Below her, the sea hurled itself relentlessly against the rocks, grasping for anything it could pull into its angry churning waves.

*This is wrong.*

She cast a look over her shoulder to track the others. It had gone all wrong from the beginning.

"Lira!"

She turned at the faint sound of her name on the wind. Was that Vaskel's voice?

Even as she snatched her gaze from the treacherous path, she knew it was a mistake. It couldn't be him. The hellkin should have been ahead of her, not behind.

Her foot missed a step, and she bobbled, her arms flailing for a moment as she attempted to right herself, her pulse jackknifing. The drop was long, and the landing sharp, and she stopped running for a beat once she'd jerked herself from the precipice.

Hells, she'd almost fallen.

She gathered a fistful of cloak at her neck, the touch of her fingertips on her throat grounding her. But she hadn't fallen. She was still alive.

"For now," she muttered, remembering why she was running along the fortress walls in the dead of night.

Despite Malek's assurances that the ancient fortress perched on the cliffs above Siren's Refuge was abandoned, her crew was scattered and on the run. He hadn't been entirely wrong. The fortress hadn't been occupied for hundreds of years—by anything alive. What their spell caster had failed to discover when he'd searched for any traces of magic was that the crumbling castle was under the control of otherworldly beings. Wraiths, to be exact.

Icy tendrils of fear slid down Lira's spine as she thought of the rotted skin dripping from exposed bones, spikes protruding from alabaster wrists that were more mist than flesh. How had Malek missed that?

She reached the end of the rampart and ducked into a corner tower, flicking a blade from her waist and holding it at the ready as she descended the foot-worn steps. The air was stale, with the faint perfume of decay, a reminder that nothing had lived in the place for centuries. No wonder the reputed treasure hadn't been found.

"It has an army of hells-cursed wraiths guarding it," Lira whispered to herself, the sound echoing in the tight, stone stairwell.

When she reached the bottom of the spiraling steps, she slipped from the arched opening and right into the keen tip of an arrow.

Her breath caught for the moment before she recognized the face beneath the woolen hood at the other end of the arrow. "Cali!"

The pantheri archer lowered her bow and released a tangled breath of relief and annoyance. "Didn't you hear me calling you?"

"That was you?" Lira gave her head a small shake. "The wind was twisting the sound on the ramparts. I couldn't tell who was calling me or from which direction. I thought it was Vaskel."

Cali shook her head, pushing back her hood to reveal soft, gray down covering her face and peaked, flat ears. Darker gray stripes converged in a point above her black nose. "The last I saw him, he was leading Rog and Pirrin out the back of the throne room."

The throne room. Bile teased Lira's throat, the tang puckering her cheeks. They'd made it all the way to the massive throne room with mirrored walls and a high, domed ceiling before encountering the wraiths. They'd almost reached the gilded chest where legend claimed that the traitorous king had hidden his treasure. Lira's fingers had tingled in anticipation of picking the lock that had glinted in the faint light, the metal surprisingly intact. Not that it would have been any match for a rogue like her.

But that had been where the ghost warriors had been waiting. The golden chest had been a trap, and now that she thought about it, not a clever one.

The chill that ran across her skin now was nothing compared to the fear that had consumed her when the wraiths had materialized, their skinless faces hollow and their royal garments hanging in wispy tatters. She glanced past Cali, bracing herself to see the misty ranks of the undead rising from the ground with an unholy wail.

But there was nothing, save the howl of the wind and the thrash of the sea.

Cali beckoned for Lira to follow her across the open courtyard, and they fell in step as they jogged toward the arched entrance of the ruined castle.

"How did Malek not know this place is overrun by wraiths?" Lira asked, as she and Cali hurried under the decomposing portcullis that sagged battered and broken halfway down the stone archway.

"How did Vaskel not sense them?"

Cali had a point. The hellkin usually picked up on any undercurrent of emotion or danger. How had he not sensed that they'd been walking into a trap?

"Over here!"

Now that they were clear of the castle, Lira spotted Rog and Pirrin waiting for them on the other side of the drawbridge. Rog's blue beard matched the cap he wore that didn't quite cover his long, pointed ears. Pirrin was at least twice the gnome's height with russet hair that sagged across his furrowed brow.

The thudding of Lira's heart slowed as they cleared the castle and passed over the long-dried moat. The gnome and ranger appeared unharmed. They looked as displeased as she felt, but they didn't boast any bloody gashes or gaping wounds. A wave of relief washed over her that her friends were safe.

Rog tugged off his cap and slapped it against his leg. "What in the moldy ogre's sack was that?"

"An army of oath-breakers," Pirrin said, pinching his brows together.

Lira looked at the grizzled ranger and wondered if he'd heard of the cursed wraiths before tonight.

"Did you know about this?" Cali asked, beating Lira to the question.

Pirrin shook his head, always better with gestures than words. "I knew the king had broken his word. Knew that the king he'd betrayed had cursed him. Didn't know it meant..." He tipped his head to the remains of the castle but didn't finish the sentence. There was no need.

"Vaskel and Malek should be here." Lira swung her head around. "Wasn't Vaskel with you?"

"Until we cleared the tower." Rog's voice was a grizzled rasp. "Then he went back for Malek. Said he had a feeling."

They all turned to the castle. Vaskel's feelings were rarely wrong.

Cali caught her eye, her whiskers twitching and the words unspoken. They couldn't leave without the last two members of their crew. They never left anyone behind.

Before Lira could suggest they go back in, a cry ripped through the night.

"Malek," growled Rog, producing a dagger with impressive speed.

Cali had notched an arrow into place and was aiming it at the walls, using the steel point as a guide as she searched for the scream.

But Lira didn't look high. She looked at the expanse of rocky ground to the right where the cliffs plunged off to the sea.

Malek.

Time slowed as she watched the young mage stagger at the edge of the drop-off. His cloak billowed behind him like a sail unfurling in a gale, as if nudging him ever closer to the sea.

She ran toward him, her only thought to catch him before he went over. But when she was only steps from him, he whirled around. She skidded to a halt, her feet slipping the last few feet, sending pebbles skittering.

Black veins were crawling up his neck and face, which was frozen in a mangled grin.

"The spell was too..." The words splintered and vanished, eaten up by the sound of the ravenous waves.

Lira knew without him saying another word. Dark magic. It was the only explanation for the infernal curse that was overtaking him. Malek had always been tempted by it, but the crew managed to keep him from delving too deep—until now.

He must have attempted dark magic against the wraiths. A dark spell that had clearly backfired onto him.

"We can fix this," Lira called over the wind that had started to shriek again.

He shook his head even as she held out her hand. "Too late."

Vaskel appeared at Lira's side, the pulse of him present even before he was. She glanced at his fierce expression, magenta skin twisted into a mask of pain. He knew what she did.

A series of hurried footsteps behind them announced the arrival of Cali, Rog, and Pirrin, but Malek didn't see any of them. His face was tipped to the sky as he convulsed, his feet dancing closer to the cliff. Then one foot met air, and his body spun away.

Without thinking, Lira lunged, snatching the cuff of his robe as he went over the side. If only she could catch him, they'd be able to save him, cure him, find a way.

Then she was jerked back, saved from following the mage into the raging sea by Vaskel's strong arm hooking her waist. The air rushed from her, the force of the hellkin's grip forcing her to slam into him as they both staggered away from the edge.

Lira's heart seized as she stared at the scrap of fabric in her hands, all that was left of Malek.

He was gone. She sagged in Vaskel's grasp with nothing to hold save a useless piece of the mage's robe.

The cold that seeped into her bones provoked a shudder that rattled her teeth. When had she last felt warm? When had she last breathed easy or slept without a dagger beneath her pillow?

Shrugging off Vaskel, she stumbled away from the crew that stood at the edge of the cliff, the crew she'd run with for years, the only family she'd known since she'd left home.

And she didn't stop walking.

# One

LIRA GLANCED over her shoulder as the mud squelched under her boots, but there was nothing in the darkness behind her aside from the winding road and the forest in the distance. No one following her. No one hunting her. At least, no one she could see.

"You're being paranoid," she whispered as she made her way through the village, the sliver of a moon shining only enough to put the thatched roof, cross-hatched buildings in shadow. She pulled her hood lower to rebuff the relentless rain and keep her face obscured. Not that being recognized was a problem here, but old habits died hard, and Lira had become very accustomed to moving through the world with stealth.

She passed the village stables, the scent of horse muck twitching her nose before she recognized the building hunched against the storm. Just past it were the shuttered market stalls, rain sluicing off folded awnings huddled tight.

It had been two years since she'd last passed through Wayside, but five years since she'd left her hometown to make it in the wider world. The village felt more changed than she'd expected. Or maybe it was just her and everything she'd seen and done in the years since that colored her memories.

"Or maybe it's this hells-cursed storm."

She cut her gaze to the castle on the high hill in the distance, sheets of rain lashing the gray stone. That had not changed, nor had the weathered stone monument standing sentry in the middle of the town square, or the apothecary with its weary black awning.

Lightning licked the sky behind the clouds, followed by a roll of thunder like a hundred trolls pounding barefoot across a wooden bridge. She allowed her gaze to linger on the darkened windows of the apothecary, her gut tightening at the memories. With a jerk of her head, she turned away from the shop and reminded herself to keep emotion out of it.

Emotion had little place in a rogue's life. She had to focus on the lock to pick and ignore the fight around her. It was her task to creep silently along a rooftop without being distracted by the guards pursuing her. Things simply went smoother if she let logic and reason take charge. They'd kept her alive this long, after all.

Not that logic was what had brought her home.

Lira passed a pair of guardsmen with swords strapped on their backs, and pulled her woolen cloak tighter around her, both to keep out the damp and to hide the fact that she wore leather armor strapped to her shoulders and arms and boasted blades hooked to her waist.

Now that she no longer traveled with a crew, she didn't want to advertise the fact that she made her way in the world with her wits, her cunning, and often her blades. Not everyone welcomed rogues with open arms. Especially not ones traveling solo.

She gritted her teeth and tried not to think about why she was alone or how her last mission had gone so wrong. There was no use dwelling on the past. It would only dull her senses, and Lira needed those to be on high alert. That is, if she didn't want to end up like Malek.

Giving her head a shake to banish traitorous thoughts from her mind, she released a breath when she spotted the tavern in the distance. The wooden sign over the door clung desperately by a single hook as it was battered by the rain and wind, but Lira would recognize The Tusk & Tail even without the weathered sign, though music no longer spilled from the windows and the savory scent of stew didn't greet her as she approached.

Lira didn't slow her pace as she shouldered open the heavy door and ducked inside the building, grateful to escape the cold, though it took her only moments to realize that being inside wasn't much warmer. She stood dripping in the doorway for a moment before scanning the interior of the tavern and sensing the hope inside her wither.

Instead of a crackling hearth and long tables filled with patrons raising tankards of ale and gnawing on crusty bread, the fire was little more than a neglected heap of smoldering ash and the tables held only a few customers. Customers who looked as sad and abandoned as the rest of the shabby place.

The floor was dirty, strewn with dried mud and bits of straw, and cobwebs clung to the corners. She wouldn't have been shocked to learn the wooden tables, smeared with grease and dusted with crumbs, hadn't been cleaned since her last visit.

"What happened here?" Lira said under her breath as she stomped her feet to rid them of any remaining dirt and damp before continuing inside and sliding into a seat at an empty table.

The last time she'd been inside The Tusk & Tail had been on the eve of her first campaign with Malek, Vaskel, Rog, Cali, and Pirrin. The six of them had enjoyed bowls of hearty stew and toasted with cold ale as they were warmed by a roaring fire and surrounded by the raucous laughter and conversation of a bustling crowd. They'd been brash and confident as they'd anticipated their success and future riches. And they'd been right—up until their last campaign.

"You drinking?"

The hard-edged voice snatched her from her memories, and she looked up from beneath her hood to the figure behind the bar. Much had changed at The Tusk & Tail, but the burly tavernkeep was the same one she remembered. Same bald head. Same thick, black mustache that was now unkempt and peppered with gray.

"No loitering!" he barked at her, the good humor she recalled from her last visit gone. "You drink or you leave." The few heads in the tavern swiveled wearily to her. "So I'll ask you again. You drinking?"

Lira cleared her throat. She hadn't uttered more than a few words since she'd started walking that morning. "I'm drinking."

He grunted and proceeded to fill a pewter tankard with something suspiciously thick and murky. He thunked it onto the long bar then turned his attention to polishing the top of it with a grimy rag that was no doubt leaving behind more dirt than it was taking.

The rest of the patrons had returned their gazes to their own drinks, which was just as Lira liked it. The less notice she attracted the better.

Lira kept her hood up as she made her way to the bar to retrieve her drink, careful not to get caught surveying the large, open room. The walls were a mix of stone and thick wooden beams, but the ceiling was vaulted with a pair of wrought iron chandeliers dangling from the crossbeams. A cursory glance overhead told her the candles slumped over in the chandeliers hadn't been lit in a good while, and it was clear the tavern relied on the squat, tallow-veined candles on tables and the meager fire for light. Even without craning her neck, she clocked the door to the cellar and the swinging half-doors leading into a back kitchen. A kitchen that was clearly not in use any longer.

The last time she'd been there, a heavy-set woman with unruly gray curls had been in the back dishing up stew and brown bread. There was no sign of the woman now, or her bellowing voice, as she'd playfully scolded the tavernkeep.

His wife, she thought as she took her drink and stole another look at the surly man with heavy lines tugging at his jaundiced skin. She might have more scars than she'd had five years ago, but the passage of time had been crueler to him. And to The Tusk & Tail.

Lira plunked a few copper bits on the bar before she made her way back to her table. She pushed back the hood of her cloak, careful not to disturb her dark red hair too much and reveal her slightly pointed ears. Folks could be quick to judge, and she preferred to keep the fact that she had some elvish blood under wraps for as long as possible—even in the village where she'd once lived. Not that anyone in the place seemed to care—or remember her.

Wasn't that what she'd wanted—to sneak in, get what she came for, and leave without being noticed? But now that she was here, could she walk away again? Or had she been drawn back for something more?

She eyed the ale in her tankard, wary of taking a sip. Instead of drinking, she slid her gaze around the room to the other brave souls who must have had nowhere else to go.

Quietly observing others was a talent she'd honed, and one that had become as natural to her as breathing. Without moving her head, she observed an old drunk slumped at the far end of the bar, his words slurred as he griped to himself. A creature she suspected was at least part troll hunched near the fire and let out the occasional startling snore. Then there was a female dwarf who appeared surprisingly tall for her kind, with light brown skin and darker brown hair that she wore in a frayed plait over one shoulder. Her clothes were well-made but worn thin and smudged with dirt. Leather armor clung to her shoulders, and Lira suspected the woman was well-armed, although she couldn't spot an axe. Lira also had a feeling that the dwarf was sizing her up, even though she hadn't caught her glancing her way.

There was that paranoia again. Her profession had made her naturally cautious, but that had bloomed into something darker lately. Her usual confidence—buoyed by the crew who'd surrounded her—had been shaken, and the comfort she'd expected by returning to someplace familiar was scant.

Observing others without drawing attention to herself had always been one of her strengths, but as she took in the lonely patrons gathered in the sad tavern Lira's heart squeezed for those who were cast out, ignored, overlooked. Perhaps it was because she was half-elf and half-human—and didn't feel fully accepted by either race—that she felt a kinship with outsiders. And anyone who'd braved the storm to take refuge in the dreary tavern clearly had no welcoming fireside to call their own.

When the door blew open, she followed everyone's gaze to track the new arrival, curious by the instant stiffening of spines and hunching of shoulders, as eyes dropped to the floor and even the faintest snippets of conversation died.

Lira instinctively flipped her hood back up as the wyvern strode into the tavern. His velvety black wings were tucked close to his body but peeked from beneath the hem of a dark green cloak that was fastened at his throat by an ornamental jeweled pin. He swiveled his long face, gold eyes narrowed and ears folded flat against the scaled skin of his head.

He didn't break stride as he headed for the bar, his arrival making even the surly tavernkeep shrink away.

"Durn." The wyvern's voice started as a hiss but descended into a growl. "You're late again."

The tavernkeep's cheeks reddened as his scraggly mustache drooped further down his face. "I told you already. I paid as much as I can."

The wyvern tipped his snout into the air, the nostrils flaring as he inhaled. "And I told you that I know you have gold here."

Lira sucked in a breath then went still, hoping that the wyvern's hearing wasn't as sharp as rumors held it was.

Durn barked out a laugh. "You think if I had gold, I'd still be here?"

The wyvern tilted his head and rested both clawed hands on the edge of the bar. "The laird appointed me to be Wayside's reeve, which means I collect the taxes. Taxes you haven't fully paid."

Durn's expression darkened. "Not even you can get blood from a stone, Rygor."

Rygor rapped his claws along the wood. "It isn't blood I want."

Lira had encountered enough wyvern to know that, while not as violent as their dragon ancestors, their desire for gold and treasure was almost as acute.

The tavernkeep shook his head and resumed his task of reapplying grime to the top of the bar. "Like I've told you before, there's no gold here."

The wyvern reeve straightened. "That's too bad. I would hate for you to lose all of..." He turned to the grim interior and his thin lips curled, "this."

Then he stomped from the great room and out the door, treating patrons to a blast of frigid air in his wake. Durn muttered to himself and kept his gaze down, but a few folks whispered to each other and even more shifted in their seats.

Lira reminded herself to breathe as she sat rigid and unmoving. Since when was the village reeve a wyvern? Her stomach snarled, a cruel reminder that it had been a day since she'd eaten, but another glance at the ale made her think better of taking a drink.

She shouldn't have come here. She shouldn't have come back.

Lira swallowed hard and attempted to push aside the guilt that had been clawing at her since their party disbanded. There were a lot of things she shouldn't have done.

"*Stop it*," she scolded herself furiously.

She took a deep breath and squared her shoulders. She didn't have time for regret. Not until she got what she came for. She'd returned to Wayside because she'd felt drawn back to the place, but she was also there to retrieve what she'd hidden in The Tusk & Tail.

Then she thought of the wyvern. She might have arrived just in time.

Lira's gaze flitted to the cellar door, and she jiggled her leg under the table. Biding her time had never been one of her talents.

# Two

THE LAST LIGHT went out inside The Tusk & Tail, and Lira released a breath as she stood under the dripping eaves of a nearby building. The entire village had gone still, enveloped in the quiet of the night and the hush after a storm. Only the mournful hoot of a distant owl and the splash of the stream running behind the tavern broke the silence.

Lira didn't move right away. She knew better than to rush it, even though her racing heart told her she was running short on time. Her hope had been to return to the tavern where she'd spent many a happy evening and enjoy another one filled with warm memories. Then she would get what she'd hidden for safekeeping and move on.

That hadn't played out the way she'd hoped, and seeing the tavern in such sad disarray had left her feeling even more unmoored. Nothing lasted forever. Not family. Not friendships. Not even simple things like your favorite drinking hole.

Lira eyed the shabby exterior of the tavern. Even in the darkness of night, she could tell that it had been neglected. The whitewashed exterior was scarred and stained, there were gaps in the wooden crosshatching, and the thatched roof appeared to be patchy and pockmarked. Not to mention the sadness that clung to the place like a heavy shroud. No, The Tusk & Tail was nothing like she'd remembered, and she would be glad to get what she came for and move on.

Once she'd waited as long as her patience would allow, Lira moved stealthily toward the building, darting from shadow to shadow. She slunk to the back door, using her metal picks to make quick work of the lock and slipping them back under her cloak before pushing open the door. She braced herself for the creak, but the hinges surprised her by making no sound.

She closed the door behind her as quietly as she'd opened it and then moved on silent feet through the kitchen that clearly hadn't been used nor cleaned in a while. The sharp bite of mildew warred with the earthier tones of decomposing garbage, and Lira pressed her lips together to keep from retching. The sticky floor pulled at the bottom of her boots, but she shifted to the tips of her toes as she crept to the cellar door.

Lira paused and listened. She knew the tavernkeep lived upstairs, but there were no sounds drifting down the staircase that opened to the side of the cellar entrance. No snoring, no heavy breathing. Was this a good sign or a bad one?

It was too late to second guess her plan now. She'd have to assume that the burly man wasn't a snorer and hope that he didn't rouse easily. Not that she intended on making any noise to give herself away. She was too good at sneaking in and out of places to do that.

Even though she'd slunk into more dangerous places than a run-down tavern, her heart thudded as she opened the cellar door just enough to slip through. This job wasn't remotely close to her most challenging ones, but her pulse quickened because she knew what awaited her downstairs. She knew what she'd come to retrieve.

Lira held tight to the wooden rail as she felt her way down the stairs in the blackness. Only when she touched the bottom did she reach inside her cloak and untie the pouch hanging around her waist. She produced a stone that was faceted with both rough and smooth sides, holding it in one hand as she whispered the elvish word she'd been taught. "Cala."

Blue light glowed from the stone as it pulsed in her hand. Lira was glad she'd endured the choppy boat ride to reach the elvish island of Lananore and procure the illumination stone, and she was even more grateful that the enchanted stone didn't require any more magic than a single word. Despite possessing elvish blood, Lira had never possessed any of the race's powers.

The dank underground space was now illuminated enough for Lira to take a quick inventory. She wouldn't have the light for long, so she swept her gaze across the barrels stacked along the walls and the empty shelves that once held stores of food.

The last time she'd been in the cellar, the baskets on the shelves had been filled with potatoes and onions, and the scent of vegetables had mixed with the aroma of ale and mead. Now the reek of rotting vegetation rose from forgotten corners, hanging over the cellar like a fog.

Lira pressed her lips together and walked forward, determined not to dwell on the cloying decay that had overtaken the storage area. It was not her business or her concern.

"Get in, get it, get out," she whispered to herself as she extended her hand holding the stone so it could light her way to the back of the cellar.

The blue light bobbled and cast eerie shadows as unseen creatures scuttled out of the way ahead of her. She ignored them and the disturbing thoughts of what else was there with her.

*You've been in dank dungeons and underground tunnels that were filled with worse.*

Lira's heart was a steady drumbeat in her ears as she rounded the shelves. She'd chosen a spot in the farthest corner of the cellar so it would go undisturbed. Who would think of poking around in the dirt walls beneath a tavern, after all?

Then she stopped short, and her breath hitched. The wall was no longer there. Well, it *was* there but it was no longer the red-brown clay of the other walls.

"Son of a wand waxer!" She forgot to keep her voice to a whisper as she stared at the wall that was now stone.

Who had stoned up the dirt wall and why? Her thoughts raced as her pulse spiked. The rest of the tavern was slowly crumbling, but the back of the cellar had been given a stone reinforcement?

Lira hurried to the wall, pressing one hand to the cool, gray stones that looked like they'd been sourced from a river. Probably the stream behind the tavern, she thought, as her muddled brain cleared, and she realized that the reason for the wall must have had more to do with shoring up the underground area than keeping her from her hiding spot.

She knelt in the corner and eyed the stones that stood between her and what she'd traveled so far to retrieve. They hadn't just been stacked one on top of the other. Mud had been spackled between them, and it had dried to make a solid wall. It would take serious effort to get through the stone, and that effort would make more noise than she could afford at the moment.

Lira glanced at the glowing stone in her hand. Not only that, but she didn't have much more light left before the stone's illumination would dim.

She mumbled a few more curses under her breath before turning away, tears of frustration prickling the back of her eyelids. She'd come all this way to finally retrieve what she most treasured just to be denied when she was so close to holding it in her hands again.

Lira swallowed hard. She'd have to adjust her plan unless she was willing to leave without getting what she'd come for, which she wasn't.

No matter. She was good at using her wits to solve problems on the fly. It was one of the skills she'd sharpened over many quests, and this hiccup was no different than a challenging lock or a mark who was reluctant to reveal his secrets. She'd simply have to hang around Wayside and The Tusk & Tail for a bit longer. Long enough to come up with a plan to break through the wall without getting caught. But not long enough to give the new reeve a chance to discover that it was her gold he was smelling under the tavern.

The gold wasn't what was most important, though. It had never been. Not to Lira.

First of all, there were only a handful of gold pieces scattered inside the iron box she'd buried. Valuable, certainly, but not as precious to her as the book the box was made to protect, the book with all her gran's handwritten recipes and the moonstone embedded in the cover.

That was why she'd come. That was why she couldn't leave. It was the last thing she had to remember her gran. It was the one possession her gran had treasured most. It was the one thing her gran had told her to keep safe. Lira had promised she would, and she had no intention of breaking her last promise to the woman who'd raised her.

Even if it meant going up against a wyvern.

Determination hardened within Lira as she paused at the bottom of the steps and the light from the stone faded. She'd had setbacks before, and she'd always overcome them. This was no different.

Lira was surrounded by darkness once more, her steady breath her only company. She tucked the stone away and groped for the handrail so she could leave the tavern as quietly as she'd entered and devise a new plan, a better plan.

Then she heard a crash from above.

# Three

LIRA STIFFENED, her entire body tingling as she stood in the dark at the bottom of the stairs. How had the tavernkeep heard her? She'd been just as stealthy as she was on missions, and she'd never been caught before. Was she losing her touch?

She shook her head roughly, casting off that thought, unwilling to admit that she wasn't the same rogue she'd been before going into the cursed castle. She might have lost a bit of her confidence, but she hadn't lost her skills.

Hovering with her foot over the first step and her hand gripping the stair rail, she squeezed the rough wood and gingerly set down the tip of her boot. Being at the bottom of the cellar steps was the last place she wanted to be found, because it was the last place she'd wanted to be trapped. She didn't know the tavernkeep well, but she couldn't guarantee that he wouldn't react badly to finding a thief in his establishment. Not that Lira had ever considered herself a common thief, but she doubted many would appreciate the difference between a rogue skilled in stealth and a basic burglar.

As she held her breath and expected to see a figure appear at the top of the steps, the rustling continued overhead. Strangely, the sounds weren't coming closer, which meant that the owner might not have heard her. It was entirely possible that he'd come downstairs to check the locks or have a drink.

Lira released a slow breath, glad that she'd pulled the tavern's back door closed behind her when she'd entered. There would be no trace that she'd broken in. Then she glimpsed the sliver of faint light peeking through the crack in the cellar door.

Orc's blood! She'd left *that* door open. She hoped the tavernkeep was as careless about shutting doors as he was about cleaning his tavern and would assume he'd left it cracked.

She crept up a few more steps, grateful that the stairs miraculously didn't creak, and when she'd almost reached the top she strained her ears. The shuffling sounds were soft, not what she'd expect from such a burly man. Maybe she wasn't hearing the tavernkeep. Maybe what she was hearing were very assertive rats coming out at night to have free rein of the place.

This thought sent a shiver down her spine. She might have preferred encountering the surly Durn over a company of vermin.

Lira placed her foot on the top step, going rigid as the wood beneath let out a groan. The sounds upstairs stopped instantly, and she held her breath and focused every ounce of self-control on remaining motionless.

A darkly muttered word was muffled behind the cellar door, but then the noises returned. Noises that Lira was sure didn't belong to the owner. For one, they were too quiet, and for another, they were furtive. Was she not the only one trying to rob The Tusk & Tail?

She slipped a dagger from her waist and held it in one hand as she silently opened the cellar door a fraction more so that she could peek out. Her eyes had adjusted to the darkness, so even without the benefit of her illumination stone, she could make out shapes in the shadows.

Someone was behind the bar, hunched over. Now Lira was sure that it wasn't the tavernkeep by the size of the figure and the desperate movements. She eased into the great room, her footsteps quiet as she moved toward the back door.

Now that she'd determined she couldn't get what she'd come for—not yet, at least—Lira had no intention of getting caught and little interest in the other robbery in progress. She sidled to one side, her gaze locked on the creature wrestling with something that would not yield, even as she moved farther away.

"Grognick's beard!" the creature muttered, with a huff of exasperation.

Lira sucked in a startled breath when she realized the voice was female—and if she wasn't mistaken—dwarven.

The dwarf spun on her heels at the sound, and Lira cursed herself for her slip. So much for escaping without notice.

"Who are you?" The female dwarf had produced a dagger with impressive speed and even in the dim lighting, the blade bared silver teeth.

Lira's own weapon remained in one hand, but she didn't raise it. "No one of importance to you."

The dwarf tossed her dark braid over her shoulder and emitted a half-snort. "It's important to me if you're poaching my mark."

Lira glanced over the female's shoulder to the wooden box on the floor, the lock dangling and the lid crooked. "I have no interest in the till."

The dwarf's eyes narrowed in obvious disbelief. She had a point. Why would Lira have broken in if she wasn't after the coin? But then her gaze slid to the back door, which was still shut. "How did you get in?"

"How did you?" Lira asked.

A low growl burbled in the dwarf's throat. "I never left."

Lira remembered seeing the dwarf at one of the sparsely populated tables earlier in the night. So she'd actually hidden after the tavern closed and waited for Durn to retire for the night? Not a bad plan, and if Lira was being honest, a part of her wished she'd thought of it. But then she would have missed out on picking a lock, and that was one of her favorite parts of the job.

She cut her eyes to the dwarf and held up her hands, flipping the blade around so that it didn't show. "I'm just passing through, so how about I leave and let you get back to your work?"

The dwarf cocked her head to one side. "Who's to say I would ever trust an elf?"

Lira bristled. "Half-elf," she muttered before she could catch herself. How had the dwarf known that?

Before she could ask, the dwarf drew in a deep breath. "I can smell an elf from a thousand paces."

Those were bold words, considering dwarves' reputations for avoiding baths. But Lira held her tongue as she took a sidestep toward the door. "You don't want to waste time killing me. Besides, it would make noise and then you'd have to clean up a body."

Despite her brandished weapon, there was no part of Lira that believed the dwarf would hurt her. Sizing up people was something she could do in an instant, and without knowing precisely how she knew, she was certain the dwarf was harmless. Scared, yes. Desperate, perhaps. But not deadly.

The dwarf bobbled her head back and forth, but she didn't lower her weapon or take her gaze off Lira. "You tell anyone you saw me here, I'll spare the noise and mess to kill you."

"Fair enough." Lira continued to edge toward the door as the dwarf followed her. She didn't break eye contact as she opened the door and stepped out into the night.

She inhaled the cool air and allowed herself a normal breath as she backed away from the tavern and the dwarf thief standing silhouetted in the open doorway. There was little doubt in Lira's mind that she could have taken her in a fight, but it was more important to get away and regroup. Only then could she formulate a plan to return and break through the wall.

Lira swiveled her head to take in the scraggly bushes between the tavern and the stream, grateful to hear nothing but the burbling water and chirping crickets. That is, until a deep-throated bellow of rage from inside the tavern tore through the quiet.

Her chest hitched as she stumbled even farther from the door and the terrifying roars.

# Four

IN THE WAKE of the shouts, the dwarf lost little time rushing from the tavern and straight into Lira, her panicked exit sending them both to the ground and into the slick, brown mud.

"Get off me!" Lira pushed the woman and tried to stand, but her hands couldn't find purchase in the sludge that was as thick as abandoned porridge. She slipped and splattered back down onto her elbows, letting loose a torrent of curses that would have made her gran smack her hand.

"You're in my way," the dwarf huffed as she used Lira for leverage to right herself.

"Only because you ran into me."

The creature muttered indignant protests that Lira would have loved to argue point by point if the hairs on the back of her neck hadn't started to prickle. As she looked up, her breath caught in her throat and her mouth went dry.

The back doorway was completely filled by the bulk of the tavernkeep who stood watching them with a hefty club in his hands. "A dwarf and an elf—together?"

Lira wanted to correct him and say that she was only half elf, but she doubted the distinction mattered to him.

"We're not—" the dwarf started to say as she took a step back.

"—sure which way he went," Lira finished the sentence, earning her a confused look from the dwarf and the human.

"Who went?" the tavernkeep growled, as he smacked the wooden club into the palm of his hand.

"The burglar, of course. Isn't that why you ran out?" Lira managed to get up and steady herself in the traitorous soup of soil.

Durn shifted his gaze from one female to the other, his brows pinched. "Aye. I heard a noise downstairs. Then I came down and saw the till laying out and you two back here."

Lira made a point of rubbing her side. "We're back here because we heard him too."

"You heard someone inside my tavern?"

"That's right." Lira waved a hand at the door. "We thought it was odd for noises to come from a darkened tavern, so we walked closer to check it out. That was when he ran out the door and flattened both of us."

"Knocked us right over," the dwarf nodded her head in agreement. "We tried to stop him, but he was bigger than either of us."

"A thief?" The man held the club suspended in the air as he seemed to consider this. "Ran out of my place and into you?"

"Why do you think we were both on the ground?" Lira opened her arms wide and glanced around her. "We would have stopped him if the ground wasn't so soggy."

The man tilted his head to one side. "You want me to believe that an elf and a dwarf are loitering outside my tavern at night because they tried to stop a thief?"

"That's right," the dwarf's voice resonated with confidence. "We would have gotten him if he hadn't been a goblin."

"A goblin, you say?" The tavernkeep lurched back and swung his head from side to side. "I've heard some rumbling about a roving goblin gang."

"Exactly." Lira latched onto this tidbit. "He must have been a part of the band of goblin thieves that's been working in these parts."

The dwarf shook her head and made tsk-ing sounds in the back of her throat. "Dangerous lot."

Durn blew out an exasperated breath. "Well, where'd he go?"

Lira made a show of peering around in the dark. "I don't know. He knocked the wind out of us."

"And he was fast," the dwarf added.

"Blood and ashes," the man's shoulders sagged. "This is the last thing I need."

"At least he didn't make off with anything," Lira offered.

The tavernkeep's glittering eyes locked on her. "How do you know that?"

Lira's pulse quickened, but she merely smiled. "I assumed, since he wasn't carrying anything when he ran into us."

"He didn't jingle when he ran," the dwarf said quickly. "He must not have gotten any coin."

"Not this time." The man heaved out a breath that ached with weariness. "If it was a goblin, he'll be back. Goblins are as stubborn as they are ugly."

Those were bold words from the jowly, bald man, but Lira refrained from commenting. Instead, she thought of the cellar and how she still wanted what was buried in it. "That's why you need us."

"What?"

Lira wasn't sure which of them had asked that, but it didn't matter. She needed to have access to the tavern, and The Tusk & Tail needed security from thieving goblins. At least, that's what its owner believed.

"We might not have stopped him this time, but that's only because we weren't prepared. If you hire us to provide security, you won't have to worry about the goblin coming back."

The man choked out a laugh. "You two? Security?"

Lira could sense the dwarf bristle beside her. "You don't think females can be deadly?"

"It's not that. It's that I don't know which I trust less—dwarves or elves."

This was fair. Elves were known for being aloof and self-interested, keeping mostly to their island kingdom of Lananore, and dwarves had a reputation for coveting the wealth of the mountains and spilling blood to keep it for themselves. Since Lira wasn't a full elf, she didn't take full offense. The dwarf, however, did not seem amused.

Lira put out a hand to keep her from charging forward. "It's clear that you need help with this place. Not only are we both trained in combat, but we can provide the feminine touch that The Tusk & Tail has been missing for..." She let her words trail off.

"Two years," the man supplied, his voice thick. "Alma's been gone a bit more than two years now."

So shortly after Lira had last passed through the village, she thought. That last visit had been so quick that she hadn't even stayed overnight or seen anyone she knew, and she'd hoped she hadn't been seen.

Then the man narrowed his eyes, latching onto Lira's face in the moonlight. "Wait a second. I know you. You're Elia's granddaughter. The half-elf one."

The *only* one, Lira thought as her throat constricted but she nodded. "Lira."

"That's right." He bobbed his head along with her. "You left after she..." Then he cleared his throat roughly and let his gaze wander to the ground. "You back now?"

Lira didn't know how to answer that. Part of her wanted to return to the village where she'd once been happy, but another part was sure that the place held nothing but memories that would remind her that those times were gone. It was hard to imagine being in Wayside with so much that reminded her of her childhood but without the most important part. Instead of answering, she gave the conversation a deft twirl.

"The Tusk & Tail isn't a one-man job," Lira told him gently. "I'd like to...*we'd* like to help you. I'm sure my gran and your wife would approve."

The man dragged in a breath as if the effort was too much. "Alma always liked Elia. Loved her baking. Said she wished she could bake as good."

"My gran used to say that no one made you feel as welcome as Alma."

Another rough clear of the throat. "Can you bake as good as your gran?"

Lira decided the truth—that she hadn't touched a rolling pin since she'd left Wayside—was not what the situation called for, so she gave the truth a spin. "I grew up baking by her side."

A rasp rattled Durn's chest as he rocked back on his heels. "It sure would be nice to serve food again. Folks like some supper with their drink." A frown tugged his mouth back down. "But I can't pay much. Business hasn't been so good since—"

"Room and board will be fine to start," Lira said, ignoring the grumble of protest from the dwarf. "And whatever supplies we need to get this place fixed up."

"Guess I got nothing to lose." The man grunted and spun on one heel. "Come on in. I'll show you where you're sleeping."

Lira waited until he was far enough inside that he wouldn't hear her before pivoting to the dwarf and holding out her hand. "I guess we're partners now. I'm Lira Redfern."

"I heard. I'm Sarsparilla. Sarsparilla Thornshield, but everyone calls me Sass." The dwarf's expression was wary as she slipped her brown, calloused hand into Lira's slender one. "That's some silver tongue you've got."

Lira wasn't sure if Sass meant that as a compliment.

"Why didn't you turn me in?" the dwarf whispered. "You weren't after the till. Does it have something to do with why you were in the cellar?"

So, she'd figured out where Lira had come from. That wasn't ideal, but Lira was sure her instinct about the dwarf was correct, and she wasn't a threat. In fact, her gut told her that Sass was going to be an asset. Or maybe it had been months since she'd run with her crew, and she missed the camaraderie. Either way, they were in it together now.

Lira shrugged and headed back inside the tavern. "You keep my secret, and I'll keep yours."

<h1 style="text-align:center">Five</h1>

LIRA'S BOOTS creaked on the narrow stairs as she followed Durn's broad back. The tavernkeep's gruff demeanor hadn't improved since their encounter downstairs, but at least he'd bought their story about the goblin burglar. And at least he'd remembered her gran.

Thanks, Gran. Lira's throat tightened as she thought of the woman who'd raised her, but she swallowed hard. The last thing she needed was to show weakness in front of the dwarf.

She cast a quick look over her shoulder as Sass trudged behind her, the dwarf's steps cautious and heavy.

At the top of the stairs, Durn shouldered open a warped door. "This'll be your room," he grunted, ducking inside.

Lira had to stoop to enter, her eyes adjusting as the candle in Durn's hand sent shadows dancing across the cramped space. Two narrow beds flanked a battered nightstand, and their frames sagged under thin mattresses. A chipped washbasin perched atop the squat dresser, accompanied by an earthenware pitcher, and a ladder-back chair with a splintered, rattan seat leaned against one wall. The fireplace beside it yawned empty and cold, only a smattering of ash in place of fresh logs or a thick chunk of peat.

The smell hit her next—the air musty and stale, with hints of mildew and mouse droppings. Lira wrinkled her nose but held her tongue. This room, as uninviting as it was, put her one step closer to retrieving what she'd buried in the cellar.

Durn used his candle to light a hurricane lamp on the nightstand, the flame dancing behind the dusty veil of glass. "There's your light. Don't burn the place down." With that, he stomped out, leaving Lira and Sass alone in the flickering shadows.

Lira's gaze slid to her unlikely companion. The dwarf's face was smudged with dirt, her clothes caked in mud from their tumble outside. Lira knew she looked no better.

Sass broke the silence first. "Well, this is right cozy." Her voice dripped with sarcasm, which amused Lira. She never imagined dwarves having much of a sense of humor.

"Beats a jail cell."

Sass lifted a brow and wrinkled her nose. "Not by much."

Lira wanted to ask how many jail cells Sass had seen the inside of, but exhaustion overtook her curiosity. The weight of her journey had seeped through skin and muscle to nest in her bones.

Things hadn't gone as planned, but they could have been worse. She was alive, she wasn't being held in a dungeon, and she was close to her gran's book and her stash of gold. A few floors above it, but that was enough for now.

"These beds don't look like much." Sass pressed one hand on the mattress closest to her and it shrank from her touch, sagging even closer to the floor from the pressure. "But I don't suppose it would be right to cover them in mud."

Lira glanced at her own cloak flecked with red-brown, shrugging it off and draping it over the ladder-back chair that blessedly did not splinter from the impact. She dropped her leather satchel on the floor next to it, grateful that she had more than just the clothes on her back.

Without a word, Sass began peeling off her muddy clothes and her shoulder armor, a startling number of blades emerging from waistbands and pockets. Lira winced as she untied her leather waistcoat, her ribs signaling that she'd bruised them at the very least. When she'd stripped down to a linen tunic, she collapsed onto one of the beds, ignoring the ominous creaking beneath her and the fact that her toes tickled the foot of the wooden bed frame.

Sass clambered into the other bed with less care, her tunic frayed at the edges and reaching nearly to her knees. The dwarf's toes were in no danger of dangling off the end.

"So—" Sass kept her eyes on the ceiling. "Why didn't you turn me in—really?"

Lira considered the question. "Call it a hunch," she finally replied. "You don't strike me as a career criminal. Figured you must have your reasons."

The dwarf grunted. "Aye, well, things have been rough since I left home. Not many crews are willing to take on an untested dwarf, much less a female one."

Lira understood feeling unwanted more than she cared to admit.

"My best gig so far was tending bar near the docks of Eldu. The place wasn't much, but I kept it looking decent." Sass's smile was fleeting. "But I had to move on."

Lira didn't ask why, but from the dwarf's stormy expression she guessed it hadn't been her choice. There wasn't much between the port town of Eldu and Wayside, which meant Sass could have been traveling through dense forest or along rocky cliffs for days.

"You come from the Ice Lands?" The mountains in the territory above the long wall were where most of the dwarves lived, mining deep under the high peaks. It wasn't far from Eldu.

Sass grunted a yes then turned her head, her long braid flopping across the pillow as she faced Lira. "Why did you say I didn't strike you as a criminal?"

A wry smile tugged at Lira's lips. "You weren't very good at it, were you? Any thief worth their salt would have just taken the box and hoofed it."

Sass's indignant splutter dissolved into a throaty chuckle. "I didn't need the box. If that wyvern was right, the box is filled with gold. I only needed a few bits to tide me over until I could get work."

Lira was certain the tavern's till wasn't filled with gold. Not if the shabbiness of the place was any indication. No, *that* wasn't the gold the wyvern smelled, but she wasn't about to correct Sass.

"Like I said," Lira cut her gaze to the dwarf and grinned, "not a real thief."

Sass opened her mouth as if to ask a question but then clamped her lips shut. Lira felt sure she was going to ask her how she knew so much about thieves, and was glad she didn't have to offer a pretty lie.

Lira couldn't tell the dwarf that she sensed other talents in her or that her instincts about people had rarely led her astray. That might lead to more questions about how she'd become such an astute observer of others and how she'd used that talent for questionable ends.

Before the dwarf could change her mind about pressing the matter, Lira leaned over and blew out the candle, soaking the room in inky darkness. As she settled back onto the bed that smelled of mildewed straw, a sigh escaped from Sass. Whether it was one of exhaustion or frustration, Lira couldn't say.

She stared into the blackness, her own weariness doing battle with the thoughts tumbling through her mind. She didn't know how she was going to break through that wall without getting caught, but one thing she'd learned during her time away from Wayside was that campaigns were not strategized in a night.

For now, no one knew where she was. No one knew her plan. Most importantly, the wyvern had no idea that the gold he sought was buried behind a wall in the tavern's cellar. Time was on her side—for now.

# Six

LIRA PUT her hands on her hips as she stood in the doorway to the tavern's kitchen. If neglect had a smell, it would be the blend of rancid grease and festering ale that greeted her now. Beside her, Sass wrinkled her nose, which Lira suspected might soon become a permanent tic.

"I've seen prettier sights in a troll's outhouse," Sass muttered.

Lira snorted, but she couldn't disagree. The kitchen was a far cry from the bustling heart of the tavern she remembered from years past. Back then, The Tusk & Tail had been known for its hearty fare and warm atmosphere. Now, neglect clung to it like a shroud.

"We have to earn our keep somehow." Lira shoved up the sleeves of her clean tunic and then gave the points of her burgundy waistcoat a firm yank.

"Aside from protecting the place from goblin burglars?"

She slid a side-eye glance at the dwarf, who wore a clean pair of brown trousers topped with a linen shirt and none of the armor she'd boasted the night before. "Aside from that."

Lira assessed the empty hearth that slumbered on one wall, its stones blackened with soot. A rustic stove squatted nearby, the iron surface rusty and flaking. At the center of the room sat a massive wooden table, its thick legs nicked from years of use and its surface piled high with teetering stacks of pewter bowls and dishes. Tarnished copper pots dangled from hooks on the walls, their once-gleaming surfaces now dull and mottled.

The floor was sticky, the counters grimy, and she could only imagine what creatures were hiding in drawers and cabinets ready to scuttle out. Yet beneath the layers of dirt and deterioration, she could see the hint of what the place had been—and what it could be again. The place had potential, just like Sass.

The dwarf snatched a bristle broom from the corner and pivoted on one foot. "I'll start sweeping the other room."

"Coward," Lira called after her.

"You're only sore you didn't think of it first," came the dwarf's muffled response along with a chuckle.

"Too right," Lira said as she pulled down a yellowed apron from a hook near the door and tied it around her waist. She moved to the wood table and ran her fingers over an exposed corner.

Unbidden, a memory surfaced. Usually, she pushed away memories of her past, but this time she closed her eyes and let it wash over her.

She was a child again, barely tall enough to see over the counter in her gran's kitchen, but clinging to the edge with small fingers. The air was thick with the scent of cinnamon and butter from the pot bubbling and hissing on the stove, its rich aroma making her mouth water.

"Come here, little one." Her gran's wrinkled hands beckoned her closer, palms chalky with flour. "It's time to roll the crust."

Lira had eagerly climbed onto the stool and let her gran guide her hands onto the mound of stiff dough. She'd been solemn and attentive, even when it pillowed between her fingers, watching in awe as her gran's deft movements transformed the lumpy mass into a perfectly flat disc.

"One day you'll make this apple tart for your own little ones."

The memories of the sticky dough, the rich sauce that was poured over the slices of apple, and the crust that became golden and flaky as it baked in the oven were so strong Lira could almost taste it.

A pang of longing jolted her back to the present, her gran's voice fading as quickly as it had appeared. She blinked rapidly, pushing away the ache of loss that always accompanied thoughts of the past. There was no time for regret or daydreaming. Not when there was work to be done.

Lira found a rag that wasn't too filthy and set to scrubbing the counters, grateful for the distraction to focus her mind. As layers of grime gave way to the worn but solid wood beneath, she moved piles of dishes, rearranged utensils, and began creating space.

From outside the swinging half-doors, the sounds of off-key humming drifted in as Sass attacked the floors with gusto. The dwarf's enthusiasm was almost comical, given how spectacularly off-key she was, but Lira didn't dare utter a word of critique. At least the dwarf was a hard worker and didn't complain.

Once the table was scrubbed clean, Lira straightened and rubbed the back of her neck, daring to let a spark of excitement creep in. "This place isn't a total disaster. There's a good set of mixing bowls, and the pans hanging overhead are good quality. They just need a decent scrubbing."

"Aye, if you say so."

Lira jumped, putting a hand to her heart. "Don't sneak up on me like that!"

Sass leaned on the knobby handle of the broom. "No one's ever accused me of being quiet enough to startle them before."

Lira remembered the clatter the dwarf had made trying to break into the till and wasn't surprised.

"You were in your own world, talking away to nobody," Sass said, although her tone wasn't judgmental.

Lira couldn't tell her that she'd been talking to her gran, running things by her like she often did, though not always out loud. Better the dwarf think she was talking to herself than communing with a woman long dead.

"What do you plan to do with this place once it's clean?" Sass asked.

"The tavern used to be known for its food. Not fancy, but solid fare. It could be again."

Sass huffed out a breath. "I hope you aren't counting on me to help with the cooking."

"Didn't you learn to bake when you were a child?"

Sass made a face. "Dwarven fare isn't known for being fancy, and I've never known a dwarf mum to relish baking. About the only thing I can make is a decent bean soup. Now, if you want to learn how to throw an axe, *that* I can teach you. My gran made sure I could split a hair at fifty paces."

"Axes, huh?" Lira grinned. "I suppose every family has their own traditions."

"Speaking of." Sass eyed Lira. "I didn't know elvish females were known for their cooking skills."

"I'm only half elf. My gran—the one who taught me to cook—was human."

Sass's face brightened. "Only half-elf? Is that so? Well, that makes me like you a bit better."

Lira couldn't help but laugh at the dwarf's blunt honesty. Despite their rocky start, she was beginning to actually like Sass. Who would have thought she'd enjoy the company of a failed thief—and a dwarf, no less?

Lira didn't think of herself as an elf, despite her lineage, but the friction between dwarves and elves went back so many generations it was almost engrained in her to be suspicious of them. Not that she didn't also have reason to be wary about the elves, who possessed natural magical abilities that they kept for themselves.

Lira pulled a copper pot from its hook on the wall and began to polish it. "My gran was a wonderful cook, especially when it came to pastries—fruit tarts, meat pies, spice cakes, scones."

"Grognick's beard, woman," Sass groaned, touching a hand to her belly. "You're making my stomach growl something fierce."

Their conversation was interrupted by Durn lumbering through the swinging doors. The tavernkeep's perpetual scowl softened slightly as he took in the improved state of the kitchen.

He grunted, which Lira took to be high praise. "Not bad. There's some bread and cheese in the pantry if you've worked up an appetite."

Sass grinned but Lira squared her shoulders. "Actually, if you could spare a few coins, I could whip up something a bit more substantial. Might be good to test out the kitchen, see what it can do after all this time." Then she slid a glance toward Sass. "Neither of us want to deal with a hungry dwarf."

Sass opened her mouth as if to protest, then shrugged and grinned. "So, you do know dwarves."

Durn's bushy eyebrows pressed together, but after a moment of consideration, he fished a handful of copper bits from his pocket and plunked them onto the table. "Find Boden in the market. He'll give you the best prices, especially if you tell him it's for the tavern."

"Boden," Lira repeated to imprint the name in her memory. She didn't remember a Boden from her childhood in the village, but that had been a while ago.

"My wife's brother," Durn added before turning and leaving the kitchen.

Sass raised an eyebrow at Lira, but neither of them commented. Lira took off the apron and draped it over the worktable, slid the copper bits off the counter and into her pocket, then jerked her head at Sass. "You staying here?"

The dwarf propped the broom against the wall and fell into step beside her eagerly. "And let you do all the picking? Not when I have some ideas for how to spruce up the main room."

Lira didn't know how far the copper bits would take them, but there was no arguing that the tavern needed all the sprucing up it could get. "You like to redecorate taverns when you aren't looking for work as a fighter?"

Sass strode out the back door behind Lira. "Let's say I've been in a few taverns, and I know what makes a good one, and I left the bar in Eldu a sight better than when I arrived."

"As long as The Tusk & Tail doesn't look like a dwarven mine."

"You've clearly never seen the inside of one," Sass said under her breath.

Lira didn't correct her. She would take the tale of sneaking into a dwarven mine to her grave.

As they walked along the stream behind the tavern and headed toward the center of the village, her own gait slow so Sass could keep up, Lira didn't care if they appeared to be an odd pairing. It had been months since she'd been in the company of a friend, or at least someone who wasn't an adversary. She'd forgotten how much she'd missed it.

*Seven*

THE VILLAGE WAS a fair sight more appealing in the day. The thatched roofs that had swollen with rain the night before were now drying under the relentless sun, and the whitewashed buildings had been scrubbed clean by the storm. But even with the blue sky and warm sunlight, the air was crisp, making Lira wish her cloak wasn't back at the tavern, covered in mud.

Wayside had always been a speck of a village with its buildings pressed together as if sharing warmth against the wilderness beyond, the high-peaked roofs facing off across the main thoroughfare. The Tusk & Tail stood weary sentinel across from the old mill, where the great wheel groaned lazily in the stream. Across the stream from the mill, the combined blacksmith and wheelwright squatted low and solid, the workshops run by an orc couple, steam and smoke rising from their forge in lazy spirals.

Lira turned away from the rhythmic clang of metal striking metal and wheel splashing water, heading toward the town square. She could already hear the chattering of vendors at their stalls and the creak of carts rolling over sodden roads.

It was all so familiar, such a powerful reminder of her childhood, that a pang twisted her heart. She'd thought she was too quest-hardened to feel nostalgia, but with each step down the road more memories rushed back, and the ache in her chest pulsed like a festering wound. Lira rubbed the spot below her collarbone as if she could smooth out the bittersweet twinge.

"So, this is home?" Sass asked, taking quick strides to keep up with Lira's longer legs.

Lira slowed her pace and glanced down. "It was."

The dwarf swiveled her head from side to side. "Not a bad place, this. Why would you leave?"

Lira thought about how much to tell. She liked Sass. She got a good feeling from her. But that didn't mean she was foolish enough to trust her fully. Not yet.

"My gran died." She kept her gaze fastened on the road. "I didn't have any coin to pay off the debt on her farm, which meant I didn't have a home. Even if I'd taken up the offer of lodging from my gran's best friend, I needed a change. I needed to see something beyond this village."

"I guess we have something in common after all." Sass didn't look at her. "I wanted to see more than what was hidden beneath the mountains."

Lira had seen enough of the Ice Lands to understand that sentiment completely. Unlike the rolling hills of Elmshire, that burgeoned with halfling holes, or the elven city of Lananore, that perched on alabaster cliffs and hid walkways and bridges beneath glittering waterfalls, the Ice Lands were merciless and unwelcoming.

As they continued down the road that was flanked by rows of shops, Lira recognized the chandler on one side, strings of tallow candles swagged across the front window, and the tinker's shop tucked beside it, its windows murky with dust and a closed sign hanging in the door.

Sass put a hand on her arm. "Do you smell that?"

Lira drew in a breath as she followed the dwarf's gaze to the shop on the other side of the road. The door was thrown open, which explained why the air was heavy with the aroma of fresh bread. "The baker, Pip Brambleheart." She remembered the baker's brother, Fennigan, or Fenni, who owned the cheese shop next door to the bakery. "And the cheese monger."

"Halflings?" Sass asked, her tone hopeful.

Lira nodded. Halflings were known for their skills as bakers and cheese mongers. Not only did they relish eating the most delicious breads and cheeses, they loved to make them.

"We need some bread and cheese, don't we?" Sass was already heading for the shops, her step quick.

They did. Even if she tried her hand at baking, Lira had no intention of attempting the rustic loaves and morning buns that were Pip's trademark. And they could hardly buy a loaf of bread without some tangy cheese to go along with it.

Lira followed Sass into the shop, tipping her head to the smiling gnome leaving with a basket hooked in the crook of her arm. Inside, the back wall was lined with shelves jammed tight with baskets turned on their sides, and those were, in turn, crowded with flour-dusted loaves. The yeasty aroma was pungent enough to make her swoon. Lira's stomach gurgled with a sharp reminder that she hadn't eaten in, well, when had she last eaten?

"Bless the stars!"

Lira couldn't see where the voice had come from, although she tracked the sound to the pine counter. Then a head popped up, revealing the baker himself. Although Pip's hair was decidedly grayer than when she'd last seen him, he looked much the same. The same oven-warmed pink cheeks, the same squat nose, the same dimple in his chin, the same flour dusting his face and hair. Even the forest-green waistcoat under his burlap apron looked like the one he'd worn so many years ago.

"Mr. Brambleheart." Lira smiled at him as memories flooded back —him sneaking her a warm morning bun or passing her a knobby loaf of bread and insisting she give it to her gran as thanks for her sharing a recipe. "It's nice to see you again."

He bustled from behind the counter, taking her hands in his small, calloused ones that were as warm as the loaves he sold. "You can call me Pip now that you're all grown up."

From this angle, Lira could see that his wiry hair was speckled with bits of uncooked dough and perhaps honey glaze.

He peered up at Lira, his eyes watering. "And look how you've grown. Your gran..." He sniffed and dropped her hands after squeezing them, hurrying back behind the counter. "Well, enough of that. What can I get you now that you've finally come home?"

Lira wanted to tell him that she wasn't home for good, that she hadn't decided if she would stay or not, that she wasn't sure if she could, but she couldn't bear to say any of that. Instead, she waved a hand at Sass. "My friend and I are helping fix up The Tusk & Tail."

Pip's already large eyes widened. "Are you now? Well, that's a job."

"You said it." Sass eyed the tray of golden-brown buns lined up at the ready on the counter. "And we've worked up an appetite."

Pip nodded as if he'd been given a particularly delightful assignment, and he rubbed his plump hands together briskly. "You'll need some honey-drizzled buns and at least one loaf of malted brown bread."

"And you can't eat brown bread without a wedge of farm cheese."

Lira twisted her head to see Fenni ambling over from the door between the two shops as he wrapped a triangle of buttery-yellow cheese in paper. His brown, brushed-velvet waistcoat hugged his belly, the wooden buttons clinging valiantly to their buttonholes. Like his brother, his hair had grayed over the years. Unlike his brother, his clothes were pristine, his hair was brushed neatly to one side, and it didn't contain bits of food.

"It's nice to see you too, Mr.— "

"Fenni," he said with a broad smile. "You know, I always knew you'd come back." He flicked his gaze to his brother. "Didn't I always say that, Pip?"

Pip bobbled his head. "He always said that."

Sass produced a net bag Lira hadn't even known she'd brought, tucking the proffered items snugly inside without question. Lira fished out the copper bits, but the halfling brothers waved her off.

"Your coin isn't good here. Not today, at least."

Lira looked from one brother to the other but they both flapped chubby hands at her. She sighed. "Thank you. I know we'll enjoy it."

"Hurry back," Pip said as the brothers waved them off, stepping outside the shops to watch them walk away.

Sass patted the bag. "I can tell already that my waist will not thank them."

As they passed the next shop, Sass inhaled sharply. Lira cut her gaze to the hats displayed in the glass storefront and then to the dwarf's curly hair she contained in a tight braid. "The haberdasher?"

"Fabric," she said. "Have you seen the moth holes in the tavern curtains?"

Lira hadn't noticed curtains at all. "Why don't I let you handle that while I pop into the shop next door?"

Sass craned her neck, her brow crinkling. "The apothecary?" Then she twitched one shoulder. "Suit yourself."

As Sass disappeared into the haberdasher, Lira pivoted to the apothecary and walked straight into someone so tall and barrel-chested she staggered back.

Hands grabbed her arms and steadied her before she stumbled, and Lira's hand went instinctively to her waist where no blades were hooked. Hells, why had she left her daggers behind?

"Apologies."

The deep voice was soft and steady, nothing like Lira would have expected from such a large creature. She tipped her head back. Correction, a large orc wearing the armor of a guardsman. His dark eyes held hers even as he released his grip on her arms.

"It's not your fault," Lira said, her breath suddenly quick. "I didn't look before I turned."

He didn't reply, but he didn't look away either. As Lira stared at the orc who was surprisingly handsome, a flicker of recognition tickled the recesses of her brain. Had she encountered him in one of her quests? She didn't remember a hot orc guardsman being stationed in the village when she'd lived there, and she felt sure she would have remembered *him*.

"Have you newly arrived in Wayside?" he asked, his black eyes never leaving hers for an instant.

Lira bobbed her head, wondering how much she should tell him. If he was asking in his role as guardsman, she didn't want to appear suspicious. "I'm helping out at The Tusk & Tail."

This prompted a quiver of his dark brows, but he made no comment. He only grunted and stepped aside as another guardsman, this one a tall woman with gold hair piled on top of her head in a messy bun, strode across the street toward him.

Lira cast a final glance at the orc, whose gaze still lingered on her, before ducking through the door to the apothecary, the bell overhead tinkling to announce her arrival. She stepped inside the dimly lit shop as her racing pulse steadied itself and her eyes adjusted to the dim interior.

How had the guardsman unsettled her so profoundly by only uttering a handful of words? Maybe that was why he'd affected her so. His penetrating gaze had done the job of an entire conversation and had left her heart pounding and her mouth dry.

Lira gave herself a mental shake. Getting rattled was not something a rogue could afford. Then she drew in a breath and was quickly grounded by the familiarity of the quiet shop.

A single sconce flickered by the door and illuminated the dark wood shelves lining the walls, the compartments holding black-glass bottles with elegantly calligraphed paper labels boasting their contents: worm wort, bone powder, newt eyes, belladonna. While the bakery had teemed with the aroma of yeast and sugar, warmth spilling from its doors, this shop was hushed and cool and smelled of a thousand different oils and potions all melded together. The cacophony of scents should have been an assault on her nose, but instead it was as comforting as a warm blanket hugging her shoulders.

The jingle of the bell drifted into silence as the door closed behind her. Lira's gaze fell on the olive-skinned woman behind the counter. Her black hair was shot through with silver strands that glinted in the candlelight and her green eyes were as shrewd as they'd ever been.

"Hello, Iris."

# Eight

IRIS KETTLEWICK RAISED her head and stopped twirling a strand of hair around her finger, before sliding a pair of half-moon spectacles down her long nose and scrutinizing Lira over them for a beat. Then her face cracked into a smile. "Lira!"

The woman hurried around the counter, her voluminous patch-work skirt billowing around her legs. She pulled Lira into a hug, the scent of herbs and fragrant oils a pungent cloud that clung to her like always. The aroma slammed into Lira, transporting her right back to being a young girl visiting Iris's dark and mysterious shop. She breathed in the memories and sank into the embrace.

But the apothecary released Lira as briskly as she'd snatched her into her arms, her smile slipping as she inventoried her at arm's length. "You've fared well then, love?"

Lira produced her own smile, even if it felt tight. "Still alive."

Iris snorted as she put her hands on her hips. "I suppose that's the important thing." The woman whipped around, her skirt following a beat behind as she returned to her counter and waved for Lira to follow. "Are you here for a visit or back for good?"

Lira didn't know how to answer that. When she'd set out for Wayside after wandering aimlessly for months, she hadn't thought about how long she'd stay or if there was even anything left for her in the village. She'd returned because it had once felt safe, it had once been home. But really, she hadn't thought before she'd started walking, her feet leading her back as if pulled by an unseen force.

She thought about what was buried under the tavern. Maybe that last part was true.

"I don't know," she finally answered, resting her hands on the polished counter.

Iris made a knowing sound in the back of her throat. "You're not with your companions any longer?"

Lira gave a curt shake of her head, hoping the woman would leave it at that.

She did.

"Well, then." Iris pushed her spectacles to the top of her head, tamping down some of her unruly curls and exposing more of the silver. "I suppose this calls for tea."

She nudged aside thick brown curtains covering a doorway, holding one side up just high enough for a person to slip through. "Come on, then. You know where I keep the goodies."

Lira didn't need to be told twice. It felt like no time had passed since Iris had first invited her into the shop's back room, but she felt just as special slipping through the curtains this time as she had when she was a girl.

Ducking her head, she passed under Iris's arm and straightened on the other side, her breath instinctively catching. Here the scent of potions was faint, replaced by the smells of old paper and crumbling leather from the hundreds of books that lined the walls and reached to the ceiling. A large, round table dominated the middle of the room, the surface cluttered with open books, empty teacups, and plates that held nothing but crumbs.

Iris stopped short when she followed Lira, resting one hand on her hip as she shook a finger in the air. "Who ate the last of my breakfast?"

Lira held her breath, her gaze sweeping the back room that was as large as the front one. A pair of overstuffed, brocade chairs hunched in the far corner, angled toward a side table that was also a jumble of books. In the other corner was a towering, gilded cage with a curved top and multiple swinging perches inside, all of them empty. Above them, a pair of skylights let in sunbeams that bounced off the gold-embossed spines of the books.

"I didn't think I'd have company today," Iris said before a flock of tiny, winged creatures emerged from within the shelves and started fluttering overhead.

Lira laughed as she watched the iridescent wings flash shades of green and pink as some soared back to their cage and others continued to dart from shelf to shelf.

Iris shook her head, but her smile was pleased. "They remember you."

"I'd hope so." Lira held up a finger so one of the bookwyrms could land on it. "I used to sneak them enough of my cookies."

Iris snorted a laugh but wagged a finger at the tiny creature perched on Lira's finger that looked like a cross between a baby dragon and a hummingbird. "If they get too fat they won't be able to fly to the top shelves."

"Then maybe someone shouldn't leave her breakfast out."

Iris slid her gaze to Lira, her eyes flashing amusement and then softening as she watched the bookwyrm nuzzle Lira's hand. "You've been missed, love."

Lira focused on the creature balanced on her finger to keep tears from springing to her eyes. She'd kept herself busy pulling off heists and quests so she wouldn't have time to miss the village, her friends here, the bookwyrms she'd adored as a child, her gran. But it hadn't taken long for her to remember all the things she'd tried to forget.

"The shop looks like it's doing well." She managed a smile as she wiggled her finger. "These little guys seem to be doing their job of keeping your books clean—if not organized."

Iris sighed. "Bookwyrms eat dust, they don't alphabetize."

Lira didn't remind the woman that the bookwyrms only existed in her backroom because they were the result of an experiment gone wrong. Luckily, the errant magic had created creatures with an innate appetite for dust and the ability to nibble it from the spines and pages of books without doing any damage. As far as Lira knew, Iris hadn't tried any magic spells since.

Iris left Lira as the bookwyrms started to land on her shoulders, slipping through an archway leading even farther back that wasn't covered with a curtain. "Good, the tea is still hot." She returned holding a copper kettle and pulled two floral teacups from a shelf. She poured steaming liquid into them and rested the kettle on a trivet waiting on the wood table. "Now where did the cookie tin go?"

Lira lowered her hand so the bookwyrm could hop off it and onto a pile of books. Then she picked up one of the teacups and blew on the steaming surface. "If I gave you a list of ingredients, could you make me a blend?"

Iris cocked her head. "A potion or a poultice?"

"A tea."

The older woman glanced at her own cup. "A tea?"

"I drank a tea blend when I was in The Wild Reach called chai." Lira shivered as she thought of the desolate lands that flanked a stormy cove called Siren's Refuge, but warmth suffused her as she remembered the spicy, milky tea that the gnomes had offered them.

"Does it have powers?"

"Not beyond warming you from tip to tail."

Iris twisted a curl around one finger. "Give me your list, and I'll find what you need."

Lira took a sip of her tea, the drink comforting, even if it was bland. "I take it your cures are still evading the notice of anyone who might object to the use of magic?"

Iris sniffed at this. "My cures aren't potions, even if they are impressively effective. Anyway, magic isn't outlawed."

Of course, it couldn't be, since some creatures naturally possessed elemental magic. Like elves, Lira thought even as she tried not to feel bitter that her elf blood wasn't enough to give her powers. Powers that would have been helpful many times over the years.

"Teaching it is, though," Lira reminded her. That was why the magical guilds had been disbanded and spell books had slipped into legend. The lairds of The Known Lands had feared the growing spread of dark magic among the mages and the potential of the magical guilds to wield more power than them. In a single proclamation, they'd disbanded the guilds, outlawed the teaching of magic, and confiscated every spell book they could find. Old mages laid low and new mages could not be trained, so their kind became as rare as the enchanted stones they'd used and potions they'd concocted.

But, as with everything forbidden, it could not be snuffed out. It only became shrouded in more secrecy, its practice the stuff of whispers and rumors. Lira glanced around her. Or back rooms.

Iris stiffened, straightening so that she looked even taller than she was. "What I taught you wasn't magic, either. It was practical." She cut a glance toward the bookwyrm cage. "Besides, I had to teach you better technique after I caught you trying to pick the lock and let them out."

Lira remembered that. She also remembered the hours she'd spent with Iris learning to pick locks, disarm traps, and even throw daggers. "Why did my gran let you do it?"

This flustered the woman, and she clattered her teacup onto the table. "I was her dearest friend. She knew I only wanted the best for you." She paused, not meeting Lira's gaze. "And she knew you would never want to run a farm like she did. Not when you were…"

"Part elf," Lira finished for her.

Iris raised her head defiantly. "Your gran knew you were special, and not only because your father was an elf."

Lira had never felt special. She'd felt different. How could she believe she was special when she hadn't been able to save her friend? But that wasn't something she wanted to tell Iris. Not yet.

"Running a farm isn't so bad," Lira said, thinking about gathering eggs from the hens and helping her gran churn butter. Things had been simple, but they'd been happy.

"But you had to leave and see what was beyond Wayside to know that."

Lira hated how the truth of that statement stung. Before she could ask Iris more, the bell in the main shop trilled and a familiar voice called out, "Lira? You here?"

She had forgotten about Sass.

## Nine

IRIS SWUNG her head to Lira. "I thought you told me you weren't with your companions."

"I'm not. This is someone I met at the tavern."

Furrows joined the worry lines on Iris's forehead. "The tavern? You went to The Tusk & Tail?"

"I did, but what in the hells happened to it?" Lira asked in lieu of an answer, hoping Iris wouldn't think to question why she'd sought out the tavern before visiting her. "When I left, it was the heart of the village. And since when is a wyvern the village reeve?"

Iris gave her a sad smile. "You left a while ago."

"Hello?" Sass bellowed, her voice getting closer. "Anyone here?"

Iris walked to the curtains, holding the two sides as she turned back to Lira. "Why is she looking for you?"

How had Lira been talking with Iris all this time and not thought to mention where she was staying or that she was roommates with a dwarf. "It's a long story, but the crux of it is I convinced Durn that his tavern needed fixing, and I was the one to do it—along with a female dwarf named Sass." She took a breath. "I'm staying at The Tusk & Tail, and she's my roommate."

Iris blinked at her and then a burst of laughter escaped her lips. "I see you've honed your skills of coercion."

"It didn't take much convincing." Lira omitted telling her that both the tavernkeep and the dwarf had been desperate.

Iris twitched one shoulder. "Spoken like a true rogue." Then her smile faded. "Do you trust her?"

Well, that was the question, wasn't it? Lira had learned not to trust anyone when she'd been tricking her way into castles, sweet-talking the keys off jailers, and convincing her marks to tell her their most precious secrets. She hadn't been someone to trust, so she hadn't dared trust. But now she was back home, and the rules were different. Weren't they?

She'd met Sass in the middle of a robbery, but it had been a pitiful one. Like she'd told her, the dwarf was obviously not a trained thief, and it was clear she didn't excel at deception. What dwarf could ever claim stealth? Lira's gut told her that Sass was exactly who she claimed to be. Not only that, but the dwarf had proven to be a hard worker, which wasn't nothing in Lira's book.

"We can trust her," she finally told Iris. "She's traveled all the way from The Ice Lands looking for a different life than mining."

Iris's brow hitched higher on her forehead. "I see you still have a soft spot for outsiders."

Lira thought of her crew, each member an outsider in their own way. Then she thought of herself straddling the elf and human worlds. "Is that so bad?"

"Not at all." Iris reached for her hand and gave it a squeeze before she held open the curtains. "She's in here, pet. Come on back."

Lira couldn't see Sass, but she could hear the dwarf's tentative steps. Then she remembered how ominous the apothecary was in the front, all flickering candlelight and murky jars of strange concoctions. Did Iris still keep the scorpion eyeballs in a jar? She definitely had a jar of beetle husks.

"It's okay," Lira called out. "I really am back here."

Sass appeared under Iris's arm, but she didn't have to duck to enter. In response to the new arrival, the bookwyrms took to the air in a flurry of fluttering wings and excited chirps.

"What in the sweet, simmering cauldrons are those?"

"Bookwyrms," Iris answered before Lira could. "They keep my books dust-free." She held out a hand to Sass. "I'm Iris."

Sass absently extended her own hand while she tipped back her head. "Sarsaparilla but everyone calls me Sass." She blinked rapidly. "I've never heard of bookwyrms."

"They're my own creation."

"Accidental creation," Lira muttered.

"They don't look much like worms," Sass said. "Are you sure a dragon didn't hump a pixie?"

"They started out as worms." Iris gave the creatures a motherly smile. "That's when I named them. Then they sprouted wings."

"You're the only one of us who's probably seen a dragon," Lira reminded Sass. "They're only found in The Ice Lands."

Sass didn't take her eyes off the flying creatures. "I've only seen one dragon, and it was only the tail as it was flying away. They're shy ones, dragons."

Lira had never thought of dragons being shy, but Sass was the only one of them with firsthand knowledge. Even though she'd traveled beyond the long wall to go to The Wild Reach and even ventured into a dwarf mine, she'd never come close to spotting a dragon.

"Would you like some tea as you admire my bookwyrms?" Iris moved past Sass, her skirts flouncing.

Sass dragged her gaze to the apothecary. "Thank you."

Iris plucked another teacup from a shelf and poured tea into it from the kettle. She handed it to the dwarf. "Lira tells me you're her new roommate."

Sass took the cup but shifted under Iris's gaze, cutting her eyes to Lira. "What else did she tell you?"

Lira took a sip of her cooled tea. "Only that we're both helping Durn get the tavern back on its feet."

Sass's shoulders lowered a touch. "That's about the long and short of it. She's taking the kitchen, and I'm taking the great room."

Lira glanced at Sass's burgeoning net bag. "Did you find what you needed next door?"

Sass gave the bag a gentle shake. "The shopkeeper had some fabric he was trying to move, so I got us a deal."

"It sounds like Durn got the best deal when he found you two." Iris shot Lira a pointed look, which she ignored.

Sass slurped her tea, and one of the bookwyrms glided down and landed tentatively on her shoulder.

Iris gave Sass an appreciative nod. "He likes you, pet."

"They took forever to warm up to me." Lira crossed her arms and narrowed her eyes at the tiny creature.

"You were a child," Iris said. "And children are too unpredictable and brash for tiny creatures."

Before Lira could argue that there was hardly anyone as brash and unpredictable as a dwarf, Sass cleared her throat. "How do you know each other, aside from being from the same village?"

Lira didn't need to exchange a look with Iris to know what to say. "Iris was my gran's best friend, so in a way, she helped raise me."

Iris's cheeks colored. "An apothecary is a wondrous place for a child."

"Especially one that has a whole bunch of these guys flying around," Sass said as she stroked one finger down the bookwyrm's green neck.

Lira took another sip of tea. "Speaking of winged creatures, tell me about Wayside's new reeve."

Iris's expression darkened. "I can't tell you how he did it, but Rygor showed up at the castle, wormed his way into the laird's good graces, and then convinced the old man that he was the best one to collect taxes from villagers who'd been holding onto more than their share."

Irritation flared inside Lira. "People in Wayside have never withheld coin from the laird."

Iris shrugged. "What better way to be sure than appoint a wyvern who can sniff out gold?"

"He thinks Durn is holding out on him," Sass said. "He said that he can smell the gold in the tavern."

Iris laughed. "If Durn had gold, the tavern wouldn't be crumbling around him."

Lira's cheeks heated as she thought of the wyvern's accusation. "Is Rygor as scary as he looks?"

"I wouldn't cross him. Not even the guardsmen can challenge his authority."

Iris met Lira's gaze, and for a moment, Lira wondered if her mentor suspected her secret. Then she brushed the idea from her mind. Iris was an apothecary, not a seer.

She put her teacup in its saucer with a clatter. "We should probably get going. We still need to get some supplies at the marketplace."

Iris made a clicking sound in the back of her throat and all the bookwyrms fluttered in a wide arc around the high ceiling and through the beams of sunlight before swirling down like a tightly spinning wind and swooping into the cage. She clicked the door closed and smiled at Sass.

"Lira says you're to be trusted, so I will trust you not to mention what you saw here."

Sass inclined her head. "I didn't see a thing but a lot of glass jars that smell funny."

Iris grinned before she shooed them both out, but it was only when she and Sass were standing outside the shop that Lira realized she'd forgotten to ask Iris the question that had been consuming her since she'd left Wayside. How had an apothecary learned all those rogue skills she'd taught her so many years ago?

# Ten

NOT ONLY WAS Sass's bag overflowing with swaths of fabric and loaves of bread wrapped in paper, Lira's arms were full of supplies that Boden had sold them for a fair price. He'd taken a bit of convincing that the pair were truly from the tavern, but then he'd recognized Lira and reluctantly accepted her tale of returning to Wayside. She was getting so good at telling it that she almost believed her own words.

Lira shifted the sack of flour on her hip as they walked back to The Tusk & Tail. She noticed Sass eyeing the jar of honey she held in her free hand. "I didn't think dwarves had much of a sweet tooth."

Sass choked back a laugh. "Shows how little you know dwarves."

Then she added. "But I got more of a taste for sweet stuff when I ventured below the long wall. Humans can't get enough of it."

"Not just humans." Lira tipped her head at the blacksmith and wheelwright shop across the stream. "The orcs who work there have a known addiction to Serena's honey, and they loved my gran's cakes."

"Seems like everyone loved your gran."

Lira's throat tightened. "They did, and they loved her baking. I don't know if I have a chance of living up to her legacy."

"I get that. If I'd stayed in the Ice Lands, I never could have been as good of a miner as my brothers. Not that I wanted to mine. But it's hard having family expectations hanging over you. Is that one of the reasons you left?"

Lira rarely spoke about why she left, but for some reason, it was easy to talk to Sass. "Once my gran passed, nothing felt right. I could only see what wasn't here anymore. I thought if I left, I wouldn't miss her so much, I wouldn't be reminded of her every minute."

Sass nodded and the two fell silent as they reached the door to the tavern, the sign still dangling overhead by one hinge even though there was no more wind to make it creak as it swung. Before Lira could push open the door, Sass put a hand on it.

"There's something I don't get."

Lira drew in a breath. "What?"

"You seem to know everyone in the village and they all like you. It seems like a nice place. I get why you left, but why stay away for so long? And why come back now?"

Lira should have known this was coming. Just like she should have known that returning would stir up all sorts of old memories. She hadn't thought about any of it in so long that dredging up the past felt like roiling up muck that had been well buried.

"The crew I joined kept busy, and we kept moving. I've been from end to end of the Ageless Lands, and I've even been as far as the Skittering Islands. I guess I got so busy I let myself forget."

Sass's expression didn't change, which meant she was waiting for Lira to tell her why she was back, which wasn't going to happen.

"All crews disband eventually, and that's what mine did. I didn't come back right away, but after a few months I decided it was time to come home."

Lira stuck as close to the truth as possible. Her crew had disbanded. She had spent some time traveling alone before she'd decided to set off for Wayside. She had been drawn back to her home, but it hadn't been because she'd missed it. At least, she hadn't thought so at the time. The sweet ache of familiarity she'd felt since she'd been back had been a surprise.

"So, you're staying?" Sass asked.

Before that morning, if she'd said yes she would have been lying. But strolling through the village and seeing those who'd been such a big part of her childhood made it hard to imagine moving on anytime soon. Besides, she was as safe in Wayside as she was anywhere, and since returning, she hadn't felt the sense of foreboding that had dogged her since Malek's death. "For the time being."

Sass hitched the net bag higher on her shoulder. "Good. Me too." She inclined her head at the tavern. "This place might not be much but it's better than sleeping under a tree."

Lira gave her a crooked grin. "Depends on the tree."

Sass was laughing as they shoved open the door and walked into The Tusk & Tail. Even though the pair had spent the morning cleaning, the place still reeked of damp and stale ale.

"I should have opened the windows when we left." Sass waved a hand in front of her face. "I think I got used to the smell when we were inside."

"I'll look for some soap as soon as I get these supplies unloaded." Lira headed for the kitchen.

"Don't worry yourself." Sass followed her through the swinging doors and dumped her armload of supplies on the newly cleared table. "I'll find it. You focus on the cooking."

"There's no rush. I'm sure no one's expecting me to have the tavern's kitchen up and running again so soon."

"Don't be so sure about that," Sass said as she opened the lower cabinet doors and began rummaging around. "Folks might come sooner than we think."

Lira set the sacks of flour and sugar on the table and then arranged the still-cool block of butter next to the bottle of cream she'd been so pleased to find. Then she let Sass's words sink in and she turned. "What do you mean?"

"Just that I might have mentioned your baking to a few people in the market." Sass's voice was muffled as she stuck her head into a cabinet.

"But you've never tasted my baking."

Sass straightened, holding a bar of soap that had seen better days. "You said you could bake. I believe you."

"But I haven't baked in ages," Lira's words spilled out in splutters. "I don't know if I even remember how, or if it'll be any good."

Sass waved away her protests. "I'm sure it's like swinging an axe. Once you know, you never forget."

Lira was sure that baking was much more nuanced than swinging an axe, but she also didn't want to argue with the dwarf. Not when she seemed to have such blind faith in her. No one had trusted her so fully other than her crew. Truth be told, she missed that.

She pushed aside those thoughts and managed a smile. "I suppose if you can get rid of the smell out there, I can figure out the food part."

Sass held up the soap. "I'm pretty sure a troll died in the great room at some point, so you might have the easier task."

Then Sass pushed through the swinging doors and was gone, leaving Lira to stare at her ingredients, trying to remember her gran's recipe for meat pie, and wondering if she could trade her job for the de-trolling.

<h1 style="text-align:center">Eleven</h1>

IT WASN'T until the afternoon that Sass appeared in the doorway of the kitchen, escaped wisps of hair curling around her face. "I'm heading out for a bit." She tucked her shirt into her pants with one hand. "Thought I'd pop into the carpenter's shop across the way."

Lira wanted to ask her why they needed a carpenter, although the answer was that there were a hundred things in The Tusk & Tail that needed fixing, but none of them were worth sparing coin on, according to the tightfisted tavernkeep. Lira suspected the man had run his business half into the ground from stinginess, and didn't have the silver even if he had thought new benches or chairs that didn't wobble were a necessity.

"I'll be here." Lira had made quick work of rearranging the pantry and storing her new ingredients, but she now had a work table filled with a bag of sugar hard enough make a fine weapon, bundles of herbs that had dried for so long they were nearly dust, and a sack of flour crawling with weevils.

Sass made a face at the kitchen that had seemed to relapse into its previous state of disarray due to the emptied pantry. "No one will blame you for taking a break."

Lira started to shake her head and say she didn't need one, but Sass had already left the kitchen.

"Hmph." Lira rested her hands on her hips as she sized up the work she'd done, wishing she had more to show for it. Then she stilled, listening for a minute to the absolute solitude of the tavern.

Sass had gone, Durn was most likely sleeping in his upstairs room, and there were no patrons to mention.

Lira glanced around, despite standing alone in the kitchen. It was as good a time as any, she thought. If the tavern started doing better, she wouldn't get many more times when she had the place to herself.

She walked on her toes so as not to make a sound, even though reason told her it was wasted effort. Old habits died hard, and Lira's rogue instincts snapped back into place the moment she slipped sideways through the swinging doors and hesitated outside the entrance to the cellar.

This time would be better. This time she wouldn't be caught off guard by the wall.

She cut her gaze to the stairs and thought of the illumination stone upstairs. She'd tucked it back into its pouch and jammed it deep beneath her mattress. By the time she retrieved it, Sass could be back or Durn could hear her moving about upstairs and emerge from his room.

She couldn't spare the time.

She changed course, taking just enough steps into the great hall to spy a lantern behind the bar. With one of the long matches placed near it, Lira lit the wick and made for the cellar door.

Remembering her last trip down, she held the rough wood of the staircase banister as she took measured steps. The yellow light from the lantern bounced off the walls, making for an easier descent, although her heart hammered just as erratically.

The fetid smell hadn't improved since her last visit, and she pressed her lips together as she took shallow breaths. Passing the baskets of rotten food reminded her that the kitchen and great room weren't the only places that needed some elbow grease, although she dreaded what she might find down there. She only hoped Sass hadn't been right about the lingering odor of dead troll.

When she reached the bottom, Lira held the lantern in front of her as she made quick work of crossing to the farthest corner. The scuttling creatures were too fast for her to see, and she told herself that they weren't anything bigger than the insects she'd encountered upstairs.

"Liar," she whispered as she located the correct spot in the stone wall. Now that there was no shock at finding her hiding spot walled up, Lira knelt and placed the lantern on the dirt floor.

She ran her fingers across the smooth stones, searching for any gap in the mortar. There was none.

She pressed on the corner stone, hoping it might give way or even shift under her pressure. Nothing.

Cursing under her breath, Lira stood. There would be no budging the rocks without a tool of some kind—or several. She bit back a groan. And it would not be quiet.

She thought about what was behind the wall. For the briefest moment, she questioned if it was still where she'd buried it, but that thought was easily dismissed. She knew it hadn't been moved from its hiding place. Even though it made no sense, she could feel its presence. Not to mention the fact that her stash was most certainly what the wyvern had detected.

A shiver slid down her back as she remembered the dark-winged creature. Durn's protests wouldn't hold him off forever. Not if he was as hungry for treasure as she suspected.

No, she needed to work fast if she was going to recover what was hers. Lira gritted her teeth with fresh determination as she wiped her hands on the front of her apron. What she needed was a plan. "And a team."

This wasn't the first time she missed her crew, and it wasn't the first time she regretted leaving them.

A creak from overhead sent a fine mist of dust over her, warning her that someone was walking above.

Lira hurried back to the stairs and headed up, keeping the lantern close to her so it wouldn't rattle as it swung. The cellar door was open a crack. Had she left it ajar—again?

She nudged the door open and slipped out, pressing it closed behind her and releasing a breath. If Sass was back, she didn't hear her heavy step or distinctive humming.

Stepping toward the kitchen doors, Lira stumbled back as they flew open, and the wyvern emerged. He stopped before walking into her, his black eyes hardening.

"Who are you?"

Lira straightened, summoning all her powers of persuasion and charm. "I'm Durn's new..." her gaze went to the freshly scrubbed kitchen, "cook."

Rygor's wings shifted beneath his cloak. "Durn doesn't serve food."

"He used to." Lira bit back the urge to remind the wyvern that he was new to Wayside. "He's decided to do it again in hopes of bringing in more business."

The creature's nostrils flared as if he was trying to detect deception from her. Finally, he huffed out a hot breath that smelled of ash. "I suppose all dying things have a few final gasps in them."

Lira pressed her lips together to keep from responding.

Rygor stepped closer, looming over her as his gaze flicked to her ears. "I have my eye on this place, which means I now have my eye on you, elf."

Lira's heart pounded as she managed a tight smile. "You're always welcome to stop by for supper once we're serving."

He released a hiss as he swept past her, his footfall heavy as he stormed from the tavern. Lira didn't breathe easily until the door thunked behind him. She was still standing outside the kitchen when Sass rushed up to her.

"Was that the wyvern I saw leaving?"

Lira nodded without speaking.

Sass's brown eyes were huge as she stared at the front door and then Lira. "What did he want?"

Lira assumed he'd been snooping around in search of the gold he was convinced Durn was hiding, and the thought of him walking out even a few seconds earlier and catching her coming from the cellar made her knees wobble. She leaned one hand against the rough wood plank of the wall. "He wanted to know why I'm here."

Sass groaned. "Durn says he has no money and then we start fixing up the place. No wonder the wyvern's suspicious."

"Maybe we should tell him that Durn's just as poor as he claims to be, and he isn't even paying us."

"And admit that we're here because fixing up a tavern beats getting thrown in a dungeon?" Sass shook her head. "No, thank you."

Lira remembered the wyvern's beady, glittering eyes. Just like she'd known instantly that Sass wasn't a deadly threat, she was certain that Rygor was.

# Twelve

LIRA TRIED NOT to let Rygor's appearance in the tavern rattle
her, but it was a stark reminder that she needed to be careful. Like he'd
told her, he was watching.

She and Sass decamped to their respective domains again, but she
could hear her through the swinging half doors that had wide openings
above and below. She was used to Sass humming and was glad that at
least the dwarf wasn't letting the wyvern bother her. Then she realized
Sass was doing more than humming. That wasn't a surprise. Dwarves
were known for mining ballads and rowdy drinking songs. But the next
time Lira got close enough to the doors to catch a few notes, she jerked
up. Was Sass singing sea shanties?

*There once was a ship went out to sea,*
*The name of the ship was the Fiddle Fi Fee,*
*The storms came up, the ship went down,*
*Lo, the Fiddle Fi Fee was gone.*

Sass's voice dropped to a throaty baritone on the last note, and Lira had to slap a hand across her mouth to keep a laugh from bursting forth. Why would a dwarf from The Ice Lands who hadn't grown up near the sea know sea shanties? Then she remembered that Sass had passed through Eldu on her way here and worked at a seaside bar. Apparently she'd encountered enough sailors to leave sounding like an old salt.

Soon enough, the sound of Sass's shanties became a comforting background to the scrape of the broom across wood planks, the clang of pots bobbing in soapy water, and the rattle of the open shutters in the breeze. So, when they stopped, Lira noticed their absence.

She stepped from the kitchen, expecting to see Sass taking a break. But instead of having her feet up and her broom quiet, Sass was using the bristly end to direct a pair of ogres who were hauling something heavy and unwieldy between them.

"Don't drop it," Sass called over their grunts and shuffling feet. "These may be castoffs, but I don't want them damaged."

"What in the hells is this?"

Sass spared Lira a brief glance as she continued to direct the ogres across the great room where the tables and chairs had been shoved aside. "Don't worry. I didn't spend any coin."

"Good, because we don't have any."

After more lumbering from the ogres and a final lurch, the sizable object draped in a tattered drop cloth thudded next to the hearth. A cloud of dust puffed up, and Lira wasn't sure if it was from the dingy cloth or what was beneath. When Sass snatched off the fabric to reveal a hulking chair upholstered in a faded brocade, she still wasn't sure.

"Ta da!" Sass waved a hand as if she'd just revealed something spectacular. Her arm holding the drop cloth fell as she caught Lira's expression. "What do you think?"

"It's a...chair."

"Nothing gets by you," Sass muttered before jutting out one hip. "Of course, it's a chair. I got it from the haberdasher. I wanted it to be a surprise."

"The haberdasher sells chairs?"

Sass huffed out a breath. "No, he was getting rid of them." She fluttered a hand toward the tavern door where the ogres had reappeared with what Lira assumed was a second chair, the massive piece of furniture swaying between them. "The previous owner was a more sizable woman." She held up a hand to her mouth and dropped her voice as if the ogres might be offended. "Part Goliath, according to Tinpin." She lowered her hand and raised her voice. "I thought we could use something to make the hearth a bit cozier. Someplace someone would want to settle in and stay for a while."

Lira eyed the second mammoth chair as it was dropped with a floor-shaking boom on the other side of the fireplace. "Someone big."

"Lots of big folks around here. Didn't you say the blacksmiths are orcs?"

Lira had to admit that the chairs didn't look too worse for wear, and she could imagine curling up on them with a good book and a cup of chai. "They don't look half bad in here."

Sass beamed, as if Lira had told her they were the most breathtaking chairs in the Known Lands. "I knew you'd like them."

"You're sure they didn't cost anything?"

Sass's brows knit together for a beat. "Nothing we'll miss." She swung her head to Lira, her braid flying behind her. "I might have told the haberdasher that he'd be welcome for supper once you get up and running." She jerked a thumb at the ogres. "Them too."

This startled Lira. "You're bribing folks with my food? Food you've never tasted?"

"You've got to have faith in something, right?" Sass shrugged. "I thought I'd start with you."

Lira didn't know what to say to that, but her throat was tight as she walked back to the kitchen.

# Thirteen

LIRA SWEPT the back of her hand across her forehead. It had taken two hard days—and two nights of collapsing into bed across from an equally exhausted and snoring Sass—but she had finally whipped the kitchen into shape, polishing all the pots and pans until they shone and scouring the surfaces until the distinctive aroma of citrus overtook the former smell of rot and mold. Even the soot-encrusted oven had been buffed clean, and Lira had the callouses on her hands to show for it.

Now it was time for the hard part. The kitchen was clean enough for her to start cooking. It had been a long time since she'd done more than warm food over a campfire. Her hands were more accustomed to lockpicks than measuring cups at this point. Not only that, but how much did she actually remember of her gran's recipes?

Lira closed her eyes, summoning visions of her gran's kitchen. The sticky dough beneath her fingers, the heft of the rolling pin, the flour drifting in the air like dust motes. If she concentrated hard enough, she could smell the yeast, the sugar, the aromatic spices that always tickled her nose.

She squeezed her eyes tight as she tried to remember the spidery script of her gran's recipes in the big leather book. She could recall the words on the yellowed parchment but couldn't remember the exact measurements.

The book. She needed the book.

"Well, you don't have it," she muttered, opening her eyes and reaching for the flour. "So, let's see how much you remember."

She slid a heavy earthenware bowl in front of her and scooped several cups of fine-milled flour into it. She eyeballed it and nodded. That looked right. Then she hacked off a chunk of the cool butter. After a pause, she reached for the two daggers she'd decided to keep tucked into her waistband after Rygor's unexpected appearance and cut the butter into the flour.

"See? You're better at this than those dull old knives," she whispered with a disdainful look at the nicked and warped knives she'd washed earlier.

A soft chittering sound in response made her spin around. There, perched on the open windowsill, sat a sleek, white stoat. It sat on its hind legs with dainty paws folded in front of its cylindrical body. His ears were rounded and pale pink on the insides, and his nose with a coal smudge on the white fur.

Lira stifled the urge to scream as she pressed a hand to her racing heart. She loved animals, she just wasn't used to them wandering into her kitchen.

His face had soft gray markings around the eyes that made it appear he was wearing a tiny mask, and the creature regarded her with what

Lira could have sworn was curiosity. Was he tame? He certainly didn't behave like a wild animal.

"Hello there." She held out a hand for him to sniff.

The fellow twitched his whiskers at her, his ink-drop eyes wide as they darted to the table and her bowl. He scampered to her, sniffed her hand, peered at the dough, and let out a gentle squeak. At least she seemed to have passed his test, although he seemed unusually curious about what was in the bowl.

"Come to critique my baking skills, have you?"

He made another series of sounds, which she could have sworn were an answer. She could have shooed him away, but she didn't mind the company. Besides, he appeared less hostile than Sass had when they'd first met, and that wasn't going so badly.

The stoat tilted his head, watching intently as Lira continued to mix ingredients. When she hesitated over adding more water to the dough, the creature made what she could have sworn was a disapproving sound in his throat.

Lira laughed as her hand hovered over the bowl. "Oh, so you're the expert, are you? Fine, we'll do it your way. But if this crust turns out to have the consistency of a crumpet, you'll have to answer to our patrons." She paused, remembering the tavern's sorry state and trickle of customers. "Well, to Sass and Durn, at least."

The creature rubbed his tiny white paws together in response, not at all bothered by Lira's empty threats. As if she could blame a dodgy crust on a woodland animal anyway.

As she worked, Lira found herself relaxing. The familiar motions of mixing and rolling out dough were soothing. She found the stoat— who was as close to tame as she'd ever seen a woodland creature— to be a reassuring presence.

"Is it because you're a rogue too?" She asked him, pointing to the pattern on his face that made a gray mask. "Is that why I don't mind having you here? Are we kindred spirits?"

It was more likely that she wasn't used to baking alone, and the creature's watchful gaze and occasional chittering helped distract her from the reminder that her gran wasn't there. She'd known baking alone would feel wrong and being in the kitchen would be when she missed her gran the most.

"But I'm not alone, am I?" she asked the creature. "I've got you."

He made a high, trilling sound as Lira chopped the meat and vegetables for the savory pie filling, which she took as wholehearted agreement.

Soon, there were several bubbling pots on the stove and the joint of beef was roasting in the oven. The rich scent of braised meat and caramelized onions mingled with the sharp, piney notes of rosemary. The aromas saturated the air and made the tavern's kitchen start to feel homey and inviting.

Lira dipped a spoon into one of the simmering fillings, blowing on it gently before tasting. Savory meat, perfectly seasoned, with just a hint of sweetness from the carrots and onions prompted Lira to close her eyes and sigh, relishing the flavors. It wasn't quite her gran's meat pie, but it was close enough for now.

She carefully spooned the mixture into the individual pie crusts and slid the pan into the oven, flinching as the heat blasted her in the face. That was the second batch in the oven, and the first pan of pies looked like they only needed a couple more minutes.

As she straightened, the swinging kitchen doors flung open. Sass strode in, holding her broom with tendrils of brown hair loose from her braid dangling over her forehead. Her brow was beaded with sweat, and her sleeves were shoved up past her elbows.

The stoat unfurled tiny wings that were as white as his fur and flew up to perch on one of the hanging copper pots. Once again, Lira suppressed the urge to yelp in surprise. Clearly, this was no normal stoat.

Sass's gaze swept across the room, landing on the winged creature, who was nibbling contentedly on a spare bit of raw pastry crust. "What in Grognick's beard is that?"

"That's my new assistant. Apparently he's not a normal stoat."

"I'd say not." Sass eyed the creature warily, taking in his distinctive mask-like markings. "Beasts in the kitchen don't seem right. Flying beasts in the kitchen are asking for trouble." She finally released a grudging breath. "I suppose he does look the part of a bandit though. Fits right in with us, doesn't he?"

Lira opened her mouth, but Sass held up a hand. "I might be from The Ice Lands, but I've seen a rogue before. You were too good at creeping into the tavern to be anything else."

Lira's cheeks warmed as she tossed the animal one of the carrot tops and he caught it deftly in one paw. "I've decided to call him Crumpet."

Sass put a hand on her hip as her eyes flared. "We're naming him?"

"He's a flying stoat. Of course, I'm giving him a name. He also has a real instinct for pastry."

"Magic?" Sass whispered the word as if the creature might transform into a dragon at any moment.

"Well, he does have wings."

Sass waved a finger at him. "And those things aren't normally winged?"

Lira had forgotten that The Ice Lands had very different animals. "I've never heard of one with wings."

This made Sass suck in a quick breath. "You don't suppose your apothecary friend made him like she made those baby book dragons?"

"The bookwyrms?" Lira shook her head. "If Crumpet was the result of one of Iris's spells gone wrong, why is he running wild? Besides, Iris hasn't cast any spells aside from the one that made the bookwyrms. She isn't a mage."

"If you say so."

The stoat nibbled away, unbothered by the two females discussing him.

"As long as you don't make up a pallet for him in our room." Sass held up a stubby finger. "I refuse to share close quarters with a beast, even if he is wee and even if he can fly."

"Agreed." Lira suspected that the tavernkeep would also object to a wild animal sharing their room. That was fine. She had a feeling

Crumpet was good at fending for himself, although she worried about him being seen by those who weren't as open to enchantments. "I'll make up a place for him in the kitchen."

Sass turned her attention fully to Lira. "While you were welcoming woodland creatures into the tavern, I was scrubbing those tables to within an inch of their lives. The floors have never been cleaner either, although I draw the line at mucking out the fireplace. There's soot in there from previous generations."

"Maybe that's where the dead troll went," Lira suggested, gaining her a dark look from Sass as the dwarf shuddered.

Lira wiped her hands on a dishrag and followed Sass from the kitchen and into the great room of the tavern. True to her word, Sass had scrubbed the tables until every sticky, congealed splotch of ale was gone and every stain buffed out. The floors gleamed and even the windows had been washed clean of the layers of grime and muck. No cobwebs hung in the corners and even the chandeliers had been polished. Gone was the pervasive odor of what Sass insisted was troll, replaced by a blend of soap and fresh air that wafted through the open windows.

Lira put a hand to the dwarf's shoulder. "Sass, the place is almost unrecognizable."

Sass shifted from one foot to the other, her cheeks mottling red. "Can't exactly serve food in a place that's filthy, can we?"

"Not if we want tips."

Sass grinned at her. "Tips? I hadn't thought about tips."

"I'll bet this job isn't looking like a bad deal now, is it?"

Sass bobbled her head from side to side. "I've had worse."

Lira gave her a teasing punch on the arm. "No time to rest on our laurels now. We have a dinner rush coming, well, hopefully one day."

As she bustled back to the kitchen, she hoped Sass's cleaning and her baking wouldn't be for naught. Maybe a rush was too much to hope for so soon. Truth be told, she'd settle for a trickle.

Then she pushed through the swinging doors and her stomach dropped.

# Fourteen

"BURNING one batch of pies isn't so bad." Sass reassured her as they both stood staring at the pan of charred meat pies, the free-standing sides golden brown but the tops as black as the belly of a cauldron.

Lira coughed and waved a dishrag at the smoke that had billowed from the oven. "It's not like we'll have so many patrons we'll need all these pies." She glanced at the other cooked meat pies cooling on the counter. "But I wanted to make sure I got the recipe right."

"I'm sure you did," Sass said through the hand covering her nose and mouth. "If it's the fault of anything, it's this old oven."

Lira eyed the stout, iron contraption that looked like it had seen better days. Even after a thorough cleaning, the iron was soot-stained with the door battered and warped. "We've only been here a couple of days. We can't ask for a new oven already."

"A new oven?"

The gruff voice made them both jump and whirl to find the tavern-keep in the kitchen doorway. He rubbed a beefy hand across his brow as he surveyed the room, his gaze sliding from the pies to the gleaming pots. Finally, he grunted. "You don't look like your gran, but I suppose you take after her in the kitchen."

Sass eyed her with curiosity but didn't speak, and Crumpet had vanished as soon as smoke had filled the room.

"I didn't think you two would be able to make much of it, but it looks like you did."

"I'm glad you approve." Lira swiped a strand of hair from her eyes. "We paid for some of the ingredients on credit—your credit."

"We ran out of copper bits," Sass added.

The man's eyes bulged, but before he could explode, the main door to the tavern thudded open.

"That would be the dinner crowd." Sass spun on one heel and left the kitchen.

Lira wasn't so sure if crowd would be the right word to use, especially since Sass promised she'd only told a handful of people, but she'd rather Durn not know that.

She waved a hand at him. "Shouldn't you be pulling pints?"

With another grumble uttered under his breath, the man stomped out.

Lira returned to her pies, touching her fingertips to the ones cooling. They were still too warm to cut, but she wouldn't have long to wait. If there were any takers. What if all her pies sat uneaten on the wooden counter? What if none of the dodgy drunks she'd seen in the tavern the night she'd arrived wanted to eat? What if her plan to rejuvenate the tavern failed? What if Durn kicked her out before she got what she'd come for?

Worry became doubt which settled like a rock in her gut. She rubbed her hands on the front of her apron and tried to convince herself that it would all work out.

"Lananore wasn't built in a day," she said, memories of the spectacular elven city making her breathe easier.

The sound of floor-shaking footfall beyond the kitchen was followed by the sound of chairs scraping. What in the hells was going on out there?

Before she could check, Sass popped her head back in. "Two meat pies, if you please."

Lira made no move toward the pies. "Really?"

Sass gave her a sly grin. "Yes, really. An orc guardsman and his cute friend, also a guard."

"And they want supper?"

Sass laughed. "You're having a tough time with this concept, aren't you?"

"Not at all."

"You want me to do it?" Sass asked, lingering in the door and giving the pies a meaningful look.

Lira gave herself a quick shake. "No. I've got it. Tell the guards their dinner is coming right out."

Sass disappeared again, and Lira busied herself with selecting the best-looking pies and sliding them onto heavy, pewter plates.

She picked up a plate in each hand then caught sight of her reflection in a polished copper pot. Her cheeks were flushed, her dark red hair escaping from her bun in wild tendrils. She looked a mess, but she also looked alive. Happy, even. How long had it been since Lira had considered herself truly happy?

Then it hit her like a punch to the gut. This wasn't supposed to happen. She wasn't here to make friends with a wandering dwarf or a flying stoat with a penchant for pie dough. She was here for one reason: to retrieve what she'd hidden. No attachments. No complications.

But as Lira headed toward the swinging doors leading to the tavern's great room, the plan didn't seem as appealing. The thought of leaving, of going back to a life of locks and shadows, filled her with a sadness she hadn't expected.

She backed through the swinging doors and almost bobbled the plates. Before when she'd seen Sass's progress, it had been daylight. Now, a fire roared in the hearth and the chandeliers flickered with fresh tapers overhead, giving the great room a warm glow. Even the simple curtains Sass had fashioned from the new fabric lent the room a fresh look. And how had she managed to make a pair of matching cushions that were now nestled in the overstuffed chairs by the hearth?

The Tusk & Tail, with its polished tables and newly scrubbed floor looked more and more familiar. She breathed in the scent of burning peat and the steam curling up from her own meat pies and fought off a wave of nostalgia. It hadn't been so long since she'd been sitting at these very tables eating hearty tavern food with her newly formed adventuring party. And now she was back.

Even though there weren't crowds of patrons yet—only one colorfully dressed gnome at a table and a couple of farmers at the bar—it wasn't hard to spot an orc towering over the other patrons at a table. Then she saw that the other guard with him wasn't an orc, or even a man, but a human female with blonde hair piled on top of her head. The same impressively tall woman with broad shoulders she'd seen in the village.

Then the orc's dark eyes landed on her and a jolt of recognition stopped her breath.

# Fifteen

AS LIRA STOOD HOLDING the tray, remembering how she knew the orc, a gruff voice snatched her attention.

"I know what you're doing."

Lira snapped her head to the graying, bleary-eyed man at the end of the bar, the one she remembered Durn talking to the night she'd arrived. Thick as thieves, they'd been.

She didn't like his tone or the way he looked her up and down with his thin lips curled into a sneer. "What am I doing?"

"Fixing this place up from the goodness of your heart?" His scowl seemed to tug his entire face down, accentuating the uneven patches of unshaved whiskers. "I don't know your game, but you've got one. You and that dwarf."

Anger sizzled through Lira at the dismissive glance the man tossed Sass's way. "There's no game, but if you don't like what we're doing, I take it you won't be eating?"

She didn't allow him to do much but grumble before turning her back on him, but her heart was pounding, and she reminded herself that he was rambling. He didn't have a clue why she was really at The Tusk & Tail. No one did.

Sass hurried to Lira, wiping her hands on an apron she must have found behind the bar. "Those look good. I'll take them over." Then she eyed Lira. "You okay?"

Lira jerked her head toward the drunk at the bar. "He's a charmer."

Sass snorted a laugh. "Silas? Durn seems to tolerate him. If you ask me, he's not worth the worry."

Lira nodded, impressed that Sass already knew names of the guests. Then she remembered that she knew one too. "I know that guy."

"Who? Silas?"

"No." Lira inclined her head toward the orc. "*Him.*"

Sass swung her head in an arc to take in the great room. "Him who?"

Lira huffed an exasperated breath. There weren't that many customers in the tavern. "The orc."

"You do?" Sass slid her gaze from Lira to the two guards in their distinctive uniforms with quilted leather breastplates and metal-studded straps crisscrossing their chests. "Did you two ever work in the same crew?"

Lira shook her head, her cheeks warming despite the fact that she'd looked away from the orc who had not yet looked away from her. "I bumped into him the other day when we went into town."

One side of Sass's mouth curled up. "Looks like he made an impression on you."

Lira ignored the warmth of her cheeks. "I didn't remember at the time, but I know him. He's from here. Remember the orcs I told you about who run the blacksmith and wheelwright? He's their son. He's younger than me by two or three years, I think. He wasn't so grown up when I left, which is why I didn't recognize him right away."

That made the dwarf's brows lift. "He's all grown up now, that's for sure." Then she elbowed Lira, but the nudge landed closer to her hip than her ribs. "What do you know about his friend?"

"Not much, but she looks familiar too."

"Is she a girlfriend?"

"No idea."

"Hmm." Sass snatched one of the pewter plates from her. "Well, we'd better take them their food before it gets stone cold."

Lira had no choice but to follow behind Sass as she wove her way through the tables to the one nearest the fire. The closer she got, the surer she was of who she was serving.

"Korl, right?" She slid a plate in front of him and let Sass give the blonde her food. "Son of Vorto and Klaff."

Korl moved his head so subtly Lira barely caught the nod. "You didn't recognize me in the village."

"Sorry." She lowered her eyes from his intense gaze. "You're... bigger."

She hadn't meant to say it like that, but the orc didn't flinch. "You used to live near here with your gran."

Lira smiled, very aware that the big, blonde guardsman was watching her intently. "That's right. I'm Lira."

"I know."

The words were so quiet she barely heard the rumble of them, but they stopped her breath. He didn't say anything else or look away, his black eyes unwavering.

The blonde cleared her throat and thrust out her hand. "And I'm Val."

Sass grabbed it first. "Sarsaparilla, but my friends call me Sass."

Lira also took her large hand and shook it, more convinced than ever that she must be part Goliath. "Welcome to The Tusk & Tail."

Val sat back and bounced her gaze between Lira and Sass. "Shouldn't we be saying that to you? You're the new ones to Wayside."

Lira felt like correcting her and saying she wasn't new, but she'd been gone so long she might as well be a stranger.

"I remember you, you know." Val picked up her fork and poked it into the flaky top of the meat pie. "And your gran. She was sweet."

Lira stared at the woman, wracking her brain to remember details. She glanced at Korl, but his attention was now on his pie.

"You wouldn't have known me," Val continued, as if reading her mind, "I lived at the castle until I didn't. Then I started spending all my time at Korl's. His dads practically took me in."

Her tone was light, but there was a story there. Not that it was Lira's place to demand it. Not when there was a temperamental oven to tend and a smartly dressed gnome trying to catch Sass's attention.

"It's nice to see you again or meet you for the first time." Lira took a step back. "I should probably get back to the kitchen, but I hope you enjoy the food."

"It's good," Korl said quietly, finally looking up again.

Lira was startled at the relief that coursed through her. Even her shoulders relaxed at his words. "Thanks. I tried to remember my gran's recipe, but don't ask what happened to the other batch."

"They burned," Sass said in a stage whisper.

"Korl wouldn't have cared," Val snorted out a laugh. "I think orcs prefer their food charred."

Korl grunted, his green cheeks mottling dark, before his eyes landed on something over her shoulder and narrowed.

Goose flesh prickled her arms as Lira turned, her spine stiffening as the wyvern strode into the tavern like he owned the place. There was always a chance that Durn was so behind on his taxes that Rygor might soon own it, but Lira didn't like the way the creature sized up the improvements.

Durn's usual frown deepened as Silas muttered some curses into his ale. The rest of the patrons went quiet as the reeve's clawed feet slapped the floorboards on his way to the bar.

"Well, Durn. Looks like you've been putting that stash of gold to use."

Durn choked on a mirthless laugh. "It's not gold. I told you I've got none."

A hiss escaped Rygor. "Then how do you explain all this?"

Behind her, Lira could sense Korl standing. She could feel the heat of him so close to her that she knew she would have trod on his feet if she'd stepped back even an inch.

Lira held her breath, certain that Durn was about to point out her and Sass and credit them for the improvements. The last thing she or Sass needed was to have the eye of a wyvern on them. Especially one in a position of power.

Durn's gaze flicked up, but Korl had pushed past her and was closing the distance between him and Rygor with Val close at his heels. The wyvern straightened at the guardsmen's approach, his slits of eyes becoming even more narrow as Korl spoke to him in hushed tones. Then he stormed off with Korl and Val trailing in the wake of a flapping cloak and rustling wings.

Lira released a breath only when they were gone, wondering what Korl had said to make the reeve leave so quickly.

"I think we owe one to your orc friend," Sass said, scooping up their partially eaten pies.

Lira nodded absently. Usually, she despised being in someone's debt, but she didn't mind so much with Korl.

# Sixteen

LIRA STEPPED GINGERLY through the windowsill of her bedroom, shooting a final glance behind her. Sass hadn't come up yet and Durn hadn't approached their room since he'd shown them to it that first night, so there was no one to witness her sneaking onto the tavern's roof.

She sat on the rough thatch and exhaled loudly into the stillness of the night, her warm breath puffing from her lips before the cloud vanished in the cold. Smoke curled from the chimney at the far end of the tavern, the sharp aroma of peat faint as it dissipated into the cool air.

For their first night serving food, it hadn't gone too badly but now that she'd stopped moving, Lira could feel the exhaustion seep into her bones. Not only that, but she was a mess. Her feet ached, her hair was a nest of frizz, and her left thumb boasted an angry red spot from where she'd touched it on one of the scorching pans. On top of it all, she was certain her hair reeked of charred pastry.

This was not at all how she'd imagined returning to Wayside.

Lira bent her knees and circled her arms around them as she shifted her weight to a less prickly spot on the thatch. She'd always heard folks say you could never go home again, and now she knew what they meant.

So much of the village was how she'd remembered it, but the one part that wasn't there, that would never be there, was her gran. Lira was doing her best to recreate those moments in the kitchen that had been the core of her happiness, but without her gran it just meant blackened pies, burned skin, and sore feet. Not to mention the wyvern who threatened to ruin everything.

Had she made a mistake coming back? Should she have forgotten what she'd hidden away and just kept moving? She could have found another crew. She could have gotten more work.

She shook her head hard. No, that life was done for her. She knew that now. As skilled as she'd become, questing hadn't been where her heart lay. Even as she'd deftly gotten her crew into impenetrable fortresses and gathered secrets that led them to hidden treasure, she'd known that it wasn't the path she was meant to traverse.

Lira scanned the rooftops of the village that now slumbered peacefully, with only the sleepy whinny of a horse or distant hoot of an owl to ripple the quiet. She'd never thought that this crumb of a village would be her destiny either, but despite a bumpy start, she didn't feel the urge to leave that she thought she would.

She unwrapped her arms and propped them behind her, closing her eyes and breathing in the crisp cool air that was so unlike the night air in Elmshire with its aroma of roasting meat seeping from every chimney, so unlike the evening air in Lananore with its heady perfume from blossoms that only flowered at night, nothing like the frigid air in Frostmoor where the smell of snow was ever-present. Lira would know the woodsy, watery, smoky scent of Wayside with a single breath.

Then her breath caught in her chest, and her eyes flared open. There was something here aside from the quiet slumber of the village. The fine hairs on her arm prickled as she scanned the village and peered beyond it into the tree line.

She wasn't sure if it was her elven blood or her years working as a rogue, but she could sense when she was being watched. And the shiver that skated down her spine told her that someone was watching her right now.

Was it Rygor? No, the wyvern was too arrogant to bother watching her in the dark. He seemed to be cunning, but she didn't get the sense that he would bother with subterfuge. Not when he'd been empowered by the laird himself.

It wasn't the wyvern, but there was someone out there. She'd bet her life on it.

"There you are."

Sass's voice ripped her from her focused scan of the hushed village, and she turned her head to find the dwarf climbing out to join her. Lira's heart hammered recklessly, and she cursed herself for thinking she was being stalked when it was just Sass. Who would be after her here?

"What are you doing on the roof?" Sass crawled on her hands and knees across the bristly thatch, wincing as she plopped herself next to Lira.

"Just getting some air. I've always been partial to rooftops for contemplation."

"Is this an elf thing?" Sass's tone told her that she considered this habit to be quite odd.

Lira smiled and shook her head. "Not that I'm aware of, but I wasn't raised by elves."

"Right." Sass snapped her fingers. "Half-elf. Human gran."

"Human gran."

Silence settled between them, and Lira thought that Sass might be absorbing the magic of perching above the world and watching it sleep.

"Smells better up here," Sass said. "You can still smell burned pie crust inside." Then she held up her hands. "Not that it was a big deal, burning one batch. The rest were enough to feed the crowd we had tonight, and not a single patron complained. Not a bad start, if you ask me."

"I'm still a bit rusty," Lira admitted. "I'm just glad they turned out at all."

Sass patted Lira's knee brusquely then pulled her small hand away. "Don't be so hard on yourself. It's a miracle you even found the oven under all that mess."

Lira laughed. "And I, for one, didn't think you'd be able to rid the place of the troll smell."

Sass shuddered. "Don't remind me."

"There's still work to do to get this place back to the way it was," Lira told her. "We only had a handful of diners tonight. The Tusk & Tail used to be packed to the rafters."

"Aye, give it time," Sass said, her northern accent thickening as she stifled a yawn behind her hand.

"You've got time?" Lira asked. "You're not eager to go find a mercenary crew?"

Sass shifted, crossing her legs in front of her. "Getting caught by you was the best spot of luck I've had since I left home."

"And you don't miss home?" Lira pressed. "You aren't ready to pack it in and go back?"

Sass gave a curt shake of her head. "That's not home anymore. Not for me. I was never going to be happy mining."

"So you truly don't mind staying for a while and trying your hand at running a tavern? Because you don't have to stay if you don't want. I have no intention of telling anyone what you were really doing here."

Sass gave Lira's shoulder a bump. "Not even the wyvern?"

"Especially not him." Lira bumped her back. "I know I got you into this, but I wouldn't hold it against you if you needed to move on."

Sass considered this for a moment. "You knowing I'd tried to rob the place was never the reason I stayed. Not really."

"Well, I know it wasn't the cushy accommodations." Lira cast a glance through the open window at their small room.

Sass laughed but not as loud. "It wasn't that, for sure. But there's something about this place, this village. Even if I'm sleeping an arm's length away from an elf—sorry, half-elf—this has been the best I've slept in ages."

Lira knew what she meant, even if neither of them could put it into the right words.

"My mum used to say that home isn't where your axe hangs, but where your heart feels light enough to set it down."

Lira tilted her head toward the dwarf. "Your mum was a poet?"

Sass barked out a laugh that startled a pair of house sparrows into taking flight from the eaves. "More like she was particular about where she hung her axe."

Lira smiled at this and rubbed her arms to rid them of chill. She glanced at the village through the darkness but didn't sense anyone watching her. Then she stretched her legs, unfolding them as she stood. "I suppose I'd better get some sleep if we're going to do this all again tomorrow."

Sass joined her, taking a step toward the window and then dropping suddenly. Lira caught her by the arm before her leg went entirely through the rotted thatch.

"Thanks for that," Sass said as Lira hoisted her back to standing.

Lira sighed and prodded the soft spot of the roof, feeling the sodden straw give. "I guess we added one more thing to our list of things to fix around here."

"As long as we didn't add 'extract dwarf from roof' to tomorrow's list, I can live with it."

As Lira followed Sass back into their room, she thought about what the dwarf had said. Could Wayside, with its crumbling tavern, make her heart feel light enough to set down all her troubles and put her past aside?

## Seventeen

**WHEN LIRA WOKE** the next morning, the bed across from hers was empty and the clothes were gone. Even the dwarf's cloak was missing.

Her heart lurched as she bolted upright. Sass wouldn't have snuck out in the night. Not after everything she'd said.

"Oh, hells!" Lira threw back the blanket and swung her feet to the cold planks, snatching her green day dress from where she'd draped it over the foot of the bed and dressing as quickly as she could with fumbling fingers.

She didn't bother to shove her feet into her boots, carrying them as she hurried down the narrow stairs and burst into the great room. The tables and chairs were neatly arranged and buffed clean, but the fire was cold, and there was no sign of Sass. She rushed to the kitchen. Nothing.

Cinders and dragon dung, where had the dwarf gone?

Lira wracked her brain for where Sass could be. It wasn't as if she knew a lot of people in Wayside. She glanced through one of the gleaming windows to see that the sun was barely warming the world. The market wouldn't even be open for business yet, so she couldn't have gone out to shop.

Lira's thoughts drifted to their conversation on the roof. Sass had claimed to be happy to stay, to like Wayside. Had that all been a ruse? But why?

Her gaze jerked to the bar, and she walked jerkily behind it to where Durn kept the till. Then she tore her eyes away. Sass wouldn't run off. Not after she'd covered for her. Lira's highly tuned instincts told her that Sass could be trusted, and Lira desperately wanted to trust her instincts again.

But if Sass hadn't run off, did that mean she was in danger? Lira had spent so long with danger snapping at her heels that it was hard not to assume that danger was around every dusty bend. Who would want to hurt Sass? Had the dwarf picked up enemies during her travels south?

Lira jammed her feet into her boots. If Sass was missing, she needed to find her. And if she'd run off, well, maybe she still wanted to find her.

Before she could take a first step, the back door scraped open and Sass ambled in carrying a pail in each hand, water sloshing over the rims, when she spotted Lira and stopped.

"You're awake." Sass set down the pails and massaged her palms where the light brown skin was rubbed pink from the handles. She shoved up the voluminous sleeves of her dark blue day dress, the full skirt almost brushing the floor.

"What are you..." Lira's words tumbled from her mouth, but she stopped as it was clear what Sass had been doing. "I didn't know... I couldn't find you."

Sass tossed her long braid over her shoulder. "Were you worried about me?" Then her grin faltered. "Did you think I'd left?"

Lira composed herself enough to shake her head. "No, of course not. I was worried something bad might have happened."

"Something bad?" Sass's smile returned at full brightness. "Here? In this little village?"

When she said it like that it did seem silly, but Lira knew better than most that evil could find safe harbor in even the loveliest of places.

Lira raised one shoulder. "You might have enemies who tracked you here."

Sass put her hands on her hips. "I wish someone thought I was deadly enough to be hunted down, but no. No one is coming after me, that, I can assure you."

Lira's breathing had returned to normal, so she nodded, as if dismissing their conversation, her fears, and Sass's disappearance in a single gesture. "I suppose I should get to work then."

The dwarf heaved one of the buckets of water onto the wooden table that took up the center of the kitchen. "We're lucky the stream is so close, since we used up almost all of the tavern's water stores. I'm going to get started with the bar. Durn didn't bother to clean it last night. Then I'm finally going to wash our muddy clothes."

So that's why her cloak had been missing.

Sass picked up the remaining bucket and headed for the swinging doors before pausing. "I don't suppose you could whip up something for us to eat?"

Lira thought about the ingredients she'd used the day before, what she'd need for that night, and what she would have left. Then she thought of what her gran loved to bake for breakfast. "Do you like scones?"

"Love them," Sass said. "What are they, exactly?"

Lira flapped a hand at her. "Don't worry. You *will* love them."

Sass muttered something about the low bar of gully dwarf porridge for breakfast as she continued into the great room. She'd barely cleared the swish of the doors when Crumpet wedged himself through the window that Lira had left open specially for him.

"Hi, there." Lira's voice softened and her mood lifted when she saw the creature somersault from the window to the counter. He sat up on his hind legs and rubbed his paws together.

"I don't have any dough for you to taste yet, but how do you feel about scones?" Crumpet chittered as if he knew exactly what a scone was. "Better than whatever gully dwarf porridge is, right?"

Crumpet made agreeable sounds as he sat back on his furry haunches and watched Lira, his shrewd black eyes following her every movement.

Lira had barely assembled her ingredients when the doors swung open again, causing Crumpet to take flight to the copper pots. "Scones take longer than that."

"I'm sure they do, love," said a voice that did not belong to Sass.

Lira almost dropped the bottle of cream as she turned to find Iris entering her kitchen.

"I hope I'm not coming at a bad time." Iris placed a basket on the table. "I thought you might be up early, and I wanted to bring you the spices."

Spices? For a moment, Lira had no idea what the apothecary meant.

"For your fancy tea?" Iris prodded.

"My chai!" Lira clapped her hands. "You sourced them already?"

Iris winked at her as she started to retrieve small burlap sacks from her basket. "Most of them I had, even if they were buried in my store-room, and the others I got from an herbalist who was passing through."

Lira picked up one bag and then the next, pressing them to her nose to inhale the spicy aroma of cardamom pods, the fresh bite of ginger, and the sweetness of cinnamon sticks. "This is perfect. Thank you."

Iris emptied the basket and then lowered it to the floor by her feet. "My pleasure, love."

Crumpet took this as an invitation to fly down and inspect the empty basket himself.

Iris didn't jump or even flinch at the creature's presence, no doubt inured by having a flock of bookwyrms. "So that's where the rascal went!"

Lira gaped at Iris. "You know him?"

The woman held out a hand and the white ermine scampered over and sniffed it before giving her fingers a little lick. "He's a flutterstoat."

"A flutterstoat?" She narrowed her eyes at the apothecary. "Should I assume he came about in much the same way as the bookwyrms?"

Iris shrugged.

"How many enchanted creatures are wandering around Wayside?"

"No comment."

Lira sighed. "Well, I call him Crumpet. He showed up when I started baking and seems to have an eye for pastry."

Iris scrutinized the flutterstoat as he leapt back to the counter. "Hmm." Then she gave herself a little shake and beamed a smile at Lira. "Now are you going to brew some of this fancy tea from The Wild Reach or are you going to make me beg?"

Lira flushed with pleasure at the request. "I'd love to, but fair warning, I've never made it from scratch."

Iris shrugged and leaned against the table. "I don't mind being your test subject. I did it enough for your gran."

Lira laughed at this as she put a saucepan on the stove and poured in equal amounts of milk and water. Then she whirled on the woman. "Do you happen to remember any of her recipes?"

Iris blinked a few times as if digesting the question. "Your gran's recipes?" She shook her head, and her curls quivered. "I'm afraid I never learned them. Not that she wouldn't have shared them. She was generous with her baking, and that included recipes. I never asked because I don't bake."

Now that she thought about it, she'd never seen Iris bake or cook. Did the woman subsist on tea alone? She was just wiry enough that she might.

"Since your gran passed, I've had to rely on Pip."

Well, that answered that.

"But he doesn't make the treats your gran did. The village keeps him busy enough doing morning buns and loaves for slicing, but I miss your gran's teacakes. They were perfect with a cup of tea, and you know I love my tea." The woman sighed, then perked up as she glanced around the kitchen. "Are you baking her recipes?"

Lira stirred the warming milk with a wooden spoon. "If I can remember them."

Iris reached for her free hand and squeezed it. "I wish I could help, love."

Lira wished she could too. She began to open the tiny bags and empty the contents onto the table, savoring the aromas wafting up. She dropped a few of the green cardamom pods into the milk along with a pinch of whole, knobby cloves and a snugly curled cinnamon stick.

Then she thought about what she'd forgotten to ask Iris when she'd been at her shop, what she'd been wondering for years. "There is one thing you can help me with."

Iris straightened.

"What is that heavenly smell?"

As Sass walked in breathing deeply, they both turned.

"Lira is making some fancy tea she tried when she was in The Wild Reach," Iris said.

"Tea?" Sass's eager expression fell.

"Spiced tea," Lira said, trying to hide her disappointment at being interrupted "You'll love it."

Sass leaned closer to the brewing chai, drawing in another long breath. "Well, it has to be better than my uncle's double fungus ale."

# Eighteen

LIRA EYED the dough as she cut the last triangle and transferred it to the baking sheet. She was reasonably sure she'd mastered the mixture for the scones, but her gran had never added cinnamon into her dough.

*It's the influence of the chai,* she thought as she glanced at her earthenware mug on the table, steam still spiraling from the hot drink.

Then she caught sight of Crumpet holding the wooden spoon she'd used to mix the scone dough, daintly licking it. "You think it's good?"

"The wee beast is the judge now, is he?" Sass asked as she and Iris walked back into the kitchen holding their own mugs of chai.

"Tease all you want, but Crumpet knows his pastry."

Iris lifted her mug. "I have to say that I'm pleasantly surprised by the spiced tea. I can see why you love it."

"Aye, it goes down easy." Sass took a long gulp from her mug. "It doesn't warm you like whiskey, but it doesn't muddle your head either."

"Let's try to limit the whiskey drinking during the day."

Sass shrugged. "As you wish."

Lira picked up her own chai and took a wary sip, careful not to let it burn her tongue as she swallowed. She closed her eyes as the milky tea slid down her throat, the spices warming her from the inside out.

"The tavern looks as good as new, pet." Iris put a hand on Sass's shoulder. "I never thought I'd see it like this again."

*Almost*, thought Lira. They might have given it a good spit-and-polish, but it still didn't have the cheerful conversation spilling from the doors or mouthwatering aromas clinging to the air. Not yet.

Crumpet let out a shrill chittering sound, fluttering his tiny paws at the oven and flapping his wings.

Lira yanked open the door, waving a hand in front of her face as acrid smoke belched from inside. "Hells and cinders!"

She snatched a rag from the counter, using it to retrieve the hot pans and clang them onto the stovetop. Crumpet had flown out the window once smoke started to fill the room, and both Iris and Sass coughed as Lira shut the oven door again.

"This oven is a menace," Lira said once she'd fanned away enough smoke to see that only a few of the scones were burned, and the ones at the other end of the pan were still pale.

"That's the gods honest truth."

The gravelly voice startled her into dropping the cloth, as she realized that Durn had entered the kitchen behind Sass and Iris.

"You gave me a fright, Durn." Iris pressed a hand to her heart as she turned to the tavernkeep.

"My Alma complained about that oven something fierce," Durn said after acknowledging Iris with a tip of his head. "She said it would be the death of her."

Iris's face constricted, and she seemed on the verge of comforting him when he turned and left as abruptly as he'd arrived. Once he was gone, she shook her head. "That man has been a right mess for too long."

"It means he loved her," Sass said, her own voice husky. "The price for sunlight is shadows."

Lira wondered if that was another of Sass's mum's sayings, but she didn't ask.

Sass drained her tea and set the mug on the counter. "I'd better get back out there. That bar isn't going to polish itself."

Lira slid the scones onto a plate and then started to tenderly scrape the bunt bits off the corners with the edge of her dagger. "I should be able to salvage most of these."

Iris eyeballed the puffy triangles. "This isn't one of your gran's recipes."

"Not entirely. These are her scones, but I added cinnamon. I thought they would go well with the chai."

Iris took one of the slightly burned scones and bit into it from the side that wasn't scorched. Then her eyelids fluttered, and she released a sound of pure pleasure. "Delicious."

Lira's pulse quickened. "Truly?"

"I could eat these all day," Iris mumbled through a mouthful as crumbs scattered from her lips. "Not that I would say no to some of her teacakes."

Crumpet had snuck back in on silent feet and was swiping each burnt bit as soon as it dropped from Lira's blade. Lira took a bite of the scone she was holding, smiling as she savored the buttery crumbly texture that was infused with the sweetness of the cinnamon.

Iris finished her scone, even devouring the burned edges, swallowing and locking her eyes onto Lira. "You've done your gran proud with these."

Lira wanted to soak that in but there was something else she wanted more. "Why did you do it?"

"Do what, love?"

"Teach me all those things when I visited you. I know my gran didn't send me to you to learn to pick locks and grapple with daggers. Did she know?"

Iris's expression twisted then her brow smoothed as she released a breath. "Elia knew everything. Do you think I would have done any of that without her blessing?"

Lira shook her head. "But she was a crofter. She taught me to gather eggs and bake. She took me in when my mother died, and my elf father was long gone. Why would she want me learning any of that?"

Iris let her gaze flicker to the doors, but whether she was hoping for a reprieve or hoping no one was behind them to hear, Lira didn't know. "It doesn't matter how lovely a village is, there will always be those who cannot stay and those who cannot leave. Your gran was one who couldn't stay until much later in life, when she needed to. She suspected that you might be the same, and she wanted you to be able to make your way in the world."

Lira scoffed at this and then pressed on, guessing at something she'd suspected for years. "Did she know you were once a rogue?"

Iris smiled and put her hand over Lira's. "Of course, she did. That's how we met, love. We ran together long before you were a thought, long before even your mother was a glimmer."

A far away ringing started in Lira's head, as if warning her not to push farther, not to ask the next logical question. The truth waited like a precipice before her; one more step and she would fall. "Ran together?"

Iris's eyes crinkled as she held Lira's, not a sliver of deception in the soft green. "We were on a crew together when we were young. I was, well, you know what I was."

"And my gran?" Lira's voice was so low she wondered for a moment if she'd only imagined asking the question. Her heart thrashed in her chest, a desperate rhythm against her ribs, as if trying to escape what was coming.

"Love, your gran was the mage."

She blinked at Iris slowly, the world seeming to blur at the edges, before giving her head a shake that felt as though it might unravel her completely. "What?"

Before Iris could repeat her words, Lira held up a hand. "No, I heard you, but I don't believe you. My gran couldn't have been a mage. She would have told me." Her voice cracked, splintering like thin ice beneath too much weight, the idea that she hadn't known such a huge part of her gran cleaving her heart in two. "She wouldn't have lied to me."

"She never lied to you, Lira." Iris's voice held an edge. "You were too young to keep such a secret. It would have been an unfair burden to tell you."

As sensible as this was, Lira didn't want to hear it. She didn't want to hear anything that would ruin the memories of her gran she'd held so tightly.

Her gran had been her gran, a warm old woman who tended chickens and baked amazing cakes. She'd been Lira's constant after her mother died, the one person she'd always been able to rely on, the only person she'd trusted with every fiber of her being. And Lira hadn't known her at all.

All the grief she'd been holding at bay for so many years came rushing to the surface. Lira pressed a hand to her mouth as a sob threatened to burst from her lips, pushing past Iris and rushing up the stairs to the small, cold room she shared with Sass. Only when she was lying face down on the bed so the pillow could muffle her cries, did she let the tears flow.

# Nineteen

LIRA PUNCHED the heel of her hand into the dough, satisfied when the elastic mixture cowered from her touch. *A mage?* Her gran had been a mage?

She scowled as she worked the dough, ignoring the warning sounds from Crumpet who sat to one side holding his tiny hands together as if in prayer. Had everything she'd known been a lie—the small farm, the cozy house they'd shared, the simple life of selling eggs and raising hens?

She shook her head like she had a hundred times since she'd run from Iris and escaped to her room. She'd cried until her eyes were sore and her chest ached, but she'd finally come back to the kitchen. There was something about baking that calmed her, and this was a time she needed calm.

Despite being steadier, questions still swirled in Lira's head. How had she not known she'd been living with a mage who'd run with an adventuring crew?

Then she thought of Iris and her bookwyrms. She glanced at Crumpet. Lira had no problem believing that Iris had been a rogue. It explained so many of the woman's skills. Skills she had no business possessing if she was truly a simple village apothecary. But if Lira was being honest with herself, it had been a long time since she'd thought Iris was simply a purveyor of tonics and tinctures. So why was it so hard to believe that her gran—the woman's best friend—would also harbor secrets?

"Because she was my gran," she said to no one.

If her gran had possessed magical skills, wouldn't she have used them? Wouldn't she have saved Lira's mother, located her father, and used her magic to make their lives easier? Why would she have lived the way they did if she had the power to change it? Was everything she'd always believed about her childhood false?

"Every memory I have is a lie," she muttered darkly.

*Not so fast, little one.*

She could almost hear her gran's soft voice, usually telling her to slow down when she was mixing ingredients, or to be more careful when she was measuring. But sometimes she'd warn Lira not to be so fast in leaping to conclusions.

*Things are rarely what they seem to be.*

Hadn't that been what her gran had told her over and over? She paused and swiped the back of her forearm across her brow, avoiding the flour coating her hands. Had the woman been talking about more than the latest drama in the village, the latest rumor to make its way through the town?

Lira was suddenly viewing everything her gran had done through a fresh lens, which meant coming to terms with a different story than the one she'd always told herself. It also meant that she needed what she'd buried in the tavern's cellar more than ever. She needed to hold the book that had been such a fixture in her childhood, the leather-bound tome that had stood propped up as she and her gran mixed up a batch of scones or teacakes. She needed it to prove to herself that her memories were real.

"They're back," Sass announced in a sing-song voice, as she strode into the kitchen and let the doors swish shut behind her.

Lira didn't even try to mask her impatient sigh. "Who's back?"

"Our regulars."

Lira knuckled the dough viciously and Crumpet squeaked. "What regulars?"

"The haberdasher and the two guards." Sass made a face. "I don't count Silas as a regular since he nurses one ale all night, but he's here too."

Lira didn't know that the town's haberdasher had become a regular, but she did know which two guards Sass meant. Her stomach did an odd flip at the thought of the handsome orc. "You'll have to tell all of them that if they want food, it will be a bit late."

Sass worked the tail of her braid as she studied Lira. "This have anything to do with your friend leaving in a flutter earlier?"

Another punch into the dough and a pained sound from the enchanted stoat. "She's not my friend."

"So, that's a yes."

Lira looked up. She didn't know Sass well, but so far the dwarf had proven to be steady and reliable, aside from her brief foray into burglary. Correction, attempted burglary, and not even a good attempt at that. "Have you ever learned something about your family that changed everything you thought you knew?"

Sass's squat, brown nose crinkled. "Can't say that I have, but that's only because I left all that behind me."

Lira had thought she'd done the same, but here she was back in Wayside, surrounded by memories she didn't even know were true anymore.

"Come to think of it, I don't know if I'd want to know everything those long-gone dwarves did. Not if they aren't here to tell me the tales themselves." Sass rested one hand on the thick leather belt that hugged her hips. "Seems a bit unfair."

Lira abandoned her assault on the pastry. "Unfair?"

Sass leaned one hand on the wooden worktable and gave Lira a pointed look. "We all have secrets, don't we? I'd hate to think of someone finding out something I did without knowing the whole story."

Lira barely flinched when Crumpet nudged her aside and started rolling out the dough with the battered rolling pin. "This is different."

"Maybe, but the past is the past. You can't forge the way ahead by looking behind you."

Lira shoved one of her sagging sleeves above her elbow. "More wisdom from your mum?"

"Dwarf mining wisdom." Sass winked. "Maybe you came back here because of your past, but you also must have come because you want a different future. Am I right?"

Lira grumbled her agreement.

"Has anything you learned change that?"

Lira had to admit that it hadn't. She still wanted a different life than the one she'd been living. She still wanted to return to the simple life she'd had before she'd left, even if that simple life might have been based on a web of secrets.

Sass straightened, not waiting for any more of an answer than Lira's gentle shake of her head. "Good. I'll keep everyone happy with drinks, and I won't tell them that their dinner is being rolled out by a furry, winged beast." She gave a wicked grin. "Or maybe I'll tell Silas that the kitchen is run by weasels, and he'll go do his scowling someplace else."

Sass swished back through the doors, and Lira turned to see that Crumpet had the pastry dough rolled to the ideal thickness. "I can't believe she called you a weasel, either."

The flutterstoat chittered his feelings about the misnaming, which made Lira laugh. Crumpet had clearly been enchanted to have wings, but she wondered about the whole story behind the little guy.

"One day you're going to have to tell me how you learned to do all this," Lira said as Crumpet flew back to the counter and sat on his haunches again, his white paws folded neatly in front of him as if he was finally satisfied that Lira could take over.

Sizing up the dough and the cooled pot of filling, Lira made the snap decision to create folded hand pies instead of freestanding ones, hoping they would bake faster. "Can't let down our regulars."

The idea of three patrons—and the grumpy Silas—making up the entirety of their "regulars" lodged a hysterical giggle in her throat. That wasn't much better than when she'd first arrived at The Tusk & Tail.

"Lananore wasn't built in a day," she told herself, although the saying was small comfort. She sincerely hoped it wouldn't take the centuries it took the elves. She might have elvish blood, but that didn't mean she'd inherited their lifespan—or their patience.

# Twenty

LIRA STOOD BACK and admired the half-moon-shaped hand-pies cozied together on a wooden tray. She'd managed not to burn a single one of them, although she'd opened the oven a dozen times to check on their progress, which had made the baking take longer than she'd hoped. She would need to figure out some way to fix the oven or figure out when it was going to belch heat and when it was going to splutter cold.

Still, she was proud of her creation as she backed from the kitchen and through the doors. Until she pivoted around and nearly bumped into Sass with her tray.

The dwarf's eyes went wide. "What are these?"

Lira wilted as Sass stared at the baked goods as if they might snap at her.

"What they are is not burned." Lira lowered the tray slightly so Sass could get a better look at the crimped crust that was the perfect shade of golden brown.

"Is this supper?" Sass fiddled with her braid, which the dwarf did when she was nervous.

"It's the same meat pie as before, but this version is portable." To demonstrate, Lira picked up one of the crescents, ignoring the intense heat seeping from the bottom.

"Because we have so much need for our patrons to walk around with their food."

Lira didn't miss the snarky tone, but she shrugged it off. "They baked faster and none of them burned." She made to turn back around. "Or should I go back and give them to Crumpet?"

Sass grabbed the edge of the tray. "Bite your tongue. That wee beast gets enough food from you as it is."

Lira let Sass flounce off with the tray, even though she could hear her muttering about pocket pies. She didn't return to the kitchen right away, though. As much as she relished her dominion over the kitchen and her relative solitude—Crumpet believed in companionable silence when he wasn't chittering his disapproval of her crust—it was nice to see her labors being enjoyed.

She had to give the dwarf credit. She might not be a fan of Lira's newest creation, but you'd never know it by how she pirouetted through the great room, lowering the tray with a flourish to show off the pies.

That must be the haberdasher, Lira thought as she spotted a gnome with distinctive pointed ears that flared to each side. She'd seen him before, of course. Not in the village, but in the tavern the night before.

His hair was silver and stood up in a tidy swirl on his head, the shape and hue mimicked by his short, pointed beard. But it was the clothes that were the giveaway to his profession. They were brightly colored and fastidiously arranged, a sea-blue shirt under a mossy-green vest with a butter-yellow ascot billowing at his neck. He hadn't always been the village's haberdasher, although her memories of the wizened old woman who'd used to run the shop were hazy.

Lira squinted across the room, even though her eyesight was perfect. Was the blonde woman who looked like she could rip a tree out by the stump knitting? And was Sass perched on the arm of her chair? Her pulse quickened as she felt Korl's gaze on her again. She was no stranger to men staring at her, but the way he looked at her didn't make her want to run him through with a dagger, which might have been a first.

She told herself that she was going over to check on Sass, but it was really her curiosity about Korl and Val that drew her.

Val grinned as she approached, holding up a hand pie. "I hear these are your idea."

Lira nodded, hoping she wasn't going to have to explain why their supper wasn't more formally presented. "Guilty."

"We love them, don't we, Korl?"

Korl flicked his gaze to her quickly then away again, making a low rumbling sound she hoped was his version of yes.

Val laughed. "See? He really likes them. You don't get a reaction like that from him every day."

A reaction like what? Lira snuck another glance at the orc, but his attention had shifted fully to the pies that were barely visible in his enormous green hands.

"That's why I usually do all the talking," Val said.

Sass hadn't moved from where she sat on the arm of Val's over-stuffed chair. "I take it he does his talking with his fists?"

That gained a bark of laughter from Val. "You'd think. No, he's just not the talking type. He might look like a brute, but he'd rather be tinkering with things than swinging his sword."

"Wish he'd tinker with our disaster of an oven," Sass grumbled.

Korl lifted his head, his black brows rising with it.

Lira laughed, the sound coming out high and chirpy. Did Sass plan on telling everyone their problems? "It's not a total disaster. It's temperamental."

"*I'm* temperamental." Sass shot a dark look toward the kitchen. "The oven is a menace. These are the first things that haven't come out half burned or half raw."

This wasn't entirely untrue, but it felt like more of a judgment on Lira's baking than the oven, and her face burned. Luckily no one seemed to be paying attention to her but Korl, whose black eyes held hers.

"So, what's all this?" Sass had already moved on and was gesturing to the knitting needles resting on Val's leg.

Val plucked the orange ball of yarn from her lap and held it up. "I like guard work more than Korl does. It keeps my mind and my hands busy, otherwise they're both too jumpy." She twisted the yarn ball as if examining it. "So, when my hands can't be busy with a blade, I do this."

"You're a knitter?" Lira felt like she needed to clarify even though it should have been obvious. She just hadn't encountered many soldiers who knit—and she'd encountered plenty of soldiers.

Val didn't seem insulted by the question. "That's right. It beats getting in trouble because I can't sit still." Her lips scrunched to one side. "I'm not good at doing much but rows, though, so everyone in my life has lots of scarves."

Korl grunted again, but this time it sounded more like an amused grunt.

"You're welcome to knit here anytime," Sass said, motioning to the basket on the other side of the chair. "You can even keep your yarn here."

When had she added that? Then Lira noticed the side tables hunched beside each chair that were polished until they shone in the dancing flames of the fire. Sass had turned the pair of weary, worn chairs someone else had wanted to discard into a cozy fireside refuge.

"Thanks." Val nudged Sass, almost knocking her off the armrest.

Lira caught her, righting the dwarf so she was standing again and tipping her own head toward the front door that had just swung open. "Looks like we have more patrons who might like some supper."

"Right." Sass cleared her throat and took a step away from the guards. When Lira turned toward the door with her, she cut her gaze to the kitchen. "You don't happen to have any more of these pocket pies in the oven, do you?"

Lira's stomach dropped. The pies. Hells and cinders!

# Twenty-One

"COULD HAVE BEEN WORSE." Sass stood with Lira in front of the cold pan and even colder oven.

Lira slid an icy glance at her. "What's worse than the oven *not* heating up?"

Crumpet let loose with a series of chitters and shook a tiny fist at the hulking iron stove.

"He knows." Sass jerked her head toward the flutterstoat. "At least the vengeful contraption didn't burn the place down."

Lira groaned. "No chance of that—or of us serving any more food."

The dwarf flapped a hand as if to dismiss this concern. "I'd say this is one advantage of not having a lot of business yet. We don't have many folks to disappoint."

"Now there's a silver lining." Lira untied the flour-smudged apron covering her clothes and tossed it onto the counter. Between Iris's visit and the temperamental oven, she was ready for the day to be done.

"I'll pop in to the tinker's tomorrow, although the shop seems perpetually closed," Sass said. "I doubt we can count on Durn to replace this monster if he hasn't yet."

Lira suspected Sass was right. The tavernkeep had generally avoided the kitchen. He went from his room upstairs to his position behind the bar, where he grumbled with Silas, and back again to his room, with not much more than a nod in their direction each evening. She was sure Sass had to be twice as boisterous to make up for the owner's dour presence.

"You know what I was thinking?" Sass asked then continued without waiting for an answer. "Durn needs a reason to get out of this place."

"Like a hobby?" Lira could hardly imagine the man doing anything but hunching over the bar.

Sass's lips curved into a wicked grin. "Like a love interest."

"You want to be a matchmaker for Durn?" Lira shook her head. "Talk about a challenge."

The dwarf did not seem dissuaded by Lira's less than enthusiastic response. "It's clear he misses his wife. It's been two years. Maybe what he needs is a new love."

Lira didn't say that she wasn't sure if Durn's relationship with his wife could be classified as a great love, but maybe Sass had a point. The man did need something, and the refurbishment of the tavern wasn't doing it for him.

"You have anyone in mind?"

"Wayside isn't bubbling over with great options, but I noticed that the chandler is single."

Lira had vague memories of the curvy gnome who had a shock of lavender hair and a bright smile. "Is she looking for someone moody and poor?"

Sass barked a laugh. "Durn is like his tavern. He just needs a bit of a spruce up."

*Spruce up?* Lira mouthed to herself. More like a total overhaul, but Sass did seem to relish a challenge.

"Ahem."

Sass swung her head to Lira, then they both looked toward the swinging doors. The polite throat-clearing came from outside the kitchen.

Sass pushed through to the great room and Lira followed her, too curious to stay behind and with no good reason to continue lamenting over raw pastries and the loveless tavernkeep. Her head instantly dropped to the smartly dressed gnome who stood outside the kitchen, his wrinkled hands rubbing together.

"Yes, yes," he said, peering up at Sass and then up even higher to smile brightly at Lira. "I wanted to bestow my compliments to the chef."

Lira flushed, although she felt it was a stretch to call her a chef. "I'm glad you enjoyed your supper."

"I hope you had enough," Sass muttered, mostly for Lira's benefit.

"Oh, yes. Plenty, plenty." The fellow had an endearing habit of repeating himself.

"Thank you for coming," Lira said, returning his smile although she got the impression that he hadn't come to stand outside the kitchen just to thank her for the food. Then she remembered the chairs. "And thank you for the chairs. They go perfectly by the hearth."

He bobbed his small head. "They do, they do." He extended a hand. "Tinpin Thistledown at your service."

Lira took his hand and shook it.

"As you no doubt know, I already met your charming business associate the other day." He inclined his head to Sass, who preened at either being called charming or a business associate or perhaps both. "She has excellent taste in textiles. Excellent taste."

Lira glanced toward the curtains, allowing that they did work well in the space. Then she looked down at the gnome again, registering his own sumptuous clothing. "How did you end up in Wayside, Mr. Thistledown? I would expect to see someone of your caliber in Hearthorn or even Frostmoor."

His friendly expression registered brief dismay. "No, no. Call me Tin. Everyone does. Everyone."

"Okay, Tin," Lira said, even though the name seemed much too casual for someone so precise about his appearance. She waited for him to tell her how he'd landed in a tiny village and not a bustling town where there was plenty of call for dress breeches and elaborate gowns.

The gnome let his gaze dart around the tavern and back to Lira. "You're right, you're right. I'm not from these parts. I hail from Port Frey in the South of the Ageless Lands."

Lira nodded, thinking of her own time in the seaside town. "Marshland and plenty of coastline. Not much like here."

Tin rocked back on his heels, and Lira noticed that his brown shoes were polished to a high shine. "Not much, not much. Port Frey is a good place to be from, but it didn't need me like Wayside does."

Lira cocked her head at him, not sure exactly what he meant.

"Don't get me wrong." The gnome waved small hands that Lira knew without asking were deft with a needle and thread. "Wayside is a lovely village, but it's lost a lot of its heart. I could sense it the moment I arrived. The very moment."

Lira thought about her gran and Durn's wife, the shuttered storefronts off the main street, the perpetually closed tinker, the vacancy sign swinging in front of the inn. She could see his point, although she never would have thought a place could have a heart.

The gnome fingered the wide lapel of his vest. "I always say that there's nothing quite as good for lifting the spirits as a new frock. Nothing as good. So that's why I'm here. That's why you're back too, isn't it?"

Lira blinked at him. "For a new frock?"

His laughter peeled high and merry. "No, no. Aren't you droll? No, you don't strike me as the frock type."

Should Lira be offended by that? Or by being called droll? Or by Sass's shoulders shaking as she tried not to laugh?

"I heard you're a local who's come back," Tin said. "You must sense the same thing about the village. Why else would you put so much into saving this tavern? Why else?"

Lira nodded, the smile frozen on her face. That wasn't why she'd come back at all, but he was right that she'd felt compelled to help The Tusk & Tail.

"That she does." Sass hooked her arm through Lira's, amusement dripping from her voice. "We all want to save the tavern."

Lira gave the dwarf a vigorous pat on the arm. "Yes, we do, and thank you again for helping us, Mr.—I mean, Tin."

The gnome grinned as he nodded, pleased that she'd called him by his name. "My pleasure, my pleasure." He turned his attention to Sass. "Now should I take at look at that room you told me about? I suspect the bedding hasn't been updated since the first dragon age."

"I don't doubt that," Sass said.

"Bedding?" Lira frowned. Did Sass mean the room they were sharing? "I think we need a new oven before we can think about redecorating our sleeping chamber."

"Of course, of course." The haberdasher bobbed his head, some of the excitement fading from his eyes. "Function before all else. That's what I always say." Then he gave Sass a knowing look. "Later, perhaps, my dear."

Lira wasn't sure if she would have called his silky ascot functional, nor the glittering pin anchoring it in place, but she couldn't help liking the fellow. Besides, he was one of their few regulars, according to Sass.

Tinpin Thistledown produced a pristine black cap and tipped it to them before he settled it onto his head, the point draping to one side. "I bid you both a good night, a very good night."

As he strode jauntily away, Lira noticed Val and Korl slipping out, Val trailing at least a foot of newly knit orange scarf behind her and the orc's gaze landing on Lira for a beat before he ducked under the doorframe.

Then Silas shuffled by, using two fingers to point to his own eyes and then at her. "I've got my eyes on you two."

All questions about Sass's plans for their bedroom flew from her mind, but the dwarf just swung a dishtowel in his direction and told him to go on home. Of course, Sass didn't have to worry about anyone keeping their eye on her.

Lira drew in a breath of peat smoke, sweeping her gaze around the now-empty tavern with the crackling fire and a few errant pewter plates and tankards scattered across the long, thick-legged tables. "So those are our regulars?"

Sass twirled the tail of her braid around one finger and her grin flashed momentarily wicked. "For now."

That gave Lira pause.

# Twenty-Two

LIRA RUBBED sleep from her eyes as she sipped her mug of chai at the stove when the swinging doors flew open the next morning. When she jumped, some of the steaming contents of her drink sloshed onto her hand and she emitted the appropriate yelp.

"Apologies."

The voice was gruff and low, and unless Sass had acquired a virulent cold overnight, it didn't belong to the dwarf. It also came from behind the swinging doors, which had swung shut again from the force of the first attempt.

A dusky, green hand appeared as an orc pushed into the room, this time more gingerly. Not just an orc, Lira realized. Korl.

Once again, she was struck by how good looking he was, especially for an orc. Not that she had anything against the looks of orcs in general. She'd known some perfectly decent ones, most notably Korl's dads, but not many she would have called handsome. But Korl's chiseled cheekbones, square jaw, and black hair that he wore in a braid made it hard for her to look away. But when her face warmed, she did.

"Did you burn your hand?"

Lira shook her head, flicking drops of spiced tea from her fingers and unable to keep the surprise from her voice. "What are you doing here? We don't open for hours."

"I didn't mean to frighten you. I didn't think you'd be here."

Lira set her mug onto the counter and patted her damp hand with a cloth. "Where would I be? What we haven't established is why *you're* here."

Korl grunted and tipped his head across the room. "Your friend said it was broken."

Lira followed his gaze to the iron stove that sat cold and sullen in the corner. "You're here to fix the oven?"

Korl shrugged. "Unless you don't want me to."

"Please, if you can make it work again don't let me stop you."

Korl lowered the metal tool caddy he gripped in one hand to the floor, the contents clattering as he squeezed past her to reach the offending contraption.

Lira sucked in to let him pass, holding her breath as his quilted leather breastplate brushed her tunic. "Have you ever fixed an oven before?"

He shook his head, not glancing back as he knelt in front of the iron beast and tugged on the handle. "Machines are machines, and all moving parts move in the same way. More or less."

That hadn't been Lira's experience, but it was safe to say that she'd never fancied herself a dab hand with gadgets. Unless the gadget was a lock, and that was more to do with listening and feeling than fixing.

Korl thrust his head inside the oven, his grunts amplified by the close quarters as he inspected the interior. When he emerged, he sat back on his haunches, jutting out his jaw and blowing a gust of air upward to remove an errant strand of hair from his eyes.

Lira pressed her lips together as she took in his serious expression and the patch of soot capping the tip of his nose. The last thing she wanted to do was laugh at him, especially since he'd come to help.

She snatched the cloth she'd used to wipe her own hand, deeming it clean enough. "Here, hold still." She knelt down in front of him and took his chin in one hand, holding his face steady as she swept the soot away in a single swipe. "That's better."

She hadn't expected him to smell so good, but she almost sighed as she breathed in his spicy, smoky scent. Lira met his eyes, which seemed to have gone even blacker than usual. He was holding his breath, his entire body rigid. Her pulse quickened, and she held up the dirty rag as explanation. "Soot."

The air between them buzzed, and even her fingers tingled from holding his chin. He still hadn't exhaled, so she rose and took a big step back. "I suppose there'll be more of that before the job's through. I'll let you get to it, shall I?" She didn't wait for an answer before beating a hasty retreat from the kitchen, and almost flattening Sass in the process.

"Grognick's beard, woman!" Sass stumbled back, almost landing on her ample rear end before Lira caught her by the arms. "What's got you in such a state?" Then her eyes went wide as her gaze danced between Lira and the kitchen doors. "It's not rats, is it? I can't abide rats."

Lira steadied her breath and released Sass. "It's not rats. It's nothing. Well, not nothing. Korl is here."

Sass gave her a blank look. "Korl?"

"Val's friend," Lira said, letting her voice drop. "The orc."

Sass's expression brightened. "Korl!" Then wrinkles crowded her brow. "Why is Korl here?"

"He's fixing the oven."

"The orc guardsman is fixing our oven?" She gave the swinging doors a pointed look. "Right now?"

Lira nodded. "Val did say he preferred tinkering to fighting."

Doubt flickered across the dwarf's face and she stepped around Lira, pushing the half doors open enough to poke her head into the kitchen. When she straightened and released the doors, she gave her head a brief shake.

"Well? I was telling the truth, wasn't I?"

"You didn't tell me that he had an assistant."

Lira cocked her head and went onto her tiptoes to peer over the top of the doors. Korl sat on the floor in front of the oven with the door open and his head inside, and balanced on the handle of his tool caddy perched Crumpet, bent over and pawing through the contents.

Lira groaned. "Crumpet!"

The creature cut his eyes to her without removing his hands from where they were buried in the tools and chittered something. Apparently, he was as fond of hammers and wrenches as he was of rolling pins.

Before she could enter the kitchen and retrieve him, Korl popped his head from inside the oven. "He's not bothering me."

"You're certain?" Lira asked, shooting a severe look at the animal.

"He's not bad at holding tools." Korl passed Crumpet a hammer, which was swiftly dropped into the caddy. The corners of Korl's mouth twitched. "Maybe he's better at putting them away."

"If you're sure..."

Korl gave her a flash of a smile. "Don't worry about us. We'll rub along just fine."

And with that, he went back to inspecting the inside of the oven and emitting curious grunts.

Lira dropped back onto flat feet. "I guess we leave him to it?"

Sass patted her on the back, steering her into the great room and toward the enormous stuffed chairs by the fire. "You and I have been so busy cleaning and cooking that we haven't gotten a moment to try out these chairs for ourselves."

Lira hadn't considered not testing out the chairs a great loss, but if she couldn't be puttering around the kitchen, she might as well have a proper sit down.

The hearth was stacked with fresh peat—no doubt done by Sass the night before to make quicker work of her morning chores—so it took only the strike of a long match and teasing the fledgling flame under some tangled kindling to get the fire going.

Lira sank into one of the chairs, her hands curling around the wide armrests to keep her from vanishing into the cushioning. The fabric smelled faintly of dust but not enough to provoke a cough.

"When did you ask Korl to fix our oven?" Lira asked once Sass had made short work of the fire and taken the chair opposite.

Sass's legs shot straight out, the chair too large for her feet to touch or even for her knees to bend. Even so, she wiggled herself to the edge of the chair and leaned forward. "Me? I was going to ask you when you did."

Lira shook her head. "It wasn't me."

"He took it upon himself then." Sass gave Lira a wry smile. "Isn't that interesting...?"

<h1 style="text-align:center">Twenty-Three</h1>

**WHEN KORL EMERGED** from the back of the tavern, Lira scrambled to rise from the chair despite the soft cushions' attempts to keep her seated. Sass managed to get up quicker by vaulting the arm, which Lira had to admit wasn't a bad strategy.

"All done?" the dwarf asked as she strode across the great room and met the orc halfway.

He set his tool caddy on the nearest table and gave a grim nod. "It'll hold for now, but it's on its last legs."

Lira wasn't surprised. She suspected the oven hadn't been replaced or even repaired since the place had opened. Still, whatever patch job Korl had been able to do, it would be better than what they had.

"No more burned pastry?" Sass cast a look at Lira. "Assuming the baker keeps an eye on it."

Lira scoffed and rolled her eyes at the dwarf as she reached Korl. "Ignore her. I won't hold you accountable for the baking that comes from my oven, but I will insist that you let me make you something for your trouble."

Korl opened his mouth, and Lira was sure he intended to protest. She held up a hand. "Do you have someplace to be?"

He clamped his mouth shut and shook his head. "Not yet."

"Then you'll let me make you some scones." Then Lira added. "They're my gran's recipe, and I'm pretty sure I got it right."

If Korl had any intention to protest more, Sass stopped him with a hand on the leather armor covering his forearm. "Please, let her make scones."

Lira grinned at the dwarf's dreamy expression. "I had no idea you were so fond of them, Sass."

"You do remember that I'm used to gully dwarf porridge, right?"

Lira had forgotten how low the bar was for Sass. Korl's expression had gone from pleased to confused, but Lira shook her head. "They're significantly better than any type of porridge."

She headed for the kitchen, pleased to see that the orc had cleaned up whatever mess he'd made while repairing the stove. Not that she should have been surprised. Soldiers were usually a regimented, orderly bunch. Now if he'd been a mercenary...

Lira shook off the shudder that swelled within her as she pulled out her mixing bowl and sack of flour. She'd barely tipped the flour into the bowl when Korl stepped into the room, his bulk seeming to take up half the space and a good deal of the oxygen.

"I'm not *that* fast," Lira said and managed a grin she hoped didn't give away too much.

"I thought I could help."

She was glad she'd already poured in the flour or she certainly would have dropped the sack. "You've already helped me by fixing the oven."

He nodded but made no move to leave. She bit back a sigh. Maybe he wanted to see his handiwork in action or maybe he wanted to make sure the oven didn't explode when she turned it on.

Despite having run with a crew, Lira was accustomed to working alone. When they'd needed to break into a locked vault, it had been nothing but her nimble fingers and silence. When they'd needed to know secrets that were whispered in the comfort of shadows, it had been her alone who'd slipped unseen through pools of darkness to gather them one by one.

But she couldn't send him away. Not when he was the reason she'd be able to bake at all, and not when he was looking at her like he might crumble at the most delicately pointed word. Besides, she didn't mind his presence. There was something tentative and sweet about him that was such a mismatch to his orc physique that she didn't mind him being in her space.

"How are you at cutting butter?" she finally asked.

"I'm good with blades."

Since he was a guardsman, Lira didn't doubt this.

She gestured to the block of butter on the counter. "Half of that in small bits, please."

He moved behind her, his body brushing hers as he took up the task. Lira focused on grating a papery cinnamon stick into the flour, the brown spice speckling the mound of white. They worked in silence until she felt his gaze on her back.

"If you're done, you can drop that into the bowl," she said, trying not to sound too commanding.

Korl was instantly at her side, his massive hands opening over the flour and unleashing a cascade of tiny yellow flakes. Lira smiled at how fastidiously he'd cut the butter. She glanced around for a pair of knives, reaching for the daggers he'd left on the counter behind her.

She deftly cut in the butter until the mixture was like sand, aware that the orc was watching her every move. He clearly wasn't one who felt compelled to fill silence, so she didn't attempt to engage him in conversation. Aside from that, the quiet in the kitchen didn't need filling.

"I've eaten these before," he said after a few minutes.

She tipped her head to meet his eyes, taken aback that he'd been the one to speak first. "Scones?"

He nodded then shook his head. "Your gran's scones. She brought some to us once after my dads fixed her cart."

Lira didn't remember this, but she now knew there was a lot she didn't remember. "Did you like them?"

Another nod and then several more moments of silence. "And we all liked her."

Lira jerked her attention back to her bowl, pouring in a glug of cream and cracking an egg as the backs of her eyes burned. She folded the batter with a wooden spoon and then slung a handful of flour onto the table, her deft movements keeping her mind busy and the tears at bay. As she flopped the dough onto the surface and worked it into a flat disc with her fingers, a wisp of a memory fluttered to the surface. "That wasn't the only time your dads fixed our cart."

Korl shook his head, as she expertly cut the dough into wedges and transferred them to a baking sheet. He opened the oven door for her and they both braved a blast of heat as she slid it inside. "One time we got an apple spice cake."

It warmed Lira's heart that he still remembered the types of baked treats her gran had used to repay them.

"We ate the whole thing instead of supper that night," Korl confessed. "I had a tummy ache the next day. So did my dads."

Lira laughed, Korl's memories of her gran's baking unlocking something deep inside her, a joy that had been bundled snugly in grief. She laughed until tears leaked from the corners of her eyes, and the velvet rumble of the orc's laugh joined hers. In that moment, Lira felt like she had when she'd baked alongside her gran. In that moment, she felt safe, she felt at home.

When she put a hand to her side, she gasped a hitching breath. "I'm not laughing at your tummy ache. I'm laughing at your dads letting you eat a whole cake."

"They ate more than I did."

She sucked in a breath. "That's what's so funny." She looked up at Korl, his smile warming her. "I can't promise that it will be as good, but I can try to make that cake for you."

"You don't have to," he said, his voice suddenly solemn again. "That's not why I told you that story."

"I know." She smiled at him, enjoying the flash in his dark eyes. "Maybe I want to."

Korl cleared his throat and looked away, glancing at the oven instead of her. "Your gran wasn't the only one who was nice. Do you remember sticking up for me?"

Lira searched her memory, vaguely recalling some bigger boys trying to provoke Korl when he'd been young and smaller. "They wanted you to fight them, right?"

He nodded. "Everyone thinks I should love to fight."

The softness of his voice constricted her chest. "Everyone thinks I should have elvish powers, but I don't, so I get it."

He lifted his gaze to her. "You told those boys to get lost or you'd turn them into newts."

"I did?" She shook her head. "I guess I was counting on them not knowing I don't have powers, or that elves can't transform people into newts. Not that I wouldn't have turned them if I could. I hate bullies, and I know what it's like to feel like you never quite fit in."

An orc who didn't relish battle and wasn't loud and raucous wasn't what anyone expected. If she was being truthful, Korl wasn't what Lira had expected.

He didn't reply but he didn't look away. Lira tried not to squirm under the intensity of his gaze and the heaviness of the air between them, wondering if she should break the silence. Then he jerked his head to the stove and released a breath. "It shouldn't burn anything else."

"Thank you again for fixing it. You really didn't have to."

"I wanted to." As Korl took a step back with his gaze fixed on the oven door, Lira busied herself with clearing up her work area and quiet settled between them once more.

"Grognick's beard, that smells good!" Sass walked into the kitchen with her nose lifted. "Are they ready yet?"

Lira had been so consumed with her conversation with Korl that she hadn't noticed the pungently sweet aroma emanating from the oven. "Not yet."

"If you have a moment before they're out, folks might not say no to some of that fancy tea to go with their scones."

Lira looked up at Korl after Sass had gone. "What folks?"

LIRA AND KORL emerged from the kitchen, the orc holding the swinging doors open for her as she wiped her hands on the front of her apron.

Lira stopped short when she saw that there were, indeed, folks in the great room. She'd expected Sass and maybe Durn behind the bar, but she hadn't anticipated Tin or the halfling baker Pip.

The door of the tavern was propped open, and Sass stood on the threshold with her hands on her hips, occasionally lifting one to throw a wave or beckon an unseen someone.

"What is she doing?" Lira asked herself more than anyone.

Korl folded his arms over his chest, the quilted leather breastplate buckling, and then grunted. "I think it's your scones that are doing most of the work."

The neatly dressed haberdasher hurried over to her, tugging on the points of his brown tweed vest that contained most of a russet-colored shirt with voluminous sleeves. "What a wonderful idea, dear. Wonderful, wonderful."

"What idea?"

He beamed up at her, lines spidering his face. "To sell your scones as an afternoon pick-me-up, of course."

"To sell—?" Lira hadn't gotten far in her spluttered question before Sass's throaty voice cut her off.

"Scones and chai," she corrected, throwing an arm as far around Lira as it could reach. "Three copper bits for the pair."

Lira opened her mouth, but nothing came out.

"I wouldn't mind trying a scone and some of the fancy tea your friend here has been telling us about."

This came from Pip, who still had his own flour-encrusted apron tied around his waist and wore the lingering scent of yeast like a signature scent. His sparse, wavy hair stood on end with bits of dried batter speckling it like doughy jewels.

"Oh, I'm sure my scones are nothing like your bread." Lira felt her cheeks blaze. The last thing she wanted was for the village baker to think she was trying to steal his business.

But Pip's grin was genuine. "That's why I'd like to try them. I don't serve scones or cakes or any of the treats your gran used to bake, and I have no intention to start."

A breath rushed from Lira as her shoulders sagged with some measure of relief. "If you're sure." She shot Sass a look. "We hadn't planned on serving anything but supper."

"Aye, but plans change.' Sass thumped her on the back. "Besides, who can resist that smell?"

Lira inhaled, the air laden with the aroma of cinnamon and sugar.

Sass nudged her. "Don't you need to put the chai on and check the scones?" She gave Korl an apologetic look. "Not that I don't trust your fix. It's the oven I don't trust."

With that reminder, Lira hurried back to the kitchen, bracing herself to find smoke snaking from the seams in the oven door. But there was none.

She allowed herself the briefest peek into the oven, blinking rapidly from the wave of heat and closing the door again. Whatever Korl had done, had worked. At least, for now, and Lira would take it.

She placed the biggest copper saucepan she could find on the stove and filled it with the milk she'd stashed in a box outside the back door to keep it cool. Opening each of the sacks of spices Iris had brought her, she dropped the whole pods, curled sticks, and black tea leaves into the milk. The fire danced beneath the copper pot as she stirred steadily, taking her cue from the scent that wafted up from the simmering chai.

Pivoting away from the chai for a moment, she opened the oven door and grinned with satisfaction. The scones were puffed up and evenly browned, the smell heavenly.

Lira used a cloth to pull the baking sheet from the oven and set it on the cool half of the stovetop. She snagged the best blue earthenware mugs from the hooks on the wall, ignoring the ones with chips, and arranged them on the wooden tray before she poured in equal measures of the steaming chai. Then she transferred the scones to the other side of the tray, standing back and admiring her handiwork for a moment.

Her gran would have been proud, she thought. Lira closed her eyes and could almost feel her gran next to her, her voice soft and her hands warm as they closed over her smaller ones.

Her gran had always been proud of her. That was why Lira had been able to go out into the world and make her way without fear. She'd carried her gran's belief in her like a talisman.

But that was also why she'd come back to Wayside. She'd wanted to feel worthy of her gran's pride again, she'd wanted to feel as happy and content as the two of them had been living in their tiny house and using cake as payment because there wasn't enough coin.

Opening her eyes, Lira looked at the scones and chai with as much pride as she had when she'd surveyed any of the treasure she'd collected or bags of gold she'd been given.

She lifted the tray and backed into the great room, careful not to move too quickly and slosh chai over the rims of the mugs. But it wasn't only Pip and Tin waiting for the chai and scones that Sass had sold them.

Val had joined Korl and the pair had taken up residency in the over-sized chairs by the fire, which was now roaring. Pip and Tin sat across from each other at the end of a long table, a curiously mismatched pair, since one was impeccably dressed and the other was wearing as much flour as fabric. Lira wondered if there might be an opposites-attract romance brewing there, which made her smile.

The two ogres who'd delivered the chairs were standing at the bar, shifting from one stumpy leg to the other. Lira suspected they couldn't sit comfortably at the tables, even the ones with long benches instead of chairs.

Then she spotted someone who almost made her bobble the tray. Lira took even steps until she could deposit the tray on the top of the bar before she focused on the gray-striped pantheri leaning against the wall with her furry arms crossed. Her feline features were schooled in an expression of calm that Lira knew all too well, and even her whiskers didn't twitch as she stared across the room.

The last time Lira had seen Cali, or Caliqua as she was formally known, had been months ago when they'd been standing on a high cliff staring at the spot in the churning sea where their friend had fallen. Lira had been certain then she would never see Cali again after she walked away.

As Lira tracked the flick of the pantheri's tabby-striped tail, she understood how wrong she'd been.

## Twenty-Five

**"COME AND GET 'EM!"**

Sass's shout gave Lira a start, and she was grateful she no longer held the tray. She stepped back as the dwarf waved their customers over, managing tight smiles as she murmured thanks for the flurry of compliments and made her way toward the pantheri.

Seeing Cali had banished all thoughts of buttery pastries and warm chai from her brain, and a chill went over her as she took wooden steps around the tables. She and Cali had always been friends, perhaps tighter than any others in their party. So why were her feet leaden as she walked toward her?

The archer wore her trademark leather pants that stopped above the knee and a vest that molded to her torso. Her claws were retracted, although she drummed them on her folded arms. Her boots were scuffed but not caked in mud, meaning she hadn't traveled through the marshlands to reach Wayside.

Lira dipped her head when she reached her. "Cali."

The pantheri's pupils flared, but not in the way they did when she was about to strike. "Is that all? After all our years together, I don't get a hug?"

Lira blinked at her. "You want a—?"

Before she could finish her question, Cali had yanked her into a ferocious embrace, holding her close enough for her whiskers to tickle Lira's cheek. Lira's entire body sagged as she wrapped her arms around her friend.

When Cali pulled back, Lira was still regaining her equilibrium. "I thought you'd be...I thought you came to..."

Cali cocked her head. "You thought I was... what? Angry that you wanted to leave our group?"

Lira gnawed at her lip without answering.

Cali threw her leg over the nearest bench and sat, waiting for Lira to join her. "No one blamed you for leaving. We were all torn up after Malek. It wasn't the same."

Lira shook her head, but it was to agree. Malek might not have been her favorite in the crew, but they'd worked together long enough that she'd felt his loss keenly.

"You weren't the only one to leave," Cali said, a flicker of something crossing her face and making her pointed ears twitch. "Vaskel followed right after you."

Lira wouldn't be surprised if the hellkin had felt guilt over losing Malek, blaming himself for not being able to sense the danger before it was too late.

"It wasn't his fault," Lira said, allowing her attention to drift to the small gathering around the scones and chai at the bar. It struck her as odd that such a deep sense of satisfaction could be swept away with a reminder of her past.

"It wasn't anyone's fault."

Cali's tone was sharp, and Lira's gaze snapped back to her.

"Malek knew what he was doing when he cast that spell. It was dangerous and risky. We'd all warned him for years not to dabble in dark magic."

Lira let loose a sharp laugh. "Malek was not one to be convinced of anything."

Cali's own chuckle was without mirth. "No, he wasn't." She put a paw on Lira's arm. "Which is why you can't blame yourself."

Lira frowned. "But I had him, Cal." She opened and closed her hand as if she could still see the scrap of Malek's cape as it tore from her fingers. "I had him, but I couldn't hold him."

A half-purr, half-growl rumbled from the feline's chest. "The spell had already rebounded on him by the time you got there. There was no saving him, Lira."

Lira's eyes fluttered closed as she fought to purge the memories of Malek's face, his shock, his horror as he'd slipped from her grasp and hurtled into the vengeful sea. Then she remembered the web of veins glowing black as they'd crawled up his arms and neck, the infernal magic consuming him with such potent power that he'd been unable to stop his inevitable plummet off the cliff.

Cali was right. He wouldn't have lived even if he'd survived. Not as he'd been before, at the very least. The dark magic they'd begged him not to dabble in would have contorted him into a creature none of them would have recognized.

When Lira opened her eyes again, it was to see Cali with her ears flattened and Korl standing beside them. He held a mug of chai and a partially decimated scone, crumbs clinging to his dusky green chin.

"You okay?" His question was directed at Lira, even though he barely met her gaze.

Cali flicked her amber gaze from her to the orc, the hairs on her slender arms rising.

"Fine," Lira said. "This is Cali, we used to run together. She's the best archer you'll ever meet."

"Caliqua." Cali extended one paw. "But if you're a friend of Lira's, which I'm guessing you are, you can call me Cali."

Korl took the paw gently in his massive hand and gave it a gentle shake. "Korl. Her gran used to make scones like this."

Cali eyed the remains of the scone in Korl's hand but didn't comment on the non-sequitur. "I've heard about this gran, but not about the scones."

"I told you she taught me to bake."

Cali shrugged. "You never mentioned specifics or that scones smelled so good." She sucked in a greedy breath. "I could smell them all the way outside the village."

Lira scoffed. "That's because you have a highly attuned sense of smell."

"Perhaps, but I would recognize the scent of that chai anywhere."

Lira grinned at the memory. "Because you were with me when we discovered it."

Cali nudged her knee with her own. "That amazing elven cafe with the hanging lanterns and cushions on the floor."

Korl scrunched his nose at this.

"You had to see it," Lira assured him. "The cushions were enormous and everyone sat on the floor drinking chai."

Korl grunted, and Lira suspected that lolling about on the floor might not be his style.

"I'll get you some chai." Lira started to stand.

Cali's ears were no longer flat against her head. "And I wouldn't say no to one of those scones."

"Sit, sit!" Sass called over. "I'll get it."

Lira noticed that the dwarf was no longer manning the tray of scones and chai at the bar but was hurrying to the tray from the hearth, patting Tin on the arm as she passed him. She also noticed Silas watching her and Cali with narrowed eyes, but she took Sass's advice and ignore the curmudgeon.

Korl grunted again. "If everything is okay here..." Then he turned and left them for his chair by the fire.

Cali twisted her head to watch his retreating back. "He's an interesting one. Quiet for an orc."

"He's on the shy side, but he's been a big help today. He fixed our oven and won't take any payment aside from free food."

"No doubt."

Lira wasn't sure what Cali meant by that or why her whiskers quivered when she swung back around.

"Too bad he's a guardsman," Cali said. "He'd make a great addition to a crew."

That thought made Lira bristle. "He hates fighting."

Cali made a face like she didn't believe her. "An orc who hates fighting?"

Lira held up one palm. "I swear on the souls of those who have gone before us. He's good with gadgets and prefers tinkering with things to killing."

"Hence the oven repair." Cali sighed. "Well, it was worth a shot."

Sass swished over, balancing a plate on her arm and holding two mugs. She dropped the mugs on the table before sliding the plate down the length of her arm. "Chai and a scone for our guest and for the baker." Sass winked at Lira. "I figure you didn't get to eat one yet."

Lira hadn't, and she was grateful that the dwarf had thought of her, even over their profits. "Thanks, Sass." She gestured to Cali. "This is Cali. We used to work together."

Sass's brows lifted. Lira hadn't told her much about her past work, but she knew the dwarf had figured out a good deal on her own. She eyed the quiver of bows on Cali's back. "An archer, eh?"

Cali smiled. "I try."

Lira shook her head at the misplaced modesty. "She's as good as they get."

Cali took a bite of the scone, and a purr rumbled her chest.

Sass grinned as if she'd come up with the recipe herself. "Good, aren't they?"

"I had no idea you could bake like this," Cali mumbled around her bite, sending a shower of crumbs cascading onto her pants.

"Your loss is our gain," Sass said with a wink as she spun around and headed back to the fire where Val was draining her chai and Korl was making little secret of watching her and Cali.

Cali took a gulp of her chai, her purring nearly rattling the plate off the table. "Why didn't you ever make these for us?"

"You mean over our campfires or in all those dodgy inns?" Lira leaned forward. "I know you didn't come here to sample my baking or even recruit more members for your crew. I also know that as much as you like me, you didn't come here for a social call."

Cali gave a curt nod. "Perceptive as always, although you're wrong about how much I missed my friend." The purring stopped. "But I did come here to warn you."

"Warn me?" Lira sat up straighter, instantly more alert.

Cali's ears folded. "Pirrin is dead."

Lira stared at her for a few beats as she thought about the Ranger she'd run with, the man who been as fierce a fighter as he'd been a loyal friend. "How?"

"No way to know. There wasn't a mark on his body."

Fear iced Lira's skin, and for the first time since she'd returned to Wayside, she wanted to run and not look back.

# Twenty-Six

"FUNNY THING, THAT," Sass said as she peeled off her boots and kicked them under her bed.

Lira was hanging over the washbasin, droplets clinging to her cheeks and nose as she shivered from splashing the frigid water on her face. She felt for the towel that was beside the ceramic bowl and patted her face dry without turning to Sass. "What is?"

"Your friend came all this way to see you, but you didn't look too happy about it."

Lira used the moments before she faced Sass to school her expression. "I was surprised to see her, that's all."

"Mmm," Sass hummed in a tone that told Lira she didn't quite believe her.

Why was Lira so reluctant to talk about her past with Sass? It didn't have a thing to do with where she was now or what they were doing. It wasn't like she'd hold it against the dwarf if she'd known Sass had run with a crew.

"She brought bad news," Lira finally said, walking toward her bed.

Sass frowned. "What kind of bad news?"

Lira stiffened, a part of her reluctant to say the thing out loud. She still hated to think about it.

"One of our crew is dead." Well, another one.

To her credit, Sass looked stricken. "That's awful. I'm so sorry."

Lira didn't meet her gaze, afraid that if she saw kindness in her eyes, she might crumble. "Thanks. Things are complicated in a crew, and you don't always like the folks you're running with, but I liked Pirrin."

She allowed a few memories of the man to resurface, and she even allowed herself a smile as she thought about laughing at his jokes that were always a touch raunchy. Pirrin hadn't minded leaning into his loner reputation, especially if it meant protecting the others, but he'd been much more than that. He'd been talented with a sword, and he would do anything for a friend. He hadn't deserved to die.

Lira shook off the worry that gnawed at her gut. Pirrin's death was a tragedy, but it didn't have anything to do with her.

"Do you mind if I ask how he died?"

Lira looked at Sass sitting on the bed across from hers, her short legs criss-crossed under the blanket. The dwarf had stripped down to her tunic, and her thick braid was curled up around her head, giving her a fuzzy halo.

"I wish I knew," Lira said, which was the truth.

The thought of Pirrin dying without a battle scar on him felt wrong in so many ways. He was a born fighter. He never would have gone down without a fight, and even she'd never been stealthy enough to sneak up on the man who was accustomed to watching his back.

How had there been no mark on his body? Pirrin was too shrewd to be poisoned. At least he had been. Lira wondered if he'd lost his edge after their crew disbanded. Had he felt as unmoored as she had after Malek's death?

Sass nodded, lips in a thin line. "It was nice of the pantheri to make the trip here to tell you."

Lira managed a weak smile. "Cali and I were always tight. She's the kind of fighter you want by your side—and the type of friend."

"It's good she's staying for a day or two then."

Sass had been the one to suggest Cali stay at the tavern—not that either of them knew if there were any more rooms with clean beds in the place—but Cali had declined with thanks, saying she already had her things at the inn.

"It is," Lira allowed, although a part of her was unsettled having her past intrude on her present.

"So, are you the last two left of your crew?"

Lira shook her head. "There's still Rog and Vaskel, but I don't know where they are."

"Your crew disbanded?"

"We did. I left first, but Pirrin was always one foot out the door." Then Lira added, as if the one word would explain it well enough. "Ranger."

Sass hummed. Either she knew something about Rangers or she'd heard rumors.

The conversation was veering perilously close to discussing why anyone left in the first place, and Lira didn't want to discuss Malek. She divested herself of her dress and swung her legs onto the bed and under the scratchy blanket. She rubbed her feet together to warm them, glad that the fire in the great room had sent heat to the second floor. Not that she would have said no to lighting the fireplace in their room, if Durn would spare the peat.

"You were right about the scones and chai," Lira said, changing the subject. "They were a hit."

Sass took the bait, straightening her legs and flopping back onto the pillow. "Who doesn't need a pick-me-up in the afternoon? You've got Pip making buns and loaves for the mornings, and most folks have their supper at home or at The Tusk & Tail, now that you can bake things without burning half of them. But there's nothing for the afternoon."

"Until now."

Sass turned her head to smile at Lira in the warbling light from the lamp huddled on the nightstand between them.

"I'll be honest with you." Sass looked up at the ceiling as if there was anything but feathery spiderwebs and water-stained wood planks to stare at.

Lira followed her lead and turned her face to the ceiling. "Please."

"I had doubts about that spicy milk tea, but it's good, and not too spicy for folks around here."

Lira was well aware that dwarves didn't employ a great deal of spice in their dishes, so she suspected that the "folks" Sass mentioned might mean her.

The corners of Lira's mouth quivered. "I'm glad you like it."

"And you can't beat those scones of yours, even with that foreign spice."

Lira rolled her head to Sass, a snip of a laugh escaping from her lips. "Cinnamon?"

Sass snapped her stubby fingers. "That's the one. Funny spice. Funny name."

Lira had never thought of cinnamon as an exotic spice, but then she'd traveled all across The Known Lands and Sass had only recently ventured south of the long wall.

Sass released a wistful sigh. "I don't know if it's because of all those funny spices or if it's the milk, but drinking chai is like drinking a hug."

Lira's chest hitched. She'd felt that same warm sensation the first time she'd had chai, like the spices were wrapping her up in a cozy cocoon. She remembered curling her hands around the mug so the heat could seep into her fingers as she'd taken small sips so she could prolong the sensation.

"Funny that a drink you've never had before can make you feel like you're home, isn't it?"

Lira didn't respond, her own throat too thick with emotion. Her gran had never tasted chai. They'd never made it in their farmhouse. Yet every time Lira took a sip of the warm drink, closing her eyes as the sweetness enveloped her, it was like her gran's arms were wrapping around her again.

"I'm not the only one who thought so," Sass continued. "That baker Pip said it made him think of growing up in Elmshire, which made him start going on and on about halfling houses. Not that Tin minded. I've never heard anyone say 'really, really?' as many times as I did today."

Lira smiled at that. She'd heard Pip wax poetic about Elmshire before. There was a time in her childhood when her greatest desire had been to go live in one of the fantastical homes in the ground that he described so eloquently. It had been all her gran could do to keep her from packing a bag and setting out for the halfling village.

"Then I suppose our plan is scones and chai in the afternoons." Lira had a firm handle on that even if she didn't have the same steady grasp on supper.

"And maybe something different for the pair of us for breakfast?"

Lira laughed out loud at that. "You don't want scones and chai morning, noon, and night?"

Sass frowned, as if not sure if she was being mocked or not. "Despite what you might have heard about dwarves, we don't eat the same thing every day. Our dishes are quite varied." She sniffed. "It just takes a dwarf's palate to discern the difference."

"Then we'll have something other than scones for our breakfast."

Lira thought about the spice cake she'd promised Korl. Then she remembered another cake her gran had made for the mornings, one with lots of cinnamon. Both of those would require another visit to the village for supplies—and another visit to Iris.

She leaned over and extinguished the flame of the hurricane lamp, plunging them both in darkness.

She would think about that tomorrow.

# Twenty-Seven

SASS WAS STILL ABED when Lira slid from beneath the warmth of the blanket and hurriedly dressed. If she was going to prepare something new for breakfast, she needed to be at the market when the vendors were first setting out their wares and unfurling their awnings.

Avoiding the creaky bottom step, Lira made her way downstairs and gave the doors to the kitchen a cursory look before continuing to the great room. The fire had burned out, but the earthy scent of peat lingered, along with what she liked to think was a hint of cinnamon. She plucked up the basket nestled beside one of the massive stuffed chairs and hooked it in the crook of her arm before slipping out the door.

Lira drew in a quick breath as the morning chill hit her, and she tugged the front of her cardigan together at her neck. Her steps were quick as she hurried along the dirt road into the heart of Wayside, sparing a glance at the waterwheel that powered the mill.

The sun was turning the world from lavender to gold as it warmed the sky and gilded the treetops. Lira breathed in the heady aroma of baking bread, another sign that it was early. Even when the rest of the village slumbered, Pip would be up feeding his dough into the ovens for morning buns and crusty loaves.

She passed the bakery with its lights on, but its door closed, and the rest of the shops that sat shoulder-to-shoulder and were dark and quiet. Although the stables were all the way on the other side of the market, she could smell the horses and hear their whinnies muffled by the thick mounds of hay and sturdy, wood plank doors.

She wasn't the only one out early, though, and her step faltered when she spotted some guardsman posting flyers on the outside of the cobbler's shop. She paused long enough to squint at the bold letters proclaiming a reward for information about the goblin gang that was roaming the area.

Was this because of the goblin she and Sass claimed had tried to rob the tavern? Was their lie the reason for the notices? She cringed, part of her awash with guilt and another part hoping the goblin gang warning was a result of their tall tale. The idea of a gang of the creatures was not pleasant.

Then a chill tickled the nape of her neck that had nothing to do with imagining goblins. She spun around, her gaze scouring the quiet street, the still windows, and then the roofline. She couldn't see anyone, but she could feel them. She was being watched. She was sure of it.

Her pulse jangled as she slowed her breath and took in everything around her. This wasn't the first time she'd felt eyes on her since she'd returned to Wayside. Of course, it could just be curious villagers peeking from behind curtains, but she doubted that would raise her hackles. Most likely, it was Rygor, although she still doubted his need to employ stealth.

Then as quickly as she'd sensed someone watching her, that feeling faded. Lira banished her worry and bustled forward, weaving her way through the village like a thread through familiar cloth, her steps keeping time with the town's awakening pulse.

She circled the stone monument that lorded over the heart of the square and reached the open-air market just when she intended to, as the vendors were putting the final touches on their displays. Wooden crates yielded up treasures of dew-kissed vegetables, jars of honey caught the newly risen sun like trapped amber, and rows of jam pots sat like jewels against rough-hewn tables.

"Aye, but you're out early," the greengrocer said as Lira picked out several glossy apples and a bottle of his cider.

She exchanged a few copper bits with him as she put the apples and cider in her basket. "Morning baking to do."

He nodded. "I heard they're serving food again at The Tusk & Tail, and you're the one making it."

"Guilty," Lira said, then remembered she should be drumming up business for them. "You should stop by. We have scones and chai in the afternoons."

"I might do," the man said, nodding again but this time with a wrinkle in his brows.

Lira was sure he was wondering what the word chai meant, but she decided she didn't have time to explain the drink to everyone she met. "The first chai's on me."

That got her a grin. He popped an extra apple in her basket. "Then you just might see me."

Lira managed to gather the rest of the ingredients she needed without much of a fuss, although she did find herself offering free chai more than a few times.

The cost of doing business, she thought. Besides, Sass had been bartering food already, so she didn't see the harm in tempting new customers to the tavern.

Once her basket was full, Lira headed out of the market. By now, the village was properly roused. The shops were lit from inside and some of the doors were propped open as customers drifted in and out.

She hesitated in front of the apothecary, her hand lingering on the door handle as she steeled herself. She hadn't spoken to Iris since she'd reacted badly to the woman's revelation. In her defense, discovering your gran had not only been part of a crew was hard enough to wrap her head around, but learning that she had also been a mage, would have been a lot for anyone.

Lira scowled at herself. She'd faced scarier things than this. Iris had practically been a second gran to her. Not to mention, she was probably the reason Lira was alive today.

Of course, that only reminded Lira that Iris had been a rogue and had never bothered to disclose that to her.

*Something you should have figured out yourself.*

She pushed the door open and strode inside with a good degree more hostility than she'd planned to bring.

Iris jumped as the bell jangled so shrilly that Lira wondered if she'd broken it. The woman's face relaxed a touch when she saw it was Lira. Then her forehead crinkled. "You still upset, love?"

Lira looked at Iris, noting all the silver glinting in her hair and the extra lines that marked the passing years. Then she thought of her gran, who was not there to take the brunt of Lira's anger or answer questions.

All the fight drained from her. "Not at you."

Iris shuffled around the counter to take Lira by the hand. "It's no use being mad at anyone. We can't reclaim the past. We can only try to understand it and move forward."

"Easy for you to say." Lira allowed herself to be led to the room behind the shop, ducking under the heavy curtain that Iris held aside for her. "Your life wasn't based on secrets."

The book-lined room smelled of tea, and Lira noticed the teapot sitting on the table. Iris poured some of the steaming brown liquid into a cup that sat waiting and handed it to her with a raised brow.

"I was a rogue. My best friend was a mage. My life was nothing but secrets." She made a clicking sound in the back of her throat, and the bookwyrms fluttered from their hiding spots. "My life is still filled with secrets."

Lira set her basket on the floor and watched as the tiny, winged creatures circled them overhead. "I guess you're right."

Iris snorted. "And these fellows aren't even really my secret to keep. Your gran was the one who made them."

Lira had raised her cup to her lips but now she almost dropped it. "She what?"

Iris flapped a hand, and a gaggle of bangles clanged on her wrist. "She was the mage, love. Not me. I forget what she was trying to create, but it wasn't these." Iris giggled. "She couldn't keep them when she took you in, so here we are."

"My gran cast creation spells?" Even though Iris had said she'd been a mage and had run with a crew, Lira had imagined her doing spells to open doors or start fires. Creation spells were both complex and frowned upon.

"She created that flutterstoat of yours, although that was less of an accident."

Now Lira did set her teacup down so she wouldn't drop it. "My gran made Crumpet?"

Iris shook her head. "Not made so much as enhanced. Why do you think he's so comfortable in a kitchen—and with you?"

Lira's head reeled at this, although she'd known there was something special about the little creature, aside from the fact that he had wings.

Iris's skirt rustled as she crossed to Lira and took her hand. "Why are you really here, love?"

Something snapped inside Lira as the woman held her gaze with her soft green eyes. She knew those eyes so well. If there was anyone she could trust it was her gran's best friend, the woman she'd run with, the woman who'd taken in a flock of enchanted bookwyrms to keep her gran's secret safe.

"Her book." The words burst from her as if they were the ones that had been trapped behind the stone wall. "The book where she kept all her recipes."

Iris's dark brows rose slowly. "The leather one with the moonstone embedded in the cover?"

Lira bobbed her head up and down. "It was the only thing she left me that I wanted to keep safe, so I hid it before I left Wayside."

Hurt flickered across Iris's face. "You could have left it with me."

"There wasn't time. I met up with my crew at The Tusk & Tail and it was either leave with them then or not go." It was hard to think back to being so reckless, so impulsive, so wracked with grief that she couldn't think straight. "I hid it where I thought no one would find it and where I could come back and retrieve it when I was ready."

Iris's shoulder's drooped. "You came back for your gran's recipes."

Lira shook her head. "That's why I thought I returned, but I came back for more than that. I came back because I wanted to be where I was happy. But I wouldn't have been happy if I'd stayed back then. I had to go away to become the version of me who can be happy here." Lira took a breath and realized she was babbling. "Does that make sense?"

"Of course it does, love."

It finally made sense to Lira too.

"So, you got the book? Your gran's recipes?"

"That's the problem. The place where I hid it in the tavern's cellar is stoned over. That's why I'm at The Tusk & Tail. I'm staying close until I can figure out a way to retrieve it."

"Then you need some help."

Lira started to wave her off, but Iris winked and steepled her fingers. "Two rogues are better than one."

## Twenty-Eight

WHEN LIRA LEFT THE APOTHECARY, she wasn't quite sure what had just happened. Had she inadvertently recruited Iris to help her break out her gran's recipe book? They might both be rogues, but the fact remained that the book was behind a stone wall and there was a tavern on top of it. Not a busy tavern, but not an empty one either. Not to mention the wyvern who was convinced there was gold hidden somewhere on the premises and would be happy to claim the coins hidden with her gran's recipe book.

It struck Lira that her desire to help The Tusk & Tail was working against her desire to retrieve what she'd hidden. The more patrons who came to sample the chai and nibble on her scones, the harder it would be to do much of anything in the cellar without being detected. Not to mention Rygor, the tavernkeep, Silas who seemed to suspect her of something, and...

"Lira!"

She'd been so lost in her thoughts that she'd almost walked right by the open door of the bakery. But it hadn't been Pip Brambleheart who'd called her name. It had been Cali.

Lira gathered herself as she stepped inside the shop where Pip was bustling behind the counter, and Cali stood on the other side of it nibbling on an enormous roll.

"You didn't tell me about these rolls," Cali said, her pink tongue darting out to lick at something sticky in the fur around her mouth.

"That's because she hasn't tried them." Pip pointed to a glass stand with a domed cover. "I was inspired to experiment after tasting your delicious scones. I hope you take these as an homage."

Lira eyed the puffy, swirled rolls under the dome and the glaze that coated them. "Those look incredible, but I don't see how they can be an homage. They look nothing like scones."

Pip flicked his fingers through his wiry hair, and bits of dough or glaze flew into the air. "I suppose they aren't. They're a yeast roll, much like my usual morning rolls. It was your unusual use of flavor that I used as inspiration."

"So, they have cinnamon in them?"

Pip scrunched his lips to one side. "No, lemon."

Lira couldn't stop herself from grinning at the nervous halfling. "I don't think you need to worry about anyone confusing these with scones, but I'm happy if I inspired you in any way."

"So am I," mumbled Cali as she devoured the last bite of her roll.

"I'd love to try one." Lira's stomach had been grumbling at her since she'd caught the first whiff of yeast that morning, and now it was relentless in its complaints.

Pip briskly lifted the glass dome and pulled a swirl onto a plate before passing it to Lira. "It's on the house." He smiled. "For the inspiration."

Lira didn't waste time in taking a bite, and she also didn't bother to hide her groan. The dough was pillowy and yeasty with a tang of lemon between the layers and a sweet glaze that was just tart enough. "Pip, these might be the best thing I've ever eaten."

"Didn't I tell you?" Cali said.

"Yes, you told me." Lira shot her a look before returning her attention to Pip. "You're a baking genius."

His smile brightened. "I haven't felt much like a genius or a baker for the past few years, if I'm being honest. It's been the same every day—up early, morning rolls, loaves, early to bed—but now I remember what it's like to feel inspired." He leveled a knobby finger at her. "Your gran and I used to do this, you know."

"Do what?" Lira asked as she swallowed the last bite of the gooey roll.

"Share ideas, swap recipes, inspire each other." He gave her a watery smile. "I didn't realize how much I'd missed it."

Lira wasn't sure what to say. She'd never thought much about how losing her gran had affected others in the village, which she now saw had been youthful arrogance and the short-sightedness of her sadness.

"That's one of Lira's true talents," Cali said as she licked one gray paw clean. "She brings out the best in others."

Lira's mouth gaped. "Do you really think that, Cal?"

The pantheri looked slightly affronted by the question. "I wouldn't say it if I didn't. You made everyone in our crew better by creating some kind of synergy. When you joined, we became greater than the sum of our parts."

Lira had never known her friend felt that way. Before she could think of something to say, Pip bobbed his head vigorously.

"Just look at all that's happened since you returned to Wayside. The tavern is no longer an eyesore, I've started creating new recipes again, and Korl is walking around humming, of all things."

"That's not all because of me," Lira protested. "Sass is a big part of the changes."

Cali's eyes narrowed. "And how did Sass become your partner in crime?"

Lira didn't answer, but she wondered if Cali used the word crime on purpose. Was it just her feline instincts?

"I'm happy I inspired you," Lira said, "but if I'm being honest, I'm still baking from memory at this point, and it's a bit hit or miss."

"Baking is all about hits and misses." Pip busied himself behind the counter again. "I heard that Korl fixed your oven."

"He did, which I hope means there will be more hits than misses now."

"Such a nice boy," Pip said more to himself than to the two friends.

"The orc?" Cali asked Lira in a whisper, clearly confused by Pip referring to the massive, full-grown guardsman as a boy.

Lira nodded, an unwanted flush warming her cheeks as she thought about Korl. "The orc."

Cali licked her other sticky paw as she eyed Lira. "Interesting."

Lira ignored the comment and lifted the basket hanging on one arm. "I'd better get these back to the tavern. I promised Sass some breakfast that wasn't scones."

Cali motioned to the lemon sweet rolls. "If she finds out about these and that you didn't bring her any...well, I wouldn't want to be on the bad end of an angry dwarf."

"How would she find...?" Lira stopped herself at the pantheri's smug smile that curved her whiskers. "You'd tell her, wouldn't you?"

"I don't think there's going to be a person I *don't* tell about these rolls."

Lira laughed as she stepped closer to the counter and tipped her head at the domed stand. "I'll take three of these to go."

Cali cleared her throat. "What dwarf would only eat three of these in a sitting?"

Pip took out a paper bag and nodded his agreement. "They wouldn't last past second breakfast in a halfling house, and our ample appetites can't hold a candle to those of dwarves."

Lira thought that they were making a lot of assumptions about Sass based on her being a dwarf, but she also knew that Sass loved pastries. "Fine. Make it six."

"I might have at least one more," Cali said.

"You're coming back to the tavern with me?" Lira kept the surprise from her voice.

"I was on my way to you when I was waylaid by this smell." Cali's ears twitched. "We didn't get much time to catch up yesterday."

Lira hoped that catching up and telling her about Pirrin were the only reasons Cali had come, but she had a growing feeling that they weren't.

Cali slapped a handful of copper bits on the counter. "Make it a dozen, and it's on me."

# Twenty-Nine

**THE MORNING BREEZE** carried the mingled scents of fresh-baked bread and wood smoke as Lira and Cali made their way back to The Tusk & Tail. Lira breathed deeply, savoring the warm, sugary aroma wafting from the paper-wrapped bundle of lemon sweet rolls tucked against her chest.

She still couldn't believe Pip had created these overnight, and she marveled at his talent for whipping up something new that was so incredible. Her baking experiments had been a bit bumpier.

"I've missed halfling bakers," Cali said, her tail swishing as she walked. "If I'd known you had baking skills, I wouldn't have had to take so many detours to Elmshire."

"Me keeping you in pastries wouldn't have done much for bringing in coin," Lira said. "Besides, you didn't need my help to obtain baked goods."

"That was one time!" Cali's ears flattened in mock outrage. "And if she didn't want someone to eat those fruit tarts, that lady shouldn't have left them cooling by an open window."

"The window was on the second floor, Cal."

"Please. As if height has ever been an obstacle for me." Cali's golden eyes flashed. "Besides, you and the rest of the crew were only upset because the tarts didn't survive the jump back down."

Lira laughed at the memory of Cali landing in a crouch with gooey fruit filling crushed under her paws and a red-faced woman shrieking from above. That had been one of their more rapid departures from a village.

"That's hardly—" Lira started, but stopped short as the tavern came into view. The steady rhythm of hammer strikes from the blacksmith rang out across the village, but there was another sound mixing with the metallic ring from the forge—a different kind of pounding, and it was coming from The Tusk & Tail.

Cali followed her gaze, putting her paws on her hips. "Well, that's something you don't see everyday."

There were two figures on the tavern's roof, one orc and one human, and Lira knew them both. Val's blonde hair caught the morning sun as she straightened and swiped her forearm across her brow, but it was Korl's dusky green arms that made the breath hitch in Lira's chest. He wasn't wearing his usual quilted chest plate, and his thin white tunic showed every ripple of his shoulder muscles as he heaved up rotten thatch.

"Well, well," Cali murmured, dropping her voice to a whisper that only Lira's half-elven ears could catch. "If it isn't your strong, silent admirer."

"Shh!" Lira hissed, though the pair was too far away to hear. "He is not my admirer. He's an old friend. Besides, he barely speaks to me."

"Exactly my point," Cali purred. "A man who doesn't talk too much sounds perfect to me. And did you see how concerned he was yesterday when I showed up unannounced? He wasn't sure if I was friend or foe, and he was ready to defend you."

"He's always with Val." Lira gestured at the tall woman. "And who could compete with that?"

Cali tilted her head, studying the broad-shouldered guard with her appraising feline gaze. "She is striking, and there's definitely some Goliath blood there, but I still think you could take her."

"I am not fighting anyone over—" Lira spluttered.

"Too bad," Cali said with a smile. "Because that would be worth watching."

Lira groaned. There was nothing Cali loved more than to tease her, and somehow Lira always fell for it.

"Morning!" Val called down cheerfully when she spotted them, pausing in her work to wave. Beside her, Korl gave a small nod of acknowledgment but kept his focus steadfastly on the task at hand.

"What brings you to our rooftop?" Lira asked, although she suspected she knew the answer.

"Oh, a little bird told us your roof might need some attention," Val replied with a knowing grin. "Or rather, a little dwarf mentioned something about nearly falling through it."

Of course, it had been Sass.

"You really don't have to do that." Lira's protests felt hollow, and she didn't want to sound ungrateful. "But it's awfully nice of you."

Val gave Korl a pointed look, but he was too busy ripping up thatch to notice. "We didn't want either of you to be in danger. Besides, if rain starts coming through this thing, none of us down below will be happy about it."

"Well...thank you." Lira gave a final wave as she continued inside with Cali a step behind her.

Sass stood arranging chairs around the freshly scrubbed tables, her long brown braid swinging as she worked. She stopped when she saw Lira and Cali. "You're back, and you brought your friend, the archer."

Lira tapped a toe on the wood plank floor. "Are you the reason Val and Korl are on our roof?"

"Might have mentioned something to Val about my foot going through that soft spot when we were sitting up there," Sass said, not looking the least bit apologetic. "Pure coincidence they showed up to fix it, I'm sure."

Lira raised an eyebrow. "Just how often do you talk to Val?"

"She's one of our regulars," Sass replied with a shrug. "I have to make polite conversation. Besides, you weren't complaining when Korl fixed the stove yesterday."

A twinge of guilt tugged at Lira's conscience. The orc guardsman had already done so much for the tavern, and so far he'd only accepted payment in baked goods.

That reminded her of the sweet rolls she'd gotten from Pip. She glanced at the bag in her arms. "I should take them some breakfast at least."

"Breakfast?" Sass's gaze went to the bag. "Is that what I smell?"

"Lemon sweet rolls," Cali said reverently. "They're heavenly."

"Did you have something to do with the tavern sign hanging up straight, too?" Lira asked as Sass and Cali followed her into the kitchen.

Sass admitted to asking the ogre chair deliverers to hook it back up, then she set about ooo-ing and ahh-ing over the sweet rolls with Cali, as Lira briskly prepared two mugs of spiced chai. The dwarf and the pantheri shamelessly stuffed their faces with gooey pastry as the warming blend of cardamom, cinnamon, and ginger rose in fragrant clouds of steam from the pot Lira left on the stove.

She shook her head at the pair. "You'd think you'd never eaten before."

Sass held up one hand. "Dwarf's honor, I've never eaten like this before." She put a hand to her stomach after her third sweet roll. "I cannot wait for afternoon scones."

Lira laughed, then carefully balancing the mugs with two wrapped sweet rolls in a bag, she made her way up the stairs and to her room. It took some effort to balance herself and the hot drinks as she hoisted herself through the window and paused on the sill.

"Hells!" Val put a hand to her heart at the sight of Lira, her shirt-sleeves pushed up to her elbows, exposing ropey forearms. "You scared me half to death appearing like that." Then she saw the mugs in her hand. "But I won't say no to a break."

Lira handed Val a chai and examined the neat rows of fresh thatch. "This is beautiful work."

"Had to strip it down to the supports in this section," Val explained as she put the mug to her lips, pointing to where they'd layered the new straw. "But it should hold now. We used the good reed thatch from upstream, not that swamp grass they've been passing off as roofing material lately."

Lira noticed Korl's quick glance in her direction before he returned his attention to his work.

"I also brought Pip's newest pastry creation." Lira held up the bag that contained two of the large sweet rolls.

"Perfect timing—I'm starving," Val said, accepting her share with enthusiasm and demolishing the roll in three bites. She washed it down with chai and then brushed the sticky crumbs from her hands. She glanced at Korl then back at Lira. "Think I'll go warm up by that lovely fire Sass has going."

She disappeared through the open window leaving Lira on the roof with the orc. Once Val was gone, Korl paused in his work, carefully wiping his hands before accepting the offered mug.

When Lira tried to hand him the sweet roll, he shook his head. "You should have some too."

"I already had one." She nudged the sweet roll toward him.

His eyes met hers for a brief moment before darting away. "You take half, and we can eat together."

Lira realized that he might not eat it if she didn't, so she tore the remaining roll into two pieces and handed him half. He took the mug from her and sat on the peak of the roof, his massive frame somehow managing to look comfortable.

Lira settled next to him, and they ate in companionable silence, the sounds of the village drifting to them along with the muffled voices of those inside the tavern below. She caught him stealing glances at her between bites, though he always looked away when she turned toward him.

"Aren't these delicious?" Lira asked, licking the last bit of lemony glaze from her fingers.

He grunted in response, although his mouth was full of sweet roll.

They'd had a nice conversation the day before, so why was he so shy again?

"Heard you and Sass were sitting up here when she almost fell through," Korl said, breaking the quiet. "Why?"

"Why what? Why did her foot go through the thatch?"

He grunted. "Why would you sit on a roof?"

Lira drew her knees up to her chest, considering. She supposed that was a valid question if you were an orc who was easily twice her size. "I've always liked roofs. It's quiet up here. You can see the stars at night, think without interruption." She gestured at the village spread out before them. "See everything and everyone without being noticed."

They watched as villagers went about their morning routines—the line snaking out of Pip's bakery, children racing hoops down the dirt road, the chandler setting up a sandwich board sign outside her shop. Korl's shoulder was close enough that she could feel the warmth radiating from him in the cool morning air.

"That makes sense. If I can't find you, I'll know to look to the rooftops." Korl's deep voice was a rasp that sent a shiver through her.

His dark eyes met hers again, holding her gaze for a heartbeat longer than Lira expected. For a moment, she thought he might kiss her, and her pulse fluttered. But then he rose in one fluid motion and disappeared through the open window, leaving Lira to puzzle over his abrupt departure.

*What in the hells was that?* Lira pressed a hand to her racing heart. She'd had less of a reaction the last time a man had actually kissed her.

Had she said something to make Korl leave? Or had he left because he was done with the job and breakfast? More and more, she was learning that Korl didn't do things the expected way.

"Oi, up there!" Sass stood outside the tavern shouting up at her. "You might have gotten out of making breakfast by bringing me the best sweet rolls in existence, but that doesn't mean you're off the hook for the afternoon rush. Those scones won't bake themselves!"

Lira laughed as she stood and balanced on the pitch of the newly thatched roof. "Rush? We have a handful of regulars."

"Building momentum," Sass called back confidently. "Mark my words—the rush is coming!"

Shaking her head, Lira took one last look at the village before heading down. Maybe the dwarf was right. Maybe something was building there.

# Thirty

LIRA'S HANDS moved with practiced ease as she measured the ingredients for the scones—flour, sugar, salt—while her mind wandered back to the roof and Korl. Just when she thought she understood the orc, he stood up and walked away. Had she said something that bothered him or worse, bored him?

She knew she should be focused on the task at hand, the scones, or the even bigger task, retrieving her gran's cookbook.

*Focus, Lira, focus.*

A soft chittering sound drew her attention to the window. Crumpet balanced on the sill, his white fur ruffled by the breeze and his whiskers dancing from side to side. His furry wings—barely larger than the leaves of a mocker nut tree—fluttered as he hopped down onto the counter.

"Well, look who's come to supervise," Lira said, reaching for the cinnamon. The flutterstoat watched her with glittering black eyes as she began cutting cold butter into the flour mixture. "I don't suppose *you* can explain why some people are so hard to read?"

Crumpet tilted his head, his intelligent face curious as he blinked at her.

"I mean, most people give you something to work with. A smile, a frown, excessive talking about themselves—" She thought of some of the more boisterous folks she'd encountered in her adventuring days. "But Korl is impossible. One day he talks, the next day he doesn't."

The flutterstoat chittered, and Lira answered in a higher-pitched voice, mimicking what she imagined would be Crumpet's response. "Maybe he's only talking to you to be nice."

"Fair point, Crump." She pointed a floury finger at him. "He doesn't have a problem talking to Val, does he?"

"No, he doesn't," she said in her Crumpet falsetto.

The flutterstoat's whiskers turned down. It was clear he was not impressed with the voice.

"Maybe that's because they work together. Guardsmen would have a lot of things to talk about."

"Or maybe it's because they're more than colleagues," she told herself in Crumpet's voice as she shaped the scone dough.

Crumpet, who was now grooming his wings with an air of skepticism that seemed far too knowing, chittered at her in what Lira would swear was a disapproving tone.

"I must be losing my mind, talking to myself in an empty kitchen—and answering."

"Yes, you must," she said in Crumpet's voice.

"What's crazy is answering yourself," Cali said from the doorway, making Lira jump. The pantheri's eyes widened as she spotted Crumpet, and he flapped his small wings. "Well, hello there. That's new."

Cali stepped fully into the kitchen and released the swinging doors, walking closer to Crumpet and extending a hand. Crumpet stood on his hind legs, assessing the feline newcomer with shrewd eyes before sniffing a paw and chirping what sounded suspiciously like approval.

"Crumpet likes you," Lira said.

Cali's own whiskers twitched. "Crumpet, eh? Well, I've always been fond of weasels."

"He's a flutterstoat," Lira corrected.

Cali held up her paws. "My mistake. I've always been fond of stoats, flutter or otherwise."

Lira stared at her levelly. "Because they taste—?"

"Nothing like that." Cali waved away the suggestion. "You know I don't catch my own food, and pantheris are more vegetarian anyway."

"Glad to hear it," Lira said, smiling at Crumpet. "I'm pretty fond of the little guy."

"You always were a sucker for an enchanted being."

"Sucker seems a bit harsh." Lira cut the scones and moved them onto a baking sheet. "Besides, we've seen stranger things in our travels."

Cali settled onto a stool she dragged over from the corner. Her tail curled around its base as she watched Lira brush the tops of the scones with cream. "Remember that talking mushroom circle in the Whispering Woods?"

"The ones that only spoke in riddles?" Lira smiled at the memory. "Pirrin was convinced they were giving us directions to ancient treasure."

"And instead, we ended up waist-deep in that fairy pond." Cali's whiskers twitched with amusement, but there was a sadness in her eyes at the mention of their fallen friend.

Lira slid the scones into the oven and didn't miss a beat before she began measuring ingredients for the spice cake she'd promised Korl. "I miss him."

Cali nodded. "He would have loved to see this place come back to life." She drummed her claws on the table. "This is where it all started. Right here in this very tavern."

"I still remember how terrified I was to approach you and Malek. I knew you must be adventurers by your clothing, but I could barely summon the courage to talk to you, much less ask to join."

"You were so green," Cali said. "But you actually turned green when Vaskel, Pirrin, and Rog showed up."

"All of you together were a lot."

"Gods, you were not the best rogue back then."

"Excuse me?" Lira pressed a hand to her chest in mock offense. "I was an excellent rogue!"

"In your first quest, you apologized to the guard captain after picking his pocket!"

Crumpet chittered what sounded suspiciously like laughter.

Lira scowled at the creature. "It was my first time! And he looked so disappointed that my flirting hadn't been genuine. I felt bad for the guy."

"We were desperate when we took you on," Cali admitted. "We were short a rogue, winter was coming on, and that necromancer's tower wasn't going to raid itself."

Lira whisked the cake batter with more force than necessary. "Always nice to know you were the desperate choice."

"Hey." Cali's paw touched her arm. "It turned out to be the best choice we could have made. You saved our skins more times than I can count."

The batter smoothed under Lira's whisk, taking on a silky sheen. "Even though I apologized to marks?"

"*Especially* because you apologized to marks. Your conscience kept us human." Cali paused. "Well, human-adjacent, in my case—and Rog's." She watched as Lira poured the batter into the pan. "Speaking of running with our crew, are you sure about leaving all that behind to come back here?"

Lira's hands stilled. Through the window, she could see the stream gurgling over rocks as it wound its way down to the waterwheel at the mill, she could hear the strike of the blacksmith's iron. The same blacksmiths who'd fixed her gran's cart, the same mill where they'd gotten their flour, the same cool water flowing the same way it had all those years ago. But it was different now. Or maybe she was the one who was different.

"I am," she said finally. "For the first time in a long while, I think I am." She turned to her friend. "What about you? What's next for the infamous Cali Quickdraw?"

Before the pantheri could answer, Sass burst through the door, her brown braid swinging. "Your scone admirers are gathering early. And by gathering, I mean there are folks outside asking for them. Folks who aren't our usual folks. Not to mention the lady chandler."

Crumpet chittered excitedly and fluttered up to perch on the rack where the copper pots hung.

"The one you want to set up with Durn?" Lira asked.

Sass hitched one shoulder. "I might have bribed her with a free scone."

"What are you using to bribe Durn to look presentable?" Cali asked.

Sass worked the end of her braid in one hand. "I hadn't thought about that. Maybe I should offer her an ale to make him look better."

"Better make it a few ales."

Sass wagged a finger at Cali. "The longest tunnel starts with a single strike of the axe."

Lira grabbed a dishcloth, grinning. "Well then, we shouldn't keep them waiting." She pulled open the oven door, releasing a wave of warm, spiced air. "Though I still think you're overly optimistic about this rush of yours."

"Mark my words," Sass called as she headed back to the dining room. "This is just the beginning!"

Cali's whiskers twitched with amusement. "You know what? I think the dwarf might be right. Not about Durn, though. That would take some powerful magic." She stood and stretched. "Need help carrying anything out?"

"Always," Lira said, and together they began loading scones onto serving plates, falling into the same easy rhythm they'd had during their adventuring days.

Lira hadn't missed everything about running with a crew, but she had missed this.

# Thirty-One

IT WASN'T until after the afternoon scone rush, as Sass insisted on calling it, that Iris appeared at the tavern. Lira heard her throaty laugh from the kitchen and emerged, wiping her hands on her apron.

"There you are, love." Iris sat at the bar facing Cali and sipping on a mug of chai, one finger absently twirling a curl of hair.

Lira clocked the half-eaten scone on her plate. "When did you get here?"

"I haven't been here long." The apothecary slid her spectacles from the top of her head where they were holding back her raucous curls and peered at Lira through them. "I've been chatting with your charming friend."

Cali smiled, raising her own mug at Lira.

She and her former colleague had never discussed how much they would share with those outside their crew, but Lira hoped Cali hadn't been telling tales about her, especially not ones about how green a rogue she'd once been.

"Have you?" Lira folded her arms across her chest.

Iris swiveled fully to face her, holding up the half of her scone that remained. "These are quite delicious. I think the addition of the spice might make them better than your gran's."

The compliment dissolved Lira's concern. "I don't know about that. I'm glad I remembered as much as I did."

"Take the compliment," Cali said.

Iris closed the distance between them and took her hand. "You haven't by chance recalled your gran's recipe for teacakes, have you?"

Lira lowered her voice and bowed her head, so it was close to the woman's. "No, but maybe if I had her book of—"

"Yes, love," Iris interrupted, tugging her hand toward the kitchen. "Of course, I'll help you. All you had to do was ask."

But Lira hadn't asked, and before she could, the woman was hurrying her from the great room. Instead of slipping into the kitchen, Iris feinted and ducked through the cellar door.

"What are you—?" Lira asked as she was being pulled down the stairs in the dark.

"What do you think, love? I'm here to inspect the wall that's keeping you from your gran's book."

At the bottom of the stairs, Iris paused. The two women breathed together, no sounds of footsteps overhead following them.

"I hate to be a spoilsport," Lira whispered, even though it was only the two of them in the dank underground space, "but there's no light down here and my illumination stone is in my bedroom."

Iris uttered a familiar elvish word and the necklace she'd worn since Lira had known her, the one with a single stone held in place within the pointed pendant, started to glow.

Lira opened and closed her mouth before finally speaking. "You wear an illumination stone around your neck?"

Iris shrugged. "You never know when you'll need light."

Lira shook her head as she pointed across the cellar. It was hard to be angry at Iris for keeping secrets when the secrets were so obvious. "It's all the way over there and around the corner."

Iris led the way, her necklace casting enough light for them to see the barren shelves and the splintered baskets. She made disapproving sounds in the back of her throat as the aroma of decay reached them.

Lira put a hand over her nose. "We haven't cleaned the cellar yet."

"Nor should you. This isn't your neglect, it's Durn's. And I hate to say that it isn't only grief that's brought this on. His wife indulged him and did too much. That man weaponized his failings until they became too much of a truth for him to undo." Something scuttled away from them, and Iris sighed. "Yet another reason I'm happier on my own."

When they rounded the corner, the woman stopped and braced her hands on her hips. "That's some wall."

Lira passed her, slapping a palm onto the smooth stone. "It's solid, too. I'd guess it was made using river rocks."

Iris joined her and also placed her hands on the wall. "Might be that Durn had to reinforce the cellar. The Tusk & Tail hasn't had much in the way of repair since he built it."

"I know. Sass almost fell through the roof."

Iris glanced at her, but she didn't ask why the dwarf had been on the roof. "I heard Korl and his friend were fixing it this morning."

"Val," Lira said, hating that her face warmed when she thought of the orc.

"Mmm. Attractive girl. Tall. But I suppose you would have to be sizable to serve as a guard."

Lira inclined her head to the wall. "What do you think?"

Iris returned her attention to the stones. "Where exactly did you bury your gran's book?"

Lira walked to the corner and squatted. "Right here. That way it would be easy to find." She produced a dagger that was tucked inside her waistband and scraped at the mortar around the stone. Only the barest amount sifted to the dirt floor. "But it won't be easy to retrieve. Not without attracting attention."

Iris knelt beside her, the light oscillating along with the pendant. She squinted at the hefty gray stone that took up a considerable share of the wall's edge. "You're sure it's back there?"

"No," Lira admitted. "I'm sure I left it there, but I have no way of knowing if it's still there." She didn't mention that she was fairly confident it was there because the box that held the book also held gold coins. Gold that Rygor smelled.

"If Durn found it when he built the wall, I have a feeling I would have heard about it."

"You think he would have told you he'd found a recipe book buried in his cellar?" If he'd found it, he would have most likely kept the gold and kept his mouth shut.

Iris made another sound in the back of her throat. "Mmm. It's a small village. Word would have gotten out."

*If he hadn't seen the book as worthless and tossed it out after keeping the gold,* Lira thought. But that brought her back to why the tavern was in such a state if Durn had gold.

Iris ran her fingers along the rough mortar, tapping her fingernails on it. "I might have something that could dissolve this enough to loosen the stone."

"A potion?"

Iris chuckled. "No, love. A solvent that removes paint."

A paint solvent? Why hadn't Lira thought of that?

The light glowing from Iris's necklace dimmed as she backed from the wall. "Even if we loosen the stone, it won't be a quiet job."

"Not even with two rogues."

Iris shot her a look, but it was laced with amusement. "Not even then. But let me think on it." Her eyes flashed. "It's been a while since I planned a heist, but retrieving items from unworthy owners used to be my specialty."

Lira trailed the woman to the base of the stairs. "Do I even want to ask?"

Iris grinned at her in the fading blue light. "Do you want to hear about your gran casting a spell to immobilize a troll, making it collapse in front of our only escape route?"

It was strange to think about her gran being young and living a life full of adventure and magic, but it gave them one more thing in common. "She didn't."

Iris took her hand as the light in her illumination stone spluttered out, leading her up the stairs to the cellar door. "Oh, she did, love."

# Thirty-Two

LIRA'S FEET ached as she trudged up the last few steps to the room she shared with Sass. The scones and chai had gained them several new customers, and half of those had returned for dinner. At the request of Val, Lira had made more hand pies.

"Easier to eat them," the guard had said, as she'd taken her usual spot by the fire and continued knitting her particularly long orange scarf.

Lira assumed it had to be for Korl or his dads. Anyone else would drown in wool by the time they wrapped it around themselves enough to keep it from dragging on the floor.

But it was Iris who occupied her mind now that she could stop working long enough to think. If Iris could help her loosen the stone and retrieve her gran's recipe book...

What? Her goal since she'd arrived had been to get the book she'd hidden, the thing she associated most with her gran. Not to mention the gold she'd tucked away so she could start fresh somewhere. But her appetite for adventuring had gone over that cliff with Malek, and she wasn't sure it ever brought her as much joy as she felt biting into Pip's lemon sweet rolls, taking her first sip of chai in the morning, laughing with Sass about her cooking misadventures, or chatting with Crumpet while she baked.

She shuffled her feet the last few steps and pushed open the door, stopping for a beat and glancing around to ensure she'd opened the right one.

"Come on in," Sass called. "You aren't seeing things."

Lira gaped at the compact room that was usually cold and dark when she entered. Tonight, a fire burned in the hearth, sending gold light dancing across the ceiling and floor.

Where the floorboards had once been bare now lay a rag rug. It was worn but it also looked familiar. Now her bare feet wouldn't freeze when they touched the floor in the mornings.

Then her gaze shifted to the beds. Sass was already in hers, tucked under a fluffy, floral coverlet that matched the one on her bed, neither of which had been there before. The fabric was a riot of enormous open blooms and vibrant colors so garish she almost laughed.

"Where did you get—?" Lira started to say before Sass held up a hand.

"Before you ask if I spent coin we don't have, Tin gave me the fabric for the coverlets at no charge. Can you believe no one in the village wanted this pattern?"

Lira could, but that didn't mean she didn't like it. The blown-open coral roses and bright yellow tulips that were splashed across her bed gave life to a room that had been utilitarian and sad.

"The rug is from Iris," Sass continued. "She said it came from your gran's old cottage."

Lira stepped forward and onto the rug. Of course. It had sat under their table in the breakfast nook, which explained why the middle was less faded than the edges.

"What do you think?" Sass's expression was hopeful as she wiggled herself upright in bed and propped her pillow behind her back.

"Honestly?" Lira cocked her head before smiling at Sass. "I think it's wonderful. Much better than sleeping in a cold room under scratchy blankets."

"It is, isn't it?" Sass patted the braid coiled atop her head. "I figured if we were making the rest of the place look so welcoming, we should get some of the love."

Lira liked the sound of that. It had been a long time since she'd allowed herself some love or even a small measure of comfort. Kicking off her shoes, she scrunched her toes on the rag rug as she made her way to her bed, sloughing off the rest of her clothes until she was in her shift. She slipped under her floral coverlet, sinking into the mattress that was still an impossible combination of saggy and hard.

"The beds are still uncomfortable and the blankets inside the new fabric are still the grays ones but—"

"It doesn't matter," Lira said before Sass could give any further explanation that might spoil the magic she'd created in their room. "It's better because you cared."

Sass scooted herself lower in the bed, not looking over. "The fire doesn't hurt either."

The warmth pulsed off the burning wood and gave the room a slightly sweet aroma. "No peat?"

Sass wrinkled her nose. "Can't stand the smell of it. The stuff is fine in the great room because there's enough space and the scent can be overpowered by other odors, your spicy tea and meat pies for instance."

"That and Durn won't pay for wood to burn in a hearth that big," Lira said.

Sass grunted. "No, he won't."

"So how did you get—?"

"Cut it myself." Sass winked at her. "I told you I was good with an axe, and that last storm took down some small trees by the stream."

"Speaking of Durn, how did it go with the chandler set-up?"

Sass released a tortured sigh. "Penny is a catch, but I'm not sure if Durn is smart enough to catch her."

That sounded about right.

"I'm not giving up, though. Everyone deserves to be happy."

Lira wouldn't mind if Durn had something to distract him from his malaise and draw him away from the tavern—and its cellar. Not that she could admit that to Sass.

She wiggled her toes under the coverlet. "When did you have time to do this between drumming up scone business and matchmaking for Durn?"

"I talked to Tin yesterday about the fabric, but I came up here when you and Iris were down in the cellar."

With that, Sass punched her pillow a few times and rolled over to go to sleep.

Lira stopped herself from groaning out loud. Sass knew she'd been in the cellar—again. If the dwarf was clever and curious—and Lira knew she was both—she'd start wondering why Lira kept sneaking into the cellar.

She lay back in bed, staring at the firelight shadows dancing across the ceiling with a sick feeling twisting her stomach.

LIRA STEWED on it all the next day, going through the motions of rolling out scones and making meat pies for their ever-growing clientele. By the following morning, she couldn't wait any longer.

The bell jangled as she burst into the apothecary, and Iris's face barely had time to register surprise.

"We should come clean," Lira said, the words tripping over each other. "*I* should come clean. I should tell Durn about the book."

When she was done with her announcement, Lira clutched her side and sucked in a breath. She'd practically run through the village to reach Iris, even ignoring the tempting smell of sweet rolls billowing from the bakery and throwing a passing wave of greeting to Pip and Fenni.

Iris's response to her outburst was a smile as she came around the counter and curled an arm around her waist. "It sounds like you've been thinking this over for a bit."

No shock. No arguments. Just a patient nod as she led Lira to the back room.

Lira flopped onto one of the overstuffed chairs as Iris opened the latch on the bookwyrms' cage, releasing them into the air to swoop overhead. Watching the tiny creatures flutter to the bookshelves and daintily brush the leather spines with their wings did make Lira smile.

Iris pressed a cup of tea into her hand. "Why don't you tell me what happened between when I saw you last and now?"

Lira sipped her tea, the sweetness of the warm drink settling her nerves almost as much as the rhythmic beating of wings overhead. "Well, Sass saw us, for one."

"Did she?"

"She saw us coming from the cellar." Saying it aloud made it sound less catastrophic than it had in her head.

Iris hitched a dark brow. "The cellar that holds the food stores?"

Lira huffed out a breath. "Sass knows there's nothing down there that isn't rancid."

"Did she say anything about it?"

"Not specifically, but she did mention seeing us coming from the cellar."

Iris poured herself a cup of tea and set the kettle on the table. "And you think that she'll think we were...what? Discussing ways to get through the wall to retrieve a book you hid years ago?"

"When you put it like that," Lira grumbled from behind her cup.

Iris laughed and shook her head. "I taught you stealth and secrecy. Don't tell me you were this nervous when you were with your crew?"

Lira released a heavy breath and sank deeper into the chair. "Of course, I wasn't. That would be a quick way to get killed." She flicked her eyes to the woman who'd taught her how to stay calm under pressure. "I'm not sure why this is so much harder."

One of the bookwyrms landed on Iris's shoulder after she shrugged it. "Maybe because this isn't any old job. This is something that matters to you. Keeping secrets from these people matters to you."

Lira frowned at this. She'd snuck into grand manors, tricked unwitting guards, charmed unsuspecting castle staff. This shouldn't be any different.

But it was.

It was one thing to divest a spoiled lady of jewels she didn't need or snatch an ancient scroll from a collector who would hardly miss it. That was work, and she'd rarely deceived anyone who didn't deserve to have their purse lightened.

Even though she'd made her way in the world as a rogue, Lira didn't like lying to friends. And, she realized with a start, she now considered Sass a friend.

Hiding the true reason she was there felt wrong, even if the true reason was no longer the only reason. She couldn't imagine getting the recipe book and gold and leaving now. Not when she and Sass had worked so hard to make the tavern flourish again, with plenty of help from Korl, Val, Tin, Pip, and even Crumpet.

Every day at The Tusk & Tail had led her farther from her original objective and closer to staying in Wayside for good. There was little reason to keep her secret any longer, if only there wasn't a wyvern on the hunt for gold.

"You're right," Lira said. "I shouldn't keep this secret from Sass—or any of my friends. I'll bet if I told Durn, he'd let us remove a few stones to retrieve the book."

Iris's teacup bobbled in her hands. "I'm not sure if that's a good idea."

Lira sat up. "I thought you were suggesting I not keep any more secrets?"

The bookwyrm took flight from Iris's shoulder as she twitched, darting to a stack of gilded-edge tomes on the table and using the flap of his wings to clear the dust.

"From Sass, no. From what I can tell, the dwarf has earned your trust." Iris gestured to the bookwyrms. "And mine. She hasn't breathed a word of my little friends."

"Or told anyone about Crumpet."

"But not everyone is so accepting of magic," Iris said, wrinkles forming around her mouth as she pursed it in disapproval.

"You mean Durn." Lira had no problem believing that the gruff tavernkeep would not be open to magic. She had a very strong suspicion he had never recognized what had been magical in his own life before he'd lost it.

Iris nodded. "He's not in the right headspace to be trusted."

"I'm not suggested we tell him about the bookwyrms or Crumpet. But the man is so distracted, I doubt he'd notice if Crumpet flew over his head." Lira gulped down the dregs of her tea and made a face. "All I'm suggesting is we ask him about removing a bit of the stone wall so I can get gran's recipe book."

Lira hoped he wouldn't think to ask if there was only a book in the metal box. She didn't believe that Durn would demand a share of the gold she'd hidden, but he might not be pleased that her stash had brought the scrutiny of the wyvern to his tavern. Still, Lira thought it was a risk worth taking.

Iris put down her teacup and fussed with the kettle. "That's the problem, love. The book."

"What about it?" Lira asked, her senses prickling the same way they had when she'd been on a job and only a breath away from cracking a lock.

"Your gran's recipe book is filled with more than just baking recipes." Iris held her gaze. "Didn't you wonder why it had that grand cover with the moonstone embedded in it? A bit fancy for a crofter, don't you agree?"

If Iris had hoped for an answer, she didn't get one. Lira was too busy slotting all her memories of the book into place. The book her gran had been so careful to wrap up and hide away after every use. The book her gran had never let Lira flip through. The book that had so many more pages than she ever saw. The book she hadn't even unwrapped from its iron box when she'd taken it from the farmhouse that last night.

Her gran had always told her that the moonstone was a family heirloom that had lost its power long ago, but it seemed her gran hadn't been completely forthright about a number of things.

"So, it's a...?" Lira's voice cracked.

"Spell book."

# Thirty-Four

LIRA GAPED AT IRIS. "Is there any other secret you want to confess or is this the last one?"

"It's absolutely the last one. I would have told you earlier, but you were so upset when you learned about your gran being a mage. I didn't want to overwhelm you."

Lira ran a hand through her hair. She guessed a mage possessing a spell book wasn't such a stretch, except for one detail. "But spell books were outlawed.'

"They were."

Iris was much too calm for Lira's liking. Then again, none of this was new information to *her*. She'd known about her gran and the spell book for... "How long?"

The apothecary blinked at her. "How long what?"

"How long did you know that my gran had a forbidden book of magic?"

Iris's brows knit together, and she opened her mouth before sighing.

"The whole time?" Lira stood and started to pace in a tight circle. "You knew that my gran was risking everything and you didn't stop her?"

Iris scoffed at this. "If you think I could have stopped Elia, then you didn't know your gran. The woman was as stubborn as the day is long. Besides, spell books themselves aren't exactly forbidden."

"You're right. Teaching magic is forbidden, which is why all the spell books were confiscated when the guilds were disbanded. You can't teach magic without books."

"Your gran didn't teach you magic from her spell book."

Lira stopped pacing and whirled on Iris. "A distinction I'm sure the enforcers would have believed when they found my gran's book and her half-elf granddaughter."

"There haven't been enforcers around these parts for ages." Iris flapped a hand in the air. "How do you think I've kept my bookwyrms secret all this time?"

Some of the fight drained from Lira. The woman was right. It had been so long since the magic guilds had been disbanded that she didn't even know if the lairds sent out enforcers anymore. If they did, they didn't reach Wayside. Besides, both the lairds of Greyhelm and Craigmire were old and hadn't been the ones to lay down the edict about magic in the first place.

Lira and her crew had only run into one enforcer—an old man who must have gotten the job when he was young and didn't have the eyesight remaining to tell a mage from a monkey—and he hadn't given Malek a second glance. Not that their crew's spell caster had looked the part, since he'd dressed more like a roaming ranger than Pirrin. But Malek also hadn't carried a spell book.

As much as the lairds of the Ageless Lands had wanted to eliminate magic from their realms, the fact remained that, even without books, spells were still passed down from mage to mage. There might not be guilds, but that didn't mean that druids didn't still harness elemental magic from the earth and seas, or that elves were any less powerful.

Not that Lira possessed any elven magic, she thought darkly, as much as she'd wished for it over the years.

The disbanding of the guilds had been intended to stop the dark magic that had been spreading throughout the lands so many years ago, and it had worked for the most part. But magic—especially the darkest versions of it—could never be wiped out entirely. Not when it held such power and possibility.

Lira took a breath. "It was still a risk to keep the book."

"Just because she was your gran doesn't mean she wasn't one bold, brash biddy."

Lira snorted a laugh at this. "I guess more than I ever knew."

Iris rested a hand on Lira's arm. "She always planned to tell you about the book. Time slipped away from her, that's all."

Lira's throat became unexpectedly thick.

"So, this means I can't tell anyone about the book?"

"That's up to you, love. I have no problem trusting your friends. If they haven't spilled the truth about all our enchanted creatures, I doubt they would tell tales about a book."

Lira thought about this as Iris poured her a fresh cup of tea. She wanted to tell Sass, and she would—as soon as she wrapped her head fully around everything she'd learned. Because she couldn't tell Sass about the spell book without telling her about her gran and about Iris. How much would unravel once she tugged at that single loose thread? But as long as secrets were being unspooled, she might as well tell Iris everything.

"Then I suppose I should tell you that it's not only the book buried behind the wall."

Iris's eyes widened over the rim of her teacup.

"There's some gold," Lira continued. "Not a lot, but some that I stashed here after a particularly successful quest. It's what Rygor's been smelling."

Iris twirled a lock of hair around one finger. "So that's why the reeve has been so sure Durn is holding out on him. You don't want the tavernkeep finding out you're the reason for that."

No, Lira didn't.

"So, I guess we don't ask Durn if we can knock down his wall," she said.

"Not unless you're ready to run again."

Lira wasn't. She sighed, disappointed that she was back to square one.

A tinkle of the bell over the door reminded both of them that it was a market day, which meant that there could be patrons wandering in to buy a poultice for their sore back or a tonic for their cough.

Iris poked her head between the curtains covering the door and then straightened, holding back one side of the velvet that pooled on the floor. "It's your friend."

Lira expected to see Sass enter the back room, but it wasn't the dwarf.

"Cali?"

The pantheri grinned, her gray-striped tail twitching as she glanced at the fluttering bookwyrms. "I didn't know you'd be here. I thought you'd be baking at the tavern."

"Not this early." Lira cocked her head. "So, you're not here looking for me?"

"She's my guest," Iris said.

Then Lira noticed the book that Cali held in one paw.

Iris took it from her with a smile. "What did you think?"

"It was a good read, although the damsel was in a bit too much distress for me."

Iris laughed. "She does veer into intolerable at some points." She dropped the book on top of a pile then bustled to get the kettle and pour the archer a cup, flicking her gaze to Lira for a beat. "Your friend is quite the reader."

Lira remembered that Cali loved nothing more than curling up with a thick book, and she'd always wanted to linger longest in villages that possessed a bookshop. "Isn't your favorite genre pirate romance?"

Cali took the tea from Iris. "I might have devoured all the pirate books that have been written in The Known Lands, so I'll read anything with rollicking adventure and a bit of romance."

Iris turned to her shelves, running a finger across the spines of the books and muttering to herself about marauders and maidens. "You only *think* you've read all the pirate romance books."

Lira eyed Cali, curious that the archer she'd run with had made such fast friends with Iris. She'd seen them chatting at the tavern, and if Cali had mentioned her fondness for books, Iris would have thought nothing of inviting her into her private library. Especially since she was a friend of Lira's.

A part of Lira questioned why Cali was still in Wayside. She'd delivered her news. Was there another reason she was hanging around aside from wanting to see Lira?

Then she shook off that thought. Cali had been nothing but a loyal friend. If she'd been charmed by the village, who was Lira to judge?

"While you're searching for buccaneer bodice-rippers, I'm going to pop into Pip's for some breakfast and head back to the tavern."

"See you later, love," Iris said as she climbed up a wooden step-stool to reach a higher shelf.

"Grab an extra sweet roll for me," Cali said.

Lira left the apothecary and stepped into the cool morning air, breathing in the smell of sugar. Then the back of her neck prickled in warning, and she swiveled her head. There was nothing but villagers meandering to the market and Tin shaking a rug in front of his shop next door.

"Morning!" the gnome said merrily, pausing his rug shaking as she passed.

Lira returned his greeting. "Good morning! I should thank you for the new coverlets for our beds."

"You're quite welcome." Tin beamed at her. "Quite welcome indeed. There's nothing like a pop of color or a bold floral to lift the mood."

Lira smiled at him. To call the fabric a bold floral might have been an understatement.

"You girls are making that tavern into quite the draw. Quite the draw." Tin tucked the rug under his arm. "One I can't seem to resist."

He ducked back into his shop, and she glanced around. The sensation of being watched had been banished by the cheerful conversation, but Lira rubbed the nape of her neck and walked faster.

# Thirty-Five

"YOU KNOW WHAT'S STRANGE?" Sass asked as Lira walked into the kitchen carrying a bag of warm lemon sweet rolls.

Lira eyed the dwarf feeding Crumpet a bit of leftover scone, his wings fluttering behind him as he hovered in mid-air. "You're going to have to be a little more specific."

Sass slid off the three-legged stool and took the bag Lira proffered, sticking her nose inside and inhaling greedily. "The smell of these rolls made me lose track of what I was saying."

She took out a fresh roll, the lemon glaze slicking her fingers as she tore off a bite. Then Crumpet chattered at her and she tore the bite into two pieces and relinquished one to the winged creature.

"Since when are you two friends?" Lira took a roll from the bag and bit into it, her teeth sinking into the pillowy sweetness.

Sass shrugged. "I figure it's best not to have an enchanted creature on your bad side."

Aside from the wings and his impressive instinct for baking, Lira wasn't sure how magical Crumpet truly was, but if it made Sass more accepting of the flutterstoat, then she wasn't going to argue.

Sass hoisted herself back onto the stool as she fed bites of sweet-roll to Crumpet between big bites of her own. "An unfortunate run-in with some water pixies in Eldu taught me that it's better to make friends than enemies."

"Well, I'm glad." Lira smiled at Crumpet as he daintily licked his paws and tucked his wings close to his furry body. Then she swept her gaze around the kitchen, noticing several bowls not where she'd left them and one of the lower cabinet doors ajar. "Did you move things around while I was out?"

Sass wrinkled her brow. "Why would I do that?"

"You wouldn't," Lira said, telling herself that Crumpet could have opened the cabinet door and Durn could have wandered into the kitchen and moved the bowls, even though she didn't believe either of those two things happened. She had the strangest sensation that someone had been snooping in her kitchen. "Rygor didn't happen to visit, did he?"

Sass made a face. "Not when I've been here. Why?"

Lira shook her head in an attempt to dismiss the uneasy feeling. "No reason. It's just been a while since he's popped in and made threats. I figure we're due."

Sass laughed darkly, swiped an errant trail of glaze on her chin with the back of her hand, and then snapped her fingers. "Speaking of popping in, now I remember what's so odd. Korl hasn't been by in a couple of days. Val stopped in yesterday for scones and she took a few to go, which I guess she took to him, but I haven't seen tusk nor tip of him." She leveled a gaze at Lira. "Any reason he'd be avoiding the tavern?"

Lira shuffled behind Sass to stand at the worktable, dodging her stare. "Why would he avoid the tavern?"

"You tell me."

Lira blew out a breath. "The last time I saw him was when he fixed the roof."

"Mm-hmm. You were up there with him for a spell, weren't you?"

Lira thought back to sitting on the roof with the orc. They'd talked, but she hadn't said anything that would make him stay away, had she? But he had been quieter than usual, quieter than the time they'd talked in the kitchen. Then there was the almost-kiss. At least, she'd thought he'd been about to kiss her, but she'd clearly been wrong about that.

"Not very long," Lira said. "I don't think I offended him by taking him a sweet roll."

Sass shook her head thoughtfully. "Couldn't have been the sweet rolls."

"To be honest, I can't get a read on the guy."

"He's shy, that's for sure, and a bit awkward around people." Sass chuckled. "I thought you were a bit standoffish, but he's got you beat."

"I'm not standoffish." Lira pulled out the saucepan and started adding the ingredients for chai by rote. "I'm selective about who I befriend."

"Mmm-hmm," Sass made a sound that told Lira she didn't see much difference in the two.

"He's all right around Val."

Sass picked up one of the papery cinnamon sticks and put it to her nose. "So the question remains. What did you do to make him avoid the tavern?"

"Why does it have to be me? Maybe you did something, did you ever consider that?"

Sass crinkled her snub nose before lowering the cinnamon stick and shaking her head. "Nope, I'm still sure this has to do with you."

Lira rolled her eyes as she stirred the spices into the milk. Crumpet flew the short distance between the counter and the worktable, pawing through the small burlap bags and producing a knob of pale yellow ginger.

"Good catch, Crumpet." Lira scruffed the fur on his head before she chopped off a sliver of ginger and added it to the chai.

Sass slid off the stool and landed on the floor with a thud. "I still don't think it's right how much he knows about kitchen work. Are we sure he isn't a runaway from Pip's?"

Lira grinned at Crumpet. "That would explain a lot, but I don't think so. If he was, why would he leave?"

"You've got a point there," Sass said. "*I* wouldn't leave."

"I guess he likes it here."

"Likes you, you mean. I don't believe for a second that he hung around here when it was Durn alone."

Lira had to agree with her. Crumpet had shown up once she'd started baking, making himself as comfortable as if the place had always been his home. She glanced at the nest of dishrags she'd made for him in the corner. Which it now was.

A thud that shook the floorboards snapped her from her thoughts about Crumpet, making both her and Sass jump. Crumpet had already flown out the window when Lira looked up.

"What in Grognick's beard was that?" Sass wasted no time hurrying from the kitchen and into the great room.

Lira turned off the flame under the pot of chai and wiped her hands on a dishtowel before taking a step. Before she could reach the swinging doors, Sass stuck her head between them, grinning wickedly.

"One of the mysteries is solved."

Thirty-Six

WHEN LIRA JOINED Sass in the great room, Korl was wrestling a massive, black iron beast through the door.

"Can you believe it?" Sass asked, rubbing her hands together.

Lira wasn't quite sure what she was supposed to believe. "What is it?"

Another orc appeared in the doorway, hefting the backend of the contraption. Unlike Korl, this orc wasn't young, but Lira recognized him. His hair boasted more silver than when she'd last seen him, and his jowls were fuller, but she would have recognized the village blacksmith anywhere. But what was one of Korl's dads doing here?

"Vorto?"

A grin split the older orc's face as he set down his end of the object. "Heard you were back in town." He glanced at his son. "Been hearing little else."

Korl grunted and put down his end, straightening and pressing his fists into the small of his back. "You needed a new oven."

Lira blinked at him, as Sass danced around the hulking stove. "But you fixed our oven."

Korl gave a rough shake of his head. "It won't hold for long. It's too old."

"I would take offense at that, since I built that old oven," his father said, "but the boy's right. If you're doing the kind of baking he says you are, you need something newer and bigger."

Lira opened and closed her mouth a few times. It was bigger, that was for sure.

"Don't worry about how big it looks," Korl said, as if he had a window into her mind, "I measured the space the last time I was here. We might have shave down the side of a cabinet, but it'll fit."

Lira finally found her voice. "You made us a new oven?"

Vorto cleared his throat. "It was a family effort."

Val strode in behind the orcs, giving them both a fond look. "I consider myself a part of the family, but I did not help with this." She held up a handful of what looked like orange knit squares. "I did make some things for you to use when you pull trays from the oven, and I made them doubly thick, so the heat doesn't seep through the yarn."

"They're perfect." Sass took them from the burly blonde as if she'd offered them bars of gold and as if Sass would be the one using them. "Thank you."

Val waved off the thanks. "It was nice to make something other than a scarf for a change." She put a hand to the side of her mouth. "But to be honest, they're really just short scarfs."

Korl picked up his side of the oven again, grunting at his father to do the same, and they started walking the heavy load toward the kitchen, the thing swaying from side-to-side like a ship being tossed by waves.

"I don't know what to say," Lira said as Korl passed her. "You didn't have to do this, but I'm grateful you did. Thank you."

His gaze met hers and one side of his mouth twitched. "You are welcome."

Then he looked down, grunted, and backed toward the swinging doors.

Heat bloomed in Lira's chest as she watched the two orcs maneuver the oven and lumber into the kitchen.

Val winked as she sauntered by. "I'll see if they need more muscle in there."

Before Lira could follow them, Sass appeared at her side.

"I guess we know why he wasn't coming around the tavern."

"I guess we do." Lira glanced at her. "Should I expect an apology now, or do you want to spend some time getting the wording right?"

Sass pressed a hand to her chest. "An apology? For what?"

"For saying I was the reason Korl wasn't coming around the tavern as much."

Sass flailed a hand at the doors the orcs had disappeared through. "But you *were* the reason."

Lira spluttered as she shook her head.

"Korl didn't have his dad help him make an oven for *me.*" Sass gave a firm shake of her head. "That was all for you."

"The oven is for the tavern."

Sass barked out a laugh. "If the oven was for the tavern, why didn't they bring it when it was just Durn here? Or when his wife was cooking, and Durn said it gave her no end of trouble?"

Lira had no answer for that.

"You use the oven." Sass held up her fingers and counted her points. "You had problems with the oven. Your life would be made easier with a new oven."

This was all true, but Lira still had a hard time believing that Korl had done it for her alone. "Maybe he likes having a place to come for supper again, and he *does* like my scones."

"Pip likes your scones and you don't see him wheeling in kitchen supplies." The dwarf patted her arm. "Some suitors bring flowers. Yours brought you a stove."

Lira swung her head to Sass then tugged her to one side and dropped her voice. "I think you've forgotten about Val."

Sass let out a wistful sigh. "I most certainly have not forgotten her."

Lira gave the dwarf a curious look, but before she could press the matter, Sass put her hands on her hips and huffed out a breath. "I don't know what to tell you, except that I think he's got it bad for you. Two-ton stove bad."

Lira groaned. As much as the orc made her pulse flutter, she didn't have time to figure out a guy who was too shy to talk to her and spent all his time with another woman. A striking, intimidating woman.

This was why she'd avoided men when she'd been part of a crew. This was why she'd spurned Malek's advances and even handsome Vaskel's attempts to become more than friends. They'd been complications she didn't need.

Just like this one.

Lira smoothed her hands down the front of her pants. "Well, we have enough to worry about with reviving the tavern without worrying about something as hypothetical as this."

Sass mumbled something about fancy words not making the big orc go away, but Lira decided there was no point in thinking about any of it.

Not with her gran's spell book still trapped behind a wall along with enough gold to make a wyvern giddy.

# Thirty-Seven

LIRA COULDN'T BAKE while her new oven was being installed, and she wasn't fond of having time on her hands. Durn had been roused by the noise and had come to observe the commotion, but had since decamped behind the bar, polishing glasses with particular menace. Sass was preoccupied chatting with Val by the fire, and Lira could swear that the guard's chair had a new decorative cushion that the large woman had tucked behind her head as she knit.

It was the perfect time to slip down to the cellar. Lira hadn't been there since she'd gone with Iris, and part of her wanted to check on the hiding place. Nothing would have changed, but it was like brushing your fingers over a touchstone in your pocket. She would feel better once she'd done it.

She slid a lantern from a hook on the wall and lit it quickly, giving a cursory glance around the great room before holding her breath and opening the cellar door. Once she was on the first step, she closed the door noiselessly behind her.

Lira stifled the urge to gag. "We have *got* to clean this place out."

It was easy to forget with all the improvements upstairs that the subterranean level had been untouched. Of course, she'd preferred it that way. The fewer people down in the cellar, the better. And with the stench, not many folks would brave more than a few steps before retreating.

She hurried down the wooden steps with a hand on the rough bannister in case one of the rickety planks gave way. When she reached the dirt floor, she released a breath and shook her head at her unreasonable worry. It didn't matter how many people traipsed through the cellar. They could even serve supper down there, although she couldn't imagine that being a cheery meal. Still, no one would imagine that anything was buried behind the stone wall.

The glow of the lantern pooled gold on the floor which caressed the walls as it swung in Lira's hand. Despite providing faint light, it didn't make the underground space any warmer, and Lira wished she was wearing more than a thin dress and simple cardigan.

Lira reverted easily to her old ways, walking on her toes and holding her breath as she listened for any sound. There was nothing aside from the scraping and clanging overhead. She crept around the corner, keeping her distance from the baskets of rotten produce, and she extended her lantern arm.

There was the wall. There were the stones, all snugly tucked into the wall. And there, on the ground in the corner, was significantly more loosened mortar than there had been when she and Iris had left.

Lira went still, swinging the lantern wide, although she was certain she was alone in the cellar. She would have felt the presence of another being bigger than a rat. The back of her neck would have pricked, and it hadn't.

"Hells and cinders," she said, taking quick steps to the wall and crouching low so she could touch the corner stones.

She remembered vividly how much mortar had been scraped free. She remembered how much of the stones had been exposed. The corner stone was still set into the wall, but notably less mortar held it in place, and significantly more dusted the ground. She and Iris had not done this, but someone had.

Lira straightened, her mind racing. Who else knew about this?

"No one. Only Iris."

Had the woman returned to work on the wall without telling her? No, she would have seen her, or Sass would have mentioned it. There was nothing that went on at The Tusk & Tail without Sass knowing.

Her stomach dropped. Sass. Had her friend been the one to venture to the cellar and try to pry out the stone? She knew that Lira had been in the cellar the first night they got caught. She'd seen her emerging from the cellar with Iris. Maybe she'd gotten curious.

As soon as the thought crossed her mind, she shook her head. Sass would have asked her. They'd become close enough that the dwarf wouldn't start hacking at a wall without mentioning something to Lira. But didn't that also mean that they'd become close enough for Lira to tell her the truth?

Her shoulders slumped. She was so used to keeping secrets and keeping to herself that it felt normal. Sharing and opening up didn't come easily to her, even when she desperately wanted to bring others into her confidence.

She stood and backed away from the wall. The only way she would know if Sass had been the one scraping at the stones was to ask her. She had no reason to think the woman would lie. There was no way Sass knew what, if anything, was behind the stones. Besides, if anyone had made an attempt, chances were high it was Rygor, although she didn't know when he could have snuck in.

Lira made her way briskly to the stairs, emerging from the cellar with considerably less stealth than she'd entered. Clangs and thumps continued to burst from the kitchen, which told her that the oven was still not fully installed.

She set the lantern on the bar, locking her gaze on Sass, who chose that moment to look up from her conversation with Val. Lira beckoned her with one finger, and Sass bustled over.

Lira jerked her head toward the door, and Sass followed her out of the tavern.

"If this is about the oven…" the dwarf started.

"It's not." Lira cut her off with an impatient wave of one hand. "It's about the cellar."

Sass tilted her head and wrinkled her nose as if she'd just taken a whiff of the dank underground storage area. "The cellar? Please don't tell me you want to clean it now."

"Hardly." Lira could think of nothing she'd enjoy less. "Have you been down there recently?"

Sass recoiled. "I've never been down there. One sniff is all I needed to keep me safe and sound upstairs." She made a face. "Besides, I've spent enough of my life underground."

Lira studied her face, detecting no evasion, no deceit. She released a breath, grateful her faith in Sass had been confirmed.

Sass tapped a foot on the dirt. "Why?"

Lira pushed aside her instinct to hide the truth. "I have a confession."

# Thirty-Eight



"SO THAT'S why you're here?"

Sass had listened to Lira's story before speaking, and even now, her tone wasn't accusatory. She sounded more curious than anything.

"That's why I'm here." Lira gave her a weak grin. "I know I should have told you sooner, but I—"

"You don't have to explain," Sass said. "You didn't know me. I didn't know you. But I don't understand why it was such a secret. So, you hid a book a bunch of years ago? Is there a demand for recipe books that I don't know about?"

Sass's perspective gave her pause. "Well, it's a very fancy recipe book with a moonstone embedded in the cover. Now I know that the book contains more than just recipes and the stone must have some kind of powers. Why else would it be on the cover of a spell book?"

Sass's eyes flared wide, and she threw up her hands. "Whoa there, what do you mean spell book?"

"I was getting to that part."

Sass stepped closer and glanced over her shoulder, even though they weren't within shouting distance of another building, and the windows of the tavern were closed. "Spell books don't exist anymore. At least, they aren't supposed to. They vanished with the magical guilds and academies."

Lira nodded. She knew all of this. "Magic itself isn't outlawed, and there's no law that says you can't possess a spell book."

"There doesn't have to be, because they're all gone," Sass whispered. "You can't outlaw magic, or you'd have to outlaw all kinds of folks." She let her gaze wander to Lira's pointed ears. "Like elves."

Lira's face burned as the familiar heat of shame flooded her. "I don't have to worry about that. I'm only half, and I've never exhibited even a hint of magical abilities."

"Oh." Sass sounded disappointed.

"You're not the only one to wish I had powers. I think my gran was always waiting for me to do something incredible."

Sass folded her arms over her chest. "Who says you haven't?"

"Something *magical*," Lira corrected.

"I'd take you over any of the elves I've met, so don't think they're better than you just because they can conjure light or hear things others can't."

Most elves possessed more powers than that, but Lira didn't want to correct Sass. Not when the dwarf was so firmly on her side. Somehow, hearing her new friend defend her lack of magic did make her feel better. "Thanks, Sass."

"You said your gran was human, right? What kind of human would want someone to be more elvish?"

Lira fought not to smile at the dwarf's clear distaste for elves. How many unpleasant elves had Sass encountered? Or was this just about the historic tension between the elves and dwarves?

"My gran wasn't any old human. According to Iris, whom I have no reason to believe is lying, my gran was a mage."

Sass let out a low whistle. "No kidding. An honest-to-gods mage? And you didn't know? She didn't teach you?"

Lira shook her head. "That would have been illegal. Besides, Iris says she stopped all that long before I came to her. Before she even had my mother."

Sass tapped a short finger on her chin. "So Iris knew?"

Lira really had left out a lot when she'd explained why she'd returned to Wayside. To her credit, she'd only recently learned a great deal of it. "They were best friends before they ended up here, and they became friends by crewing together when they were young. Back then, Iris was a rogue."

Sass eyed her and nodded, as if it all made sense. "Is that why you became a rogue?"

"She trained me. It's not like my gran could have trained me to be a mage. That would have been too risky."

Lira thought back to growing up outside of Wayside in the little cottage with chickens that meandered around the backyard. "I think she thought that the middle of nowhere was a safe place for us. We weren't near any cities. The laird who presides over Grayhelm Castle was already old when I was a child. Now, I hear he's at death's door and barely cares about fortifying his walls, much less sniffing out magic, which is why he has that wyvern working for him."

"I suppose it would be hard to find a safer place, unless she raised you among the halflings in Elmshire."

"Yes, a human and a half-elf wouldn't have stood out there at all," Lira drawled sarcastically.

Sass shot her a look, the corners of her mouth quirking. "I take your point. So, your gran must have settled here when she decided to lay low. Not a bad plan, if I'm being honest."

Lira thought back to her gran's soft eyes that sharpened when she was thinking. "She was smarter than I knew." A pang of nostalgia tightened her throat. "I wish I could talk to her now that I know more about who she was. I spent too many years thinking I knew everything about her, and that there wasn't much more to know."

"I think we've all been guilty of that." Sass shifted her weight from one foot to the other, her gaze dropping. "Suddenly, everything my mum told me that I brushed off makes a whole lot of sense." She snapped her head up. "But don't you ever tell her I said that."

"Never," Lira promised, holding up a palm as if making a solemn vow.

They both laughed.

"So why did you finally tell me all this?" Sass asked.

"I realized that I don't like keeping secrets from you. I know we haven't known each other for long, but you've become—"

"I feel the same way about you," Sass said gruffly before Lira could finish. "In spite of the bubbly personality I show our patrons, I don't make friends easily. I supposed it's because dwarves aren't trusting."

"Especially of elves?" Lira teased.

Sass's grin was wide. "Especially."

"So much of being a rogue is keeping secrets and being a bit of a loner, even on a crew, that I got used to solitude. Too used to it. Then I left my crew and almost forgot what it was like to have friends." She gestured to the village. "Or community."

Lira's heart squeezed as she looked at the road leading into the heart of the village, the stream meandering past the mill, the open-air blacksmith and wheelwright workshops perched on the other side of the stone bridge. Then she turned back to Sass.

"There's one other reason I told you why I came back," Lira said. "The book isn't the only thing I buried. There's some gold with it, and that why Rygor keeps sniffing around here."

Sass's mouth gaped. "So, he isn't wrong about knowing there's gold here?"

"He's not wrong but he doesn't know where it is. At least, I hope he doesn't. I need you to help me get it before the wyvern, or someone else, gets to it first."

Sass's expression hardened with determination. "I've never been on a heist crew before. Count me in."

# Thirty-Nine

LIRA TOOK long steps to keep up with Sass, even though she should have easily outpaced the dwarf. "Slow down, will you?"

"Not on your life." Sass shot her a worried look as they hurried through the village. "Not after what you told me."

Both women waved absently as they passed Pip's bakery and Fenni's cheese shop, even though Lira's stomach protested that they weren't stopping. She was more surprised that Sass didn't want to stop.

"If you're right about more mortar being loosened, then that means someone aside from you or me knows what's behind the wall."

"I've only told you and Iris."

"That's it? You're sure?" Sass paused with her hand on the door to the apothecary shop.

That question didn't take long thought. "Positive. The only thing I can think is that Rygor is behind the attempt."

Sass frowned. "I would have noticed him in the tavern and so would you. He smells of brimstone."

The dwarf had a point. Rygor was imposing, but he was not easy to miss.

Sass sniffed. "Maybe you don't think you told anyone else, but I'm here to tell you that you talk in your sleep."

Lira's jaw dropped, and it took her a beat to follow Sass as she entered the dimly lit shop. She talked in her sleep? Why had no one ever mentioned this before?

By the time they were inside and wrapped in the myriad exotic scents of oils and potions, she'd regained her ability to speak without stammering. "Does that mean you heard me talking about hiding the book or the gold?"

Sass waited until the door glided shut behind them both and the jingling bell stopped. "No, but that doesn't mean someone didn't."

Before Lira could stumble too far down the rabbit hole of who might have heard her talking in her sleep, Iris's head poked from between the velvet, brown curtains leading to the back. Her face relaxed into a smile when she saw who it was.

"Come on back, girls." She waved a beckoning hand and then vanished behind the fabric wall.

Sass parted the curtains and held them open for Lira. The book-wyrms were fluttering inside the closed cage, and Cali sat in an over-stuffed chair with an open book in one hand and one leg crossed over the other at the knee.

Sass stopped short and glanced at Lira, her expression questioning. She was clearly letting the rogue decide how much to tell and to whom.

The pantheri grinned over the top of the leather-bound book. "This is a nice surprise."

"I'm the one who's surprised." Lira shouldn't have been though. Cali had always loved books, and there was no one in Wayside who had as many as Iris.

"I found a pirate romance your friend hadn't read," Iris said with notable glee.

Sass shifted from one foot to the other, her impatience hard to miss.

Iris's expression clouded in an instant. "Everything okay, love?"

Lira took a breath and jumped in. "You haven't been back to the cellar, have you?"

Iris frowned. "The cellar in the Tusk & Tail? Of course not. I assumed we'd take care of our project down there together."

Lira had suspected as much. She flicked her gaze to Cali. "Have you been to the tavern's cellar?"

The pantheri blinked in obvious surprise. "Why would I go into the cellar of the tavern?"

Lira held her golden eyes for a several breaths. She'd known the archer long enough to know she wasn't lying. Cali had never been a good liar, anyway.

Iris closed the distance between them and took Lira's hands. "You're scaring me, love. What's going on?"

"She's been betrayed, that's what's going on," Sass said with an angry flutter of her hands.

Iris gaped, and Cali stood quickly, dropping the book into the chair.

"We don't know it's betrayal," Lira said, her calm tone in sharp contrast to Sass's heated one. "But someone has been to the cellar and tried to loosen the rocks in the corner."

Iris sucked in a sharp breath. "You're sure?"

Lira gave the woman a curt nod. "Mortar doesn't scrape itself onto the ground."

Cali looked between the three women. "Would you mind filling me in?"

Lira did, compressing the information into as few sentences as possible and avoiding her friend's gaze. When she'd outlined everything from stashing the recipe book and gold in the tavern to coming back and finding it walled over to discovering that the book was much more than a recipe book, including the revelation that her gran had been a mage and Iris a rogue, Lira finally looked up. "I'm sorry I didn't tell you sooner."

Cali's tail quivered behind her as she stared at Lira for entirely too long. "That's okay. There's nothing wrong with having things you keep only for yourself, even if that thing is a spell book the likes of which hasn't been seen in a century."

Lira's vision swam for a moment as she nodded at her friend. "Thanks, Cali."

"Now that we all know," Sass said, "what are we going to do? Someone who isn't one of us must know about the book."

"Did you tell anyone else?" Cali asked.

"No, just us three, but she talks in her sleep," Sass answered for her.

The archer's whiskers twitched, and Lira wasn't sure if it was from amusement or surprise, or a bit of both. "Does that open the field of candidates much wider?"

Lira narrowed her eyes. "You know it doesn't, but our crew did sleep rough together."

Cali shook her head. "Rog snored too loud to ever hear one of us talking in our sleep, and Vaskel...?"

Lira understood the questioning tone as her words drifted off. Despite Vaskel being a hellkin and the reputation of the devilish creatures, she had never believed him to be dishonest. In fact, he was scrupulously direct. When you were that devilishly attractive, you could be.

Iris sighed, as she twirled a strand of dark hair around one finger. "Rygor already suspects gold is somewhere in the tavern. We did leave the mortar I scraped on the ground."

Lira could have kicked herself. She was too good a rogue to be that sloppy, but it hadn't occurred to her that anyone else, including the wyvern, would brave the dank darkness of the cellar. "We can't be sure Rygor tried to loosen the wall, but we do know that someone did."

Iris glanced at the group. "Which means we need get the book and gold ourselves—and soon."

# Forty

LIRA SWEPT the back of her hand across her damp brow as she pulled a cake pan from the new oven, setting it on the top of the stove with a satisfied clatter. There was no smoke, no smell of soot, no odd clang as it heated.

She used one of Val's knit squares to transfer the pan to the worktable, pleased by the brown, crackled top of the cake. The blast from the oven had brought with it the aroma of apple cider, and Lira felt reasonably confident that she'd replicated her gran's apple cider cake recipe.

"Yes, yes," she muttered to Crumpet as he sat grooming his fluffy white tail on the windowsill. "I made the cake that Korl mentioned." She held up a finger. "But don't you start too."

Crumpet chittered at her, chittered at the oven, and then twitched his whiskers at the cake.

"It's good to have something else to serve now that I've gotten meat pies and scones well in hand." She wilted under Crumpet's gaze. "But yes, the first cake is going to Korl and his dads for the new stove, especially since they refused payment."

Korl and his father had been leaving the kitchen when she and Sass had returned to the tavern. She and Sass had both tried to offer payment to Korl and Vorto, but neither had entertained the thought.

"It's a gift," Korl had insisted. "You don't pay for a gift."

Sass had elbowed her, and she'd elbowed the dwarf back hard enough for her to stumble through the swinging doors.

Maybe her friend was right. Maybe Korl was trying to woo her by repairing the oven and mending the roof and making her a new stove. Then again, it could just be him being nice. Either way, they were the nicest things anyone had done for her in a long time, and if Lira had been in the right headspace to think about being wooed, she'd be flattered. But she'd been on her own for so long that it was hard to imagine any other way.

Even when she'd run with a crew, she'd stayed free from attachments. Pirrin might have taken up with a buxom widow or strapping sailor in almost every village they passed through, and Rog had a wife tucked away safe in a gnome enclave, but she'd never formed attachments. She knew all too well that loving someone meant risking your heart, and she had her fill of risk on their quests.

"So, that's what smells so good." Val pushed through the doors, her ball of yarn and knitting needles in one large hand.

Lira tried to mask her surprise at seeing the woman venture beyond her seat at the hearth. She held up the knit squares. "Your short scarves work like a charm. Thanks again."

Val nodded and gestured to the cake. "No scones today?"

"Don't worry. There will be scones. This is a cake that my gran made for Korl and his dads years ago. I made it as a thank you for the new stove since they won't take payment." Lira looked back at the cast iron oven. "I think I'm going to need to make a lot more cakes to properly thank them."

Val rested her palms on the worktable. "I'm sure they'll love the cake, but Korl didn't do it for baked goods."

Lira hesitated as she grasped the sides the cake with the short scarves so she could flip it over onto a plate.

"He did it because he likes to see you happy."

Now this surprised Lira, and she stared at Val. "He told you that?"

Val let loose a throaty laugh. "He doesn't have to. We've been friends so long that I know what he's thinking, which is good because he isn't much for talking."

"I guess he isn't."

"Don't be fooled by his quiet ways." She tapped her temple with one finger. "Korl has a lot going on up there. It just gets muddled going from his brain to his mouth. That's why he doesn't talk much. That, and he gets nervous around people he doesn't know well or apparently women he likes."

"You mean...?"

Val straightened and folded her arms across the quilted armor covering her chest. "Are you saying you haven't figure it out?"

There had been few times in Lira's life when she'd felt truly foolish, but this was one of them. "I thought that you two might be—"

Before she'd finished her sentence, the woman slapped a hand on her knee and cackled. "Me and Korl? Not likely. I love the orc like a brother, especially since we grew up together. We stick close because he doesn't understand social niceties, so I try to smooth the way." She gave Lira a sly wink. "Besides, Korl isn't exactly my type."

Suddenly, it all made sense to Lira, and her cheeks flamed with embarrassment for ever thinking Val was anything but a friend to Korl. The fact that she'd been jealous of his best friend made her want to sink in to the floor.

"You aren't the first person who's thought we were together, though," Val said. "It took the other guards a while to get that we were nothing but best mates. I get it. I finish the guy's sentences for him."

Lira gave her a grateful smile. "I think I might owe you a cake, too."

Val threw back her head and laughed at this. "You don't, but I won't fight you about it."

Then Val caught sight of Crumpet, who hadn't run from the kitchen when the woman had entered, although his wings were tucked flat enough to his side that they weren't noticeable. "So Korl wasn't making it up when he said you had a furry assistant. I thought he might be casting unfair aspersions on Sass."

Lira couldn't help grinning at that. "That would be unfair, since Sass doesn't even sport a small beard."

"If anyone could pull it off, though…" Val hiked a thumb toward the great room. "Well, I'd better be off." She held up the orange ball that was significantly smaller than it had been a few days ago, no doubt thanks to making the oven scarves. "Think about what I said. Korl might take more effort, but he's worth it."

"Thanks, Val."

The woman glanced at the cake. "You want me to take that to Korl and his dads? I'm on my way there now."

"Would you?" Lira would have preferred to deliver it herself, but she still had supper to get through.

Val took the cake but paused in the doorway between the kitchen, letting out a low whistle as something caught her eye in the great room. "Now if I was the kind of woman who fell for men, he would be one I'd fall for."

"I thought you weren't into Korl."

"I'm not talking about Korl. I'm talking about the hot hellkin who just walked in."

Lira stiffened. *Hellkin?*

# Forty-One

LIRA FOLLOWED Val from the kitchen, muttering to herself. Was every member of her former crew going to descend on Wayside?

Every living member, she reminded herself, thoughts of Pirrin dampening the sharp edge of her frustration.

She shouldn't have been surprised to see that the great room wasn't empty, but the steady presence of patrons continued to give her a pleasant jolt. Sass moved confidently around the tables, refilling pewter tankards and gathering empty chai mugs as villagers sat in conversation or deep in thought.

Val slipped out the front door, holding the cake in one hand and sliding a questioning look at Lira. At least Korl wasn't there.

It took no more than a breath to spot the hellkin Val had noticed, and another to raise an eyebrow at him.

Vaskel sauntered toward her with an arch grin. His magenta skin was hidden partially under the hood of a black cloak, but he flipped it back as he closed the distance between them. His ice-blue eyes; short, pointed beard; long, slashing tail; and horns that curled back from his forehead were all as she remembered, but the scar that split one dark slash of an eyebrow was new.

A few patrons' eyes followed the hellkin, but Lira wasn't sure if it was because the fiendish creature wasn't something frequently spotted in this part of the Known Lands, or if they were struck by his wicked good looks. Either way, Vaskel didn't seem to mind.

He swept her into an embrace without a word, and Lira inhaled the faintest scent of ash that her friend covered with a liberal application of sandalwood. Despite his appearance, Lira had never found Vaskel as irresistible as most females who encountered him. Of course, Vaskel was charming, but he'd never been able to seduce Lira with his silky words and seductive moves. Maybe it was one of the few ways in which her elven blood came in handy.

His hug was fierce and his voice a velvet purr as he whispered in her ear, "You don't get to walk away, Lira. Not after all we've been through."

For the briefest moment, Lira worried that the hellkin's visit was not a friendly one. Did he hold a grudge against her for leaving like she had? She wouldn't blame him, although she didn't want to have Vaskel as an enemy. When he pulled back and held her at arm's length, he smiled, melting all her fears in a heartbeat.

Her breath rushed from her as swiftly as her words. "I'm sorry I left like I did, Vask. It didn't have anything to do with you, with any of you."

Vaskel shook away her apology with his head, his hands still on her waist. "I never took it personally. We were all a mess after Malek, and I know how much you adore me."

Lira laughed. "Since you're the one who tracked me down, it looks like the adoration goes the other way."

His light eyes flashed heat. "I would never deny that."

She shook her head, almost relieved that her friend hadn't changed one bit. "Tell me, is there a town crier somewhere spreading the news of my new address and vocation?"

He gave a throaty laugh. "Word does travel, especially if you're listening for it."

"Cali didn't tell you?" Lira swept her gaze around the great room, noticing for the first time that the pantheri wasn't there.

"Cali?" Vaskel's brows pressed together, which made him look both more sinister and more smoldering. "I haven't seen our archer friend since we disbanded. Have you?"

Lira wondered if there was a reason her friend didn't want the hellkin to know her whereabouts. She decided not to continue discussing their crew and her past life in full view of everyone, taking him by the arm and pulling him to the small round table in the farthest corner where two wooden chairs huddled across from a pair of short stools. A single taper burned in a wrought iron candleholder.

"Did you two fall out?"

Now Vaskel looked affronted. He tossed his long, dark hair, as the tail he'd tucked to one side lashed. "Never. We all parted as friends."

Even though he had many impish qualities, lying wasn't one of them.

"She's here," Lira said. "I thought that was why you'd come. I thought she might have mentioned searching for me."

"I suspect we've all been searching for things we lost." He glanced around the tavern. "Although it seems you returned to where it all began."

Lira's gaze wandered to the long table where they'd all first met. "I did, although it's taken some work to get this place back to what it was when we were here."

"Oh?" Vaskel's scarred brow twitched.

"When I arrived, the place was a mess. It's taken a good deal of work for me and Sass to get it even close to its former state."

"Sass?"

She thought of how she and the dwarf had met. She couldn't tell him that. It wasn't that she didn't trust Vaskel, but the fewer people who knew her secret, the better. Especially since her secret was even more important than she'd known.

Instead, she gestured toward the dwarf who was bustling around the tables refilling mugs of chai. Her braid was frayed with wispy curls sprouting from her hairline, and her apron had seen better days. "She's better at sprucing things up than you'd guess by looking at her."

"You know I hesitate to judge others by their appearance," he said with a silky smile.

"Too true. You would never have been a part of our motley crew if you only kept to your kind."

Vaskel waved a hand and leaned back in his chair. "Too boring." Then he winked at her so quickly she almost missed it. "Besides, too many hellkins means too much competition."

Lira grinned at this, but the grin slipped from her face when she thought of Pirrin and how the two had always served as wingmen for each other. "You haven't heard then?"

He bristled, the blue in his eyes flashing heat. "So many questions you seem to know the answer for already. Why do I get the feeling I'm late to the proverbial party?"

She put a hand on his arm, the warmth from his skin pulsing through the cloak. "I thought maybe you'd been with him—"

"You going to introduce me to your friend?"

Sass's appearance made Lira drop her hand, and Vaskel swung to face the dwarf with a fierce expression. To Sass's credit, she didn't so much as flinch as she leaned a hand on the table. "You another one of Lira's old crew?"

"This is Vaskel," Lira said before he could speak.

"Pleased to meet you." Sass flipped her braid behind her, but her grin wasn't a simpering one. "You thirsty?"

The hellkin blinked at her, the fire in his gaze dimming. "I am."

"You look like you could do with a cold ale." Sass nodded decisively. "I'll bring one right over."

As she left, he studied her retreating back as if attempting to puzzle out why she hadn't been charmed by him.

"She's as immune to your seductive powers as I am," Lira whispered.

Vaskel hummed at this, the sound rough and gravelly. "You're half elf, and you aren't fully immune."

Lira laughed as the hellkin squared his shoulders. "Believe what you wish."

He cut her a look, his lips twitching. "I will admit that you always made a valiant effort to resist me."

Lira sat back and folded her arms over her chest. "It wasn't the effort you thought it was."

His laugh was full-throated and drew some stares. "I *have* missed you, Lira." He allowed his eyes to move across her face and down to her waist, but it wasn't remotely predatory. "I'll be the first to admit that it's unsettling to see you in an apron and not your rogue's attire. You're not the Lira I remember."

"I'm the same Lira I always was, but you never got to see this side of me."

He leaned forward, his elbows on the table. "You don't miss it?"

"What? The danger, sleeping rough, being chased?"

"The excitement, nights under the stars, the treasure."

Fond memories tugged at her, as if they could pull her back if they cast themselves in a flattering light. "I won't lie. There are things I miss about that life, but one of them is sitting across the table from me. Another is already in this village. I hope the other is tucked away safe and sound in the gnome enclave with his wife."

Vaskel's brow creased as he stroked one hand down the point of his short beard. "And Pirrin?"

"I wish it was not me telling you." Lira swallowed the lump that lodged in her throat every time she thought of the Ranger who was such a dab hand with a sword.

Vaskel's tail went rigid. "How?"

"I don't know," Lira admitted. "Cali told me, but she said she didn't know how he died either. She said there were no marks on his body."

The hellkin reared back as if she'd struck him. "He didn't die by the sword?"

Lira shook her head. "I've told you all I know."

Vaskel hunched forward with both forearms on the table, his head bowed between them. "First Malek and now Pirrin."

She put a hand over one of his. "It's bad luck."

Vaskel growled at this. "Like hells it is. It's those wraiths."

The tankard that Sass had been lowering to the table bobbled and thunked, some of the foam sloshing over the side. "I'm sorry. Did you say wraiths?"

# Forty-Two

SASS PULLED a cloth from her waist and dabbed at the foam she'd spilled on the table. "Wraiths?"

Lira shot Vaskel a warning look, but the hellkin only crossed his arms, his magenta skin darkening with conviction.

"Wraiths," he repeated, his icy eyes glinting in the low light of the tavern. "The oath-breaking spirits we encountered in the ruins."

"He's not serious," Lira said quickly, her voice carrying more confidence than she felt. "Vaskel is just upset about our friend Pirrin, which is understandable."

But even as she spoke the words, a shiver slithered down her spine. She pushed away the memory of those ghostly warriors with their translucent bodies and rotting armor, the way their hollow eyes had locked onto her as they'd materialized in the throne room of the cursed castle.

"Those wraiths were bound to the castle, cursed to remain where they betrayed their oath." She leaned forward, lowering her voice. "They can't just travel across the Known Lands, killing off members of our former crew. That's not how curses work."

Sass hadn't moved, and her head swung between the two as they argued.

Vaskel's tail lashed against the wooden chair leg, his sharp teeth pressing into his bottom lip. "Then how do you explain what happened? Pirrin was a fighter, one of the best swordsmen I've ever known. He wouldn't just die without a mark on him."

"People die mysteriously all the time," Lira said, though the words sounded hollow even to her own ears.

"Not Pirrin."

Vaskel was right. Pirrin's death didn't make sense, and it unnerved her.

She put a hand over his, the flesh so hot she almost flinched. "I miss him too, but us fighting won't bring him back."

Vaskel's shoulders sagged, the tight set of his jaw relaxing. "I shouldn't have snapped at you. You aren't the reason he's gone."

Lira wasn't, but she couldn't help wondering if Pirrin would still be alive if their crew had stayed together. The pain of that thought made her jerk her head away. Her gaze caught on Durn standing behind the bar, and she nearly did a double take.

The tavernkeep's usually wild mustache was neatly trimmed and combed, and his typically stained shirt looked freshly cleaned. Even more surprising was the sight of Penny, the chandler, leaning against the bar, her ample curves accentuated by a dress that certainly hadn't been made for working with tallow and wax.

"Speaking of working miracles." Lira caught Sass's eye and nodded toward the bar. "Your matchmaking seems to be paying off."

Sass followed her gaze, and a triumphant grin split her face. "Would you look at that? Durn actually took my advice about grooming that mop on his face." She gave a self-satisfied nod. "The man just needed a reason to care again."

"And it looks like Penny might be that reason."

She could see the gnome's lavender hair coiffed in an elaborate updo, and even from this distance, the sparkle of what might be a new brooch pinned to her bodice.

The pleasant warmth of the scene evaporated instantly as the tavern door swung open with enough force to rattle the hinges. The buzz of conversation dropped to a murmur, then to silence as Rygor stepped inside, his black wings tucked close to his lanky frame but still visible beneath his cloak.

Penny's face blanched, and she scurried away from the bar as the wyvern stomped across the tavern floor, his clawed feet scraping against the wooden planks. Durn's newly groomed mustache did nothing to improve his scowl as Rygor planted both hands on the bar and leaned forward.

"I warned you, Durn," the wyvern's voice carried easily in the hushed room. "I said you couldn't hide it from me."

"And I told you," Durn retorted, his shoulders bunching with tension, "I'm not hiding anything."

"You expect me to believe that The Tusk & Tail suddenly started thriving because of a few meat pies and fancy tea?" Rygor hissed, his nostrils flaring. "The laird will hear about this."

Lira stiffened as Silas slid from his stool at the far end of the bar and shuffled up to Rygor, his thin lips stretched in a smile that made Lira's skin crawl.

"The reeve is right to be suspicious," Silas said, his voice carrying just enough for Lira to hear. "The place was barely staying afloat, and then these two show up, start making changes…" He flicked a glance toward their table, his gaze hardening with unmasked disdain.

"Who is that?" Vaskel asked quietly.

"The wyvern is Rygor, the village reeve." Lira kept her voice low.

"He collects taxes for the laird. The man next to him is Silas. He doesn't appreciate what Sass and I have done with the place."

"That's putting it mildly," Sass said.

Rygor's head swiveled toward their table, his eyes narrowing as they landed on Vaskel. The wyvern straightened, leaving Silas mid-sentence, and began stalking toward them.

"You have new friends," Rygor said to Lira, his wings twitching beneath his cloak as he approached. "How interesting."

Vaskel stood in one fluid motion, his height nearly a match for the wyvern. The hellkin's tail slashed behind him, and though his posture appeared casual, Lira recognized the coiled readiness in his stance. She'd seen him like this before fights.

"I don't believe we've met," Vaskel said, his voice lower than usual, velvet wrapped around iron. "I'm an old friend of Lira's."

Rygor's scaled lips pulled back, revealing teeth that were just a bit too pointed for comfort. "But not from around here."

Vaskel returned the smile with one equally as menacing. "I roam where I please."

Lira held her breath, aware that everyone in the tavern was watching.

"I was just reminding the proprietor of this establishment," Rygor said, still addressing Vaskel but now looking at Lira and Sass, "that the laird owns a share of their success."

"Does he now?" Vaskel's voice dropped even lower, the hint of a growl rumbling beneath his words. "Funny, I wasn't aware that collecting crumbs from honest work would interest a laird."

Rygor's clawed hands flexed at his sides. "The laird's business is whatever the laird deems it to be."

"Perhaps," Vaskel stepped closer, his tail carving an angry arc through the air, "the laird should find his crumbs elsewhere."

The wyvern's wings strained against his cloak, but after a tense moment, his posture eased slightly. He swept his gaze around the tavern, taking in the watching faces. Then his eyes returned to Vaskel, reassessing.

"Another time, then," Rygor said, his voice calmer, though his eyes remained cold. "But remember, the laird's due will be collected one way or another."

With that, he turned and swept from the tavern, his cloak billowing behind him. Silas lingered at the bar, his sour expression focused on Lira, before he too slunk out the door.

Conversation slowly resumed, though at a more subdued volume. Vaskel sat back down, adjusting his cloak with a casual flick of his wrist, as Sass hurried off to refill ales.

"You may have just made an enemy," Lira said.

Vaskel laughed, the sound warm after the cold exchange with Rygor. "I'll add him to the list. Besides, I've faced worse than an overgrown lizard with delusions of grandeur."

Lira shook her head but couldn't help smiling. Vaskel had always been like this—quick to dive into danger, quicker to brush it off afterward. It was part of what made him both infuriating and endearing.

"You know," Vaskel said after a moment, his expression growing more serious, "I meant what I said earlier. About us still being a family." He reached across the table and touched her hand lightly. "You leaving didn't change that."

The warmth of his touch brought a lump to Lira's throat. "I'm glad you found me, Vask."

## Forty-Three

"ARE YOU STILL GLAD YOU CAME?" Lira asked Vaskel as they walked along the dark, dirt road leading to the heart of the village and toward Wayside's only inn. "Even after learning about Pirrin?"

She'd thrown on her old rogue's cloak to walk with him, and even though she'd arrived in it, she hadn't worn it since she'd started reviving the tavern. It felt strange to wear it again, but she was glad for the added warmth on the crisp night.

His nod was curt. "I'd rather know, even though I wish I didn't."

Lira sighed and her breath made a cloud in front of her face. "I know. Malek was bad enough, but Pirrin...?" She let her words trail off. "But you know as well as I do that it couldn't be wraiths."

He raked a hand through his dark hair, the movement harsh. "Then how do you explain it? Did our crew get cursed by them?"

Lira hadn't thought of that, but she was pretty sure wraiths who were trapped by a curse couldn't inflict curses on others. She shook her head. "The rest of us are all right, aren't we? Rog's safe with his wife. You and Cali are here with me."

Vaskel turned his head, his pale blue eyes practically glowing in the faint moonlight. "I hope you're right."

Guilt twisted Lira's gut. Should she tell Vaskel that she'd felt like she was being watched lately? That would do nothing but confirm his worst suspicions, and he was already more on edge than she'd ever seen him. The last thing she wanted to do was add fuel to the hellkin's fire—literally. He already ran hot, with passions that he fought to control.

An owl hooted in the distance, and Lira gathered her cloak tighter around her neck. The village was quiet, all the storefronts dark and the market stalls empty. When they reached the inn on the other side of the open-air market, a figure was hanging halfway out of a second-floor window.

"I knew I smelled you," Cali called down, her grin wide.

"I hope she's talking to you," Lira said.

Vaskel chuckled, not remotely offended by the pantheri's comment. "She can probably smell both of us."

Cali beckoned him with one arm. "Come on up, you wastrel."

"See?" Lira gave his arm a squeeze. "Things aren't so different."

Vaskel took a step toward the inn then paused. "Thanks, Lira." He gave her a grin that made his scarlet face even more handsome. "It's good to see you again."

"You, too." She shooed him with both hands. "Now don't keep Cali up too late."

Lira watched him disappear through the door to the inn, turning and heading back the way she came. As soon as she passed the stone monument that centered the village, her neck prickled.

*Son of a wand waxer! Why hadn't she sensed this when she was with Vaskel?*

Picking up her pace, she darted to the potter's storefront and pressed herself to the door. She held her breath, listening for footsteps or the rustle of clothing. Nothing.

*You're as paranoid as Vaskel,* she told herself as her shoulders crept down from her ears. *There's nothing stalking any of us. There's no one out there.*

If anything, it was Rygor watching her, and as much as she disliked the reeve, she didn't believe he would attack her. With renewed confidence, Lira darted to the next storefront and then the next, until she hurried under the awning for the chandler and almost ran straight into someone.

Hands closed around her arms as she stumbled back, but her breath lodged in her throat and prevented her from screaming. Then the figure stepped into the moonlight.

"Korl?" Lira didn't bother to keep her voice low. "What are you doing here?"

He released his grip on her, his gaze sliding to the ground. "I went to the tavern to thank you for the cake, but Sass said you'd left."

Lira had almost forgotten that Val had delivered the cake for her earlier.

"So, you followed me?" She hadn't meant her tone to sound quite so accusatory, but she blamed it on the fact that her heart hadn't resumed its normal pattern.

He jerked his head up, shaking it. "I was walking back when I saw you running through the village like you were being chased. I wanted to make sure you weren't."

Lira released a breath, kicking herself for jumping to the wrong conclusion. Then she grinned at him. "That might have been the most words I've ever heard you say at once."

He grunted. "If you're okay…"

She caught his sleeve as he turned to go. "Wait, I'm sorry. I'm not teasing you. It's nice hearing you talk." She glanced over her shoulder. "And I did think I was being followed, or at least watched. Not that this is the first time I've had that feeling in Wayside."

He scowled, then took her by the elbow and hurried her away from the village.

"Where are we…?" She started to ask before she saw exactly where they were going.

They walked past the mill on one side and the tavern on the other then across the stone bridge that crossed the stream. Korl didn't bother knocking on the door that led into the house attached to the blacksmith and wheelwright workshops.

Lira might not have been surprised when they entered the orc's home, but Korl's dads were. They turned abruptly from where they sat at a massive iron table, and both had a slice of Lira's apple cider cake in their hands.

"Well, this is a nice surprise," Vorto managed to say while Klaff only stared with cake-stuffed cheeks.

"Lira needs a weapon," Korl said without preamble.

Her mouth fell open as he led her to the table. "I don't need a—"

"You do if you're being followed," Korl insisted.

Both his orc dads bristled at this, even as Lira smiled at Korl, touched that he'd believed her without question.

"Is this true? Are you being followed?" Klaff asked, having finally swallowed.

"It's a feeling I've had, that's all." Lira had learned to trust her instincts, but she also was used to dealing with danger on her own. "But no weapon is necessary."

"Cake then." Vorto held out the plate. "It's delicious. Just as good as your gran's."

Lira flushed at the compliment, but Korl spluttered.

"You aren't going to help her?"

Vorto smiled at Lira as he shifted his considerable bulk in his orc-sized chair. "I suspect Lira doesn't need a weapon because she already has some. Am I right?"

# Forty-Four

SILVER MOONLIGHT PAINTED the dirt road with broad strokes, as Lira walked beside Korl away from his home. She was acutely aware of his massive presence—the measured rhythm of his breathing, the subtle scent of smoke and metal that clung to him, the way he purposefully shortened his steps to match her pace.

Though she was grateful for his company, Lira couldn't shake the prickling sensation at the nape of her neck. She scanned the tree line, the darkened storefronts, the shadows between buildings, looking for any sign of movement. There was nothing, but the feeling of being watched was like a shadow she couldn't outrun.

"You keep looking back," Korl said.

"Just seeing if your dads are watching," she lied.

He twisted, grunting when he spotted the massive figures backlit in the doorway, thick arms wrapped around each others' waists. Lira didn't mind that Vorto and Klaff were watching. She thought their protectiveness was sweet.

As they approached the stone bridge that would take them back to The Tusk & Tail, Lira slowed her pace, reluctant to reach the tavern so soon. Korl matched her, coming to a stop in the middle of the bridge.

Without speaking, they both leaned against the low stone wall. Below them, moonlight danced on the rippling surface of the stream.

"I should have told you sooner," Lira said finally, her voice barely louder than the water below. "About being a rogue."

Korl's massive shoulders lifted in a shrug. "It's all right. I'm used to my dads picking up on things I don't."

Something in his tone made Lira turn to study his profile—the strong jaw, the slight tilt of his head as he gazed at the water. It struck her then, how often she'd cataloged the details of others, tucking the information away for later.

"Sometimes noticing everything is exhausting," she confessed. "Sensing tension, picking up on hidden agendas, always being aware of every exit in a room. It's become second nature, but sometimes I wish I could just *be*."

The orc turned to face her, his dark eyes reflecting the moonlight as he waited for her to continue.

"Observing quietly has always been one of my talents," she said, her fingers tracing the rough stone beneath her hands. "But I think that's one of the real reasons I wanted to come back to Wayside. It was the last place I remember where I didn't have to be on my guard all the time."

A fish jumped in the stream below, creating a splash that momentarily silenced the crickets.

"I missed just being the Lira who baked with her gran, instead of Lira the rogue who dwelled in shadows. Don't get me wrong—I was good at what I did. But what I really loved was the camaraderie of my crew. When that was broken..." She paused, swallowing hard. "So was I."

Korl remained silent, but Lira could sense his attentiveness in the way his body angled toward hers.

"Seeing my old crew again has reminded me how much I missed that feeling," she said. "But now I'm starting to feel it with the tavern, with all our regulars. It's becoming a community. Maybe not quite a family yet, but it's getting there."

The words hung in the air between them, honest and unvarnished in a way Lira rarely allowed herself to be. Korl grunted softly, a sound she was beginning to recognize as acknowledgment rather than dismissal.

After a moment of companionable silence, the orc pushed himself away from the wall and began walking again. Lira fell into step beside him, crossing over the bridge to the gravel road again.

"I understand not being able to be yourself," Korl said. "I never wanted to be a guardsman."

Lira looked up at him, not terribly surprised by the admission. But like he'd let her talk, she gave him space to continue.

"I did it because Val needed a partner, and because it made my dads proud. But I've always wanted..." He trailed off, as if embarrassed.

"Wanted what?"

"To be a tinker," he said, the words coming out in a rush. "I like fixing things. Understanding how they work, making them better."

"Like our oven."

A small smile tugged at the corner of his mouth. "Like your oven."

They walked in silence for a few more steps before he spoke again. "If you can go from a rogue to a baker, maybe I could leave the guards. But Val..."

"You're worried about leaving her," Lira finished for him.

He nodded, his brow furrowed.

"I'm sure Val wants you to be happy," Lira said, remembering the way the tall guardswoman had spoken about him. "She thinks the world of you."

"She'd be fine," Korl admitted, his voice tinged with what might have been guilt. "She's always been the stronger one. I just..." He struggled, his hands opening and closing at his sides. "It feels like abandoning her."

"It's not abandonment to follow your heart," Lira said softly. "Besides, she wouldn't be alone. She'd still have you, just not as her partner in the guard."

They'd reached the tavern now, the weathered sign creaking gently in the night breeze. Lira turned to face Korl, suddenly aware of how close they were standing. The tavern was dark and quiet, likely everyone inside asleep by now.

The glowing moon overhead illuminated half of Korl's face, casting the other half in shadow, but his eyes were fixed on her. Lira felt herself leaning toward him almost imperceptibly.

Korl's gaze dropped to her lips for the briefest moment, and her breath caught in anticipation of him kissing her.

Instead, he cleared his throat and took a small step back. "Sleep well, Lira."

Before she could respond, he turned and strode away, his large frame melding into the shadows.

What had just happened? Or more accurately, what hadn't?

# Forty-Five

## "SO, YOU TOLD HIM EVERYTHING?"

Sass hadn't been asleep when Lira had slipped into their room, the fire still crackling in the hearth and the candle flickering on the bedside table, so Lira had told her what had happened, from walking Vaskel to the inn, to thinking she was being followed and running into Korl, to him taking her to his dads' home and her telling them of her life after leaving Wayside.

Sass fiddled with the end of her braid. "And the book? Did you tell them what it is?"

Lira divested herself of her thick cloak and day dress and then sank onto her bed in her shift, the weariness of the day replacing the heaviness of the garments. "Not that it's actually a spell book and that my gran was a mage. I couldn't bear to spoil their memories of my gran. They knew her as a sweet old lady who baked them cakes."

"You reckon they'd think differently if they knew?"

Lira shrugged. "Probably not, but I'm still coming to terms with it. Besides, Iris hasn't given me leave to tell folks in the village her part in this. She might not want everyone knowing what she was and how she knew my gran."

Sass moved her head up and down thoughtfully. "People are entitled to their secrets."

"That's what I think."

Lira did believe that, even though learning that her gran had kept so many secrets from her had been a shock. She'd wanted to hold onto her memories of her gran as they were, warm and sunny, but now she feared that every time she thought about her gran, the thoughts would be tainted by everything she hadn't known.

Lira gave her head a shake and shoved her feet under the brazenly floral coverlet, as Sass snuggled deeper beneath her own covers.

"So, what did Korl say when he found out you were a rogue?"

"What do you think he said?"

Sass gave her a crooked grin. "Not much."

"I will say that I'm starting to get pretty good at deciphering his different grunts and growls."

"We do love a good growl."

Both women laughed, and Lira reached over and blew out the candle.

"At least I know that he and Val are just friends," Lira said through a yawn.

"How do you know that?"

Lira punched her pillow a few times to get it to the right shape. "Val told me. They're best friends but that's all."

"I could have told you that," Sass muttered through the shadowy darkness only lit by the firelight.

"I think you did tell me that."

Sass sighed heavily. "If you want a guy who's going to profess his love to you and sweep you off your feet, I don't think Korl is it. Your friend Vaskel would probably be that guy. He looks the type to be a feet-sweeper-offer."

Lira laughed darkly. "You have no idea."

"I think I can guess, and I think he'd be more than happy to have you be the object of his attentions." Sass sat up in bed again and propped herself up on one elbow, her face partially illuminated by the dying fire. "But I also think if you wanted the hellkin, you wouldn't be here."

"Vaskel and I are nothing but friends," Lira said.

"Smart." Sass flopped back onto her pillow. "I think he'd be a whole lot of work."

Lira chuckled at this, thinking of Vaskel's dramatic shifts in mood. No, the passionate but volatile fighter had never been her type.

She stared at the beams in the ceiling. With everything that was going on and as much change as had happened in her life, the last thing she should be thinking about was love. But as she drifted to sleep, Lira hoped it was what occupied her dreams.

# Forty-Six

LIRA BLEW a strand of hair off her forehead as she pulled a tray of hand pies from the oven, setting in on the top with a clatter. She fed Crumpet an overly browned corner of crust as he sat patiently on the counter, his soft chittering providing a comforting backdrop.

Then the doors swung open, Crumpet flew to the hanging copper pots, and Sass strode into the kitchen.

"They're here."

The dwarf didn't need to explain further. *They* were Cali and Iris, and as previously planned, they'd come to try Iris's solvent to dissolve the mortar.

"Cal is keeping Durn distracted at the bar while Iris sneaks down below."

Knowing Durn, Cali had the harder task.

Lira wiped her hands on the front of her apron and gestured to the cooling pies. "The second batch is ready, so I'm going to pop down with Iris."

Sass bustled forward and used the knit short scarves to move the hand pies from the hot pans to a large wooden tray. "I'll get these served while you two try your luck downstairs. Folks who are busy eating and drinking are plenty distracted."

Lira hoped she was right. She met Iris outside the cellar door, and Sass passed them on her way to the great room with the tray held overhead. Iris held a lantern at the ready, and her dress pockets bulged.

Iris gave Lira a solemn nod, and the two former rogues opened the door and slunk downstairs. They made quick work of getting to the corner of the cellar, with Lira too nervous to pay much mind to the fetid odor and dank cold this time.

Iris emitted a disapproving sound when she saw the mortar on the ground. "No rat did that."

She produced a brown glass bottle from her pocket and then a rag from her other pocket. "Don't stand too close to me. This might make you lightheaded."

Lira took a step back as Iris uncapped the bottle and poured a generous amount of solvent on the rag. She pressed the wet cloth to the mortar, burying her nose in the crook of her arm.

The sharp chemical smell bit the back of Lira's throat even though she wasn't close to the wall. She put a hand over her nose and mouth as she battled the urge to cough.

After a few minutes, Iris tossed the cloth on the ground and stepped back. "It isn't working."

Lira blinked rapidly as she leaned closer to the wall. "Not even a little bit?"

"Not enough." Iris waved her hands in front of her face. "The amount we'd need to use to dissolve it might kill us."

Lira was sure her gran would not want her and Iris dying over the spell book.

"I brought something else in case the solvent didn't work." Iris reached into her apparently bottomless pockets and pulled out a chisel.

Lira had barely opened her mouth to register hesitation when Iris thrust the sharp end into the mortar. The sound was anything but quiet, but bits of the mortar did flake away.

"When there's a will..." Iris muttered, striking the point into the mortar again, the metal clanging as it slipped and struck one of the stones.

Overhead, someone belted out what was undeniably a sea shanty. Lira put a hand over her mouth to keep from laughing, knowing exactly who it was.

Quick footfall descended the steps behind them, and Cali's voice cut through the darkness. "What's going on down here?"

Iris paused with the chisel suspended in mid-air. "Can you hear me?"

Cali stepped into the circle of warm light. "Why else do you think Sass is leading everyone in a song? A very strange song, I might add."

"I think she makes up her own sea shanties," Lira said.

"Goblin's spawn." Iris stamped her foot and stepped back from the wall. "We're going to need a bigger distraction."

"Bigger than a dwarf leading the tavern in song?"

Iris gave the wall a grim look. "If we want to get through all that mortar and rock without poor Sass running out of breath."

Or without Rygor catching wind of unusual sounds coming from the tavern's cellar. If the wyvern was the one who'd tried to get through the wall, he'd be watching for anything suspicious.

"Maybe we should do it when the tavern is empty," Cali suggested.

"That means we'd have to get Durn off the premises." Lira wasn't sure how possible that was, considering how much the man slept. "It also means anyone passing by could hear the racket."

"Like Rygor," Iris muttered.

Cali swung her head from rogue to rogue. "Who's Rygor?"

Iris made a disapproving sound in the back of her throat. "The wyvern reeve."

Cali's ears twitched. "Vaskel mentioned him—not favorably, I should add."

"He knows there's gold on the premises," Lira said, "but he doesn't know where."

Iris flicked a hand at the mortar on the ground. "Or maybe he does."

Lira's pulse spiked at the thought of the greedy beast getting his claws on her gold or her gran's book. "We have to get through the wall before he does."

"But when?" Cali's tail swished behind her as she paced a small circle. "There's never a time when this village isn't peaceful and quiet."

Iris's face brightened. "You are a genius, love."

"I am?" Cali looked to Lira, but the woman could only lift her shoulders.

"The village wasn't always so quiet, especially not during festivals," Iris said.

Lira snapped her fingers. "Does Wayside still have Night Faires?"

Iris's smile slipped, and there was sadness in her eyes. "Not in a long time."

"Night Faires?" Cali asked.

"Celebrations that used to be held one night a month, on the night of the new moon. Luminaries lit the roads, the market was open and lit by lanterns, the shops set up outside, and special vendors sold decorated paper lanterns."

"There was music and dancing and then at midnight, all the paper lanterns were released into the sky," Iris added.

"Sounds like a good distraction," Cali said.

There was a determined glint in Iris's eyes. "Now we just have to convince the village it's time for another one."

Lira thought about the moon cycle. "And plan it in two days."

# Forty-Seven

"WELL, THAT'S IT." Sass sank into the chair usually occupied by Val and blew out a breath that ruffled the wispy curls that had sprung loose from her braid. "Everyone's gone, Silas slunk off, and Durn wandered off to bed."

Despite the night being a busy one with more patrons than ever, Sass had wiped down every table and swept the floor clean of all the dirt the new business dragged in. For Lira's part, the dishes had been washed, and you never would have known from the spotless counters and worktable, that she'd turned out a record number of meat pies, courtesy of their new oven.

Iris cut her eyes to the back of the tavern, shaking her head as she stood in front of the hearth and warmed her hands. "At least he isn't complaining about all the changes. Before you came, I would have said he'd have been as excited to improve the place as a dire cat being tossed into a room full of rocking chairs."

"I'm not sure if excited would describe him." Lira understood Iris's point, and she wondered why the tavernkeep had all but abdicated control of his place to their improvements. "He spends too much time listening to Silas, who doesn't like me or Sass."

Iris shook her head. "Silas is a harmless old fool."

Lira wasn't sure she agreed with that. She'd seen words work on people as effectively as any poison. For a second, she wondered if Silas could be the one who'd been in the cellar. But when? Besides, how would he know what she'd buried or where?

"Durn does seem to be enjoying Penny's company, even if he's neither here nor there about the tavern," Sass said, her smile smug.

Lira hadn't spent much time in the great room, but even she'd noticed that the chandler had been at the bar for a good part of the evening.

Cali leaned forward in the chair across from Sass and braced her elbows on her knees. "As much as I love discussing the romantic lives of grumpy men, tell me more about this festival and how we're going to pull it off before I fall asleep from exhaustion."

"It shouldn't be hard to get the village behind it," Iris said. "We used to hold the Night Faires monthly, so we'd only be reminding folks about them."

"Why did the faires stop?" Sass asked.

"They were still happening when I left," Lira said.

A frown tugged at Iris's lips. "A lot happened after you left, love. Your gran had passed, you up and left, Durn lost his wife and stopped serving food, the old haberdasher moved on and the shop sat empty for more than a few seasons, and the laird stopped sending crews to keep up the roads, so some of the vendors from outside the village stopped coming in to set up their stalls. If you ask me, I don't think the village was in much of a mood to celebrate."

"You think they will be now?" Lira asked.

Sass sat forward. "Sure, they will. Things have changed. Good things have come to Wayside." She winked. "If I do say so myself."

"I won't argue with you there." Iris twirled the usual strand of hair around one finger. "You girls have brought some energy back to the village. Why, you even inspired Pip to create lemon sweet rolls."

"That's worth a party by itself," Cali said.

Sass got a faraway look in her eyes. "You can say that again."

Lira joined Iris to stand in front of the low fire. "You're sure we can convince the village to have a Night Faire so soon?"

"How soon are we talking?" Sass asked.

"We don't know how long we have before whoever tried to get through the wall will do it again." Lira exchanged a nervous glance with Iris, thinking of the sinister Rygor. "The Night Faires were always on the night of a new moon, and that's this Saturni."

Sass let out a low whistle. "You're sure we can pull this off?"

Iris tightened the curl around her finger as she considered it. "I do, and we only have to get a few more vendors onboard to make it happen."

"We already have the tavern and the town apothecary," Sass said.

"Then we divide and conquer to get everyone else."

Sass's arm shot into the air. "Lira and I volunteer to talk to Pip and Fenni."

"Cheat," Cali mumbled with a grin.

Sass smirked at her. "Never let it said that a dwarf passed up a chance for food."

"We'll go first thing in the morning," Lira added. "I need to go to the market anyway."

"And I can talk to Tin," Sass said.

Lira shook her head at the dwarf, certain that another visit to the haberdasher would mean more cushions for Val's chair. "Then I can stop by the blacksmith and wheelwright workshops later. I need to stop by anyway."

Sass arched a brow. "Do you?"

Lira ignored the burn of her cheeks.

"I can talk to the innkeeper since I'm staying there," Cali offered. "She seems a friendly sort."

Iris nodded. "Ginnie won't say no. She loves a good party. I'm happy to visit the shop owners across from me and talk to the stall owners I know. I'll also need to talk to someone about paper for the lanterns."

"What about the laird?" Cali asked. "Won't the castle want to take part?"

Iris frowned. "Not much of a staff left anymore, and the old laird stopped taking part in village happenings a long time ago."

"What do you think Rygor will say when he finds out?" Lira asked.

Sass slipped off the end of the chair and yawned. "Hopefully he won't find out until it's too late to do anything about it. It's always easier to ask forgiveness than permission anyway."

"Why do you need to be forgiven?"

Their faces swung toward the doorway, startled that Vaskel had slipped inside. Between her own weariness and the crackling of the fire, Lira hadn't heard a thing. Was she slipping?

Cal and Lira exchanged a speaking look, both nodding. They couldn't keep the plan from their friend. Not when he could be put to such good use.

Lira walked toward the hellkin. "Are you up for one last heist as a crew?"

Vaskel's eyes flashed interest.

"If we pull it off, it will enrage the wyvern," Cali added.

Vaskel's grin was almost feline. "Name the time and place."

# Forty-Eight

THE NEXT MORNING, Lira had already finished shopping in the marketplace when she met Sass at the stone monument centering the town square.

"Tin's in!" Sass's voice carried in the fresh morning air as she hurried toward Lira, who'd hooked the basket filled with her purchases in the crook of her arm. "He was opening his shop as I walked by, so I popped in. He'd never heard of a Night Faire, but he's delighted at the thought. Delighted."

Lira grinned at the dwarf's spot-on impersonation of the gnome. "One down. You ready to talk to Pip and Fenni?"

"If you're done with your shopping."

Lira told her she was, cutting her gaze to the bag of apples the cider seller had sold her for a song. "I have everything I need."

Sass cocked an eyebrow as they walked side-by-side toward the bakery. "That goes in a cake?"

"It's for something special to sell at the Night Faire, and I'm almost certain I remember the recipe."

"When we get the book, you'll have all the recipes you've been trying to remember."

"Even before I knew the book was…" Lira swung a furtive glance around them, but the village was still rousing itself and there was no one to hear her, "…special, I wanted to get it back because it's the only thing I kept that really reminds me of her. Besides, it would be nice not to guess on the measurements. I'm almost certain I didn't put enough spice in the apple cider cake."

Sass gave her a nudge with one shoulder. "Don't worry. We'll get the book."

The bakery had been closed when Lira walked by earlier in the morning, even though all the lights had been blazing, and she knew Pip had been baking away in the back. She was also aware that the halfling baker often got so caught up in his baking that he forgot to open his doors. That was when Fenni would open them for him, bustling about scolding his brother and laughing in equal measure.

But the door was open now, as evidenced by the hypnotic scent of sugar and yeast that hit Lira and made her eyelids flutter.

"Sweet simmering cauldrons," Sass said the curse like a prayer. "You might have to do all the talking. I'm going to be too busy eating."

"A fine morning to you both," Pip called from behind the counter as they walked inside the warm shop.

As was usually the case, his hair stood on end and was dusted with so much flour it looked white. Today, he even had a glob of glaze trailing down his cheek.

Sass wasted no time walking to the counter, her eyes locked onto the sticky sweet rolls stacked high under a glass, domed stand. "It's getting better by the second."

"Sweet rolls for you both?" Pip lifted the dome and grabbed his tongs.

"Two for me," Sass said, her tone dreamy.

Lira nodded at the baker. "The same for me."

"Up early to do your shopping?"

Lira turned at the sound of Fenni stepping inside from the interior door separating the two shops. The cooler air, pungent with the tangy aroma of cheese, wafted in, but was soon overwhelmed by both the warmth of the bakery and the scent of the breads.

"Yes, but we mostly came to see you two."

"Two?" Fenni's neat brows popped high. "Both of us?"

"Both of you," Lira said with a smile to the halfling brother with not a smudge on his three-piece suit or a hair out of place.

Fenni tugged at his spotless, white apron. "Usually, it's Pip who gets the callers in the morning and me in the afternoon."

"Mmm," Sass mumbled through a mouthful of sweet roll. "There's nothing like some soft cheese with supper."

Lira shook her head at the dwarf, although her stomach was growling in protest. "Do you remember the Night Faires?"

Pip's eyes sparkled as he bounced on his heels. "Oh, they were wonderful. All those lanterns floating into the air."

Fenni nodded. "Good for business too. I used to invite the beekeeper to set up with me outside the shop. Honey and cheese are the perfect combination."

Another moan from Sass, but this time there were no words.

"What would you say to another Night Faire?" Lira asked, looking from one brother to the other. "This Saturni."

Pip clapped his hands together and a cloud of flour billowed over his head. "I think it's a marvelous idea."

Fenni worked the edge of his apron with his hands. "Do you think it can be planned so quickly?"

"Tin has already signed on," Sass said with a swipe of her hand across her sticky mouth.

"Not to mention the tavern and Iris," Lira added, hoping her smile was bright enough to mask her worry that they would say no.

"Count us in!" Pip thrust one arm into the air with his thumb up. "A Night Faire is just the thing Wayside needs."

Fenni muttered some mild protests about the time he typically needed to arrange the perfect pairings but they were drowned out by his brother's exuberance.

Pip was hurrying back and forth behind the counter waving his hands. "I must come up with something new and exclusive for the Night Faire."

"New?" Sass had already started on her second sweet roll and almost choked at this proclamation. "No sweet rolls?"

Pip stopped and spun toward them, pointing a dough-stained finger at first one and then the other. His eyes were wide as he dropped his voice to a whisper. "Better than sweet rolls."

When the women left the bakery, with Pip exclaiming about his Night Faire creation and Fenni muttering about his cheese and honey pairings, Lira opened the paper bag Pip had given her and inhaled deeply. Better then sweet rolls?

The Night Faire could not arrive soon enough.

# Forty-Nine

CRUMPET EYED the mountain of apple peels Lira had created, plucking up one strip of red peel and nibbling on it cautiously.

"Be careful." Lira grinned at his pinched face as she poured water and sugar into a saucepan. "They're tart now, but just wait until they're wrapped up in pastry dough and baked."

The flutterstoat discarded the apple peel and chittered at her.

"I told you, I'm making apple dumplings for the Night Faire." She gestured to the rows of neatly peeled apples on the worktable. "The cider seller had a bunch he wanted to move, and I remembered that my gran would save aging apples by making them into apple dumplings."

Crumpet flew to the counter and sat on his hind legs with his tiny arms crossed.

"Don't look at me like that." Lira stirred the sugar slowly as the granules dissolved. "I'm making more than apple dumplings. I'll have our usual scones and hand pies, too. The first batch of scones is already in the oven."

Crumpet seemed slightly appeased by this, curling his fluffy white tail around himself and grooming it daintily.

Lira glanced at the oven and inhaled deeply. She'd learned to time the scones to the smell in the air, and if her calculations were right, they had a few more minutes to bake.

"You can't blame me because you were gallivanting about." Lira added a generous spoonful of cinnamon to the simmering sugar water. "I've been baking since the small hours of the morning. The Night Faire is tonight, after all."

Crumpet emitted what she could have sworn was a huff and flounced his tail in her direction. Lira only laughed.

Despite the rush to pull together the Night Faire so quickly, they'd managed to build up quite a bit of excitement and get the entire village behind it. Well, the entire village aside from Silas, who'd remained content to prop up the far end of the bar and mutter to himself about the fuss.

Tin and Sass had nominated themselves for the joint task of coordinating the village decorations, which meant that Tin had created festive pennants from scrap cloth and they'd strung them crisscrossed between storefronts and from the top of the town monument down to the nearest buildings, making it look a bit like a Maypole.

The market was hung with lanterns, and Penny had provided luminaries that lined the main road that wound through Wayside. Even though it wasn't yet dark, Lira's heart had skipped when she'd seen how the village was decked out earlier.

On her morning walk to get the final few ingredients for her baking, she'd noticed that Pip's door had been closed, but his windows shone with light. She'd even seen his brother Fenni wearing a baker's apron and piling fresh loaves into the baskets behind the counter.

The town was brimming in anticipation, and Lira couldn't help sharing in the excitement. She had such fond memories of childhood Night Faires that she had to remind herself many times that this would be different. She couldn't wander the stalls feasting on culinary delights or spend an inordinate amount of time decorating a paper lantern. The rest of the village could indulge themselves, but despite the happy thrum in her chest, she needed to focus on the reason they'd thrown together the event in the first place.

Iris had it all worked out. While the Night Faire was in full swing with musicians playing and people laughing and wandering from shop to shop and stall to stall through the village, she and Lira would slip away and sneak down to the cellar. They'd use the cover of the festivities to mask the sound of breaking through the stone wall.

If all went according to Sass's plan, Penny would entertain Durn away from the tavern while Cali stood watch to ensure that no one approached The Tusk & Tail. Korl hadn't been told about the plan because if he was told, Val would need to know, and Iris had argued that the more people who knew, the greater a chance of a slip-up. Plus, they were guardsmen and letting them know of a potential crime would put Korl and Val in a tenuous position. The last thing anyone wanted was to get the guards fired.

Lira didn't like keeping things from Korl, especially after he'd been so kind to them—to her. He hadn't scoffed when she'd told him she thought she was being followed, and he hadn't judged her when she'd revealed what she'd been doing for all her years away. She hadn't seen him since then, but that was only because in the days since she'd done nothing but prepare for the Night Faire. She hoped his and Val's absence from the tavern meant that they were busy with work or perhaps preparing for the upcoming festivities as well.

As Lira was thinking that she missed seeing Val and Korl in their usual chairs by the fire, the kitchen doors flew open, and Sass burst in.

"This is a disaster!"

Lira almost sloshed some of the bubbling syrup onto the floor, and Crumpet flew to the hanging pots. The dwarf braced two fists on her hips and blew an errant curl from her forehead.

"What's a disaster?' Lira asked, instinctively cutting her eyes to the stove. No smoke billowed from the door, so at least the disaster wasn't from her kitchen.

"How is this plan going to work if Durn is too thick to know that Penny wants him to ask her to the faire?"

Crumpet flapped his furry wings and fluttered down from the top rack, landing on the worktable and shooting Sass a scathing look.

"Relying on Durn's sensitivity should never have been Plan A."

Sass crossed her arms over her chest. "You're right. We should just lock him in a closet somewhere." Her eyes brightened. "Or we could drug him. Could you make one of those apple things with some of Iris's sleeping tonic in it?"

Lira shook her head at the exasperated dwarf. "Let's call that Plan C."

"Maybe this is why I never made it onto a crew. Contingency plans make me too nervous."

Strategizing came as naturally to Lira as baking, with a good deal fewer burns. "Why does Durn need to ask her or the other way around, for that matter? They only need to think they've been asked by the other."

Sass bobbed a nod. "We trick each into thinking the other asked."

"A pair of notes delivered to each should do the job." Lira lifted the spoon, pleased with the amber syrup coating it. "Cali is good at mimicking handwriting. You should ask her to help."

Sass bounced on the balls of her feet. "I knew you would have a solution." Then she eyed Lira. "Should I be worried you're so good at trickery?"

"Not when I'm on your side."

A grin teased the edges of the dwarf's lips, and she drew in a long breath. "Any chance of something to munch on while I'm working with our forger?"

"Not unless you consider raw apples a treat."

Sass grimaced, backing from the kitchen as quickly as she'd arrived, leaving the doors swinging in her wake.

Lira winked at Crumpet as she took the fragrant cinnamon syrup off the stove. "Now where were we?"

Fifty

LUTE MUSIC GREETED Lira as she stepped outside the tavern holding a tray of scones in one hand and a platter of baked apple dumplings in the other. Even though the sun had barely set, people were already milling about and drifting over the stone bridge toward the heart of the village. Luminaries spilled puddles of yellow light along both sides of the hardpacked dirt road, and even the bridge had been strewn with fabric pennants.

Her pulse quickened, and for a moment she was transported back to being a girl and walking to the Night Faires with her gran, her small hand nestled safely in the old woman's soft one. She'd barely been able to contain her excitement as a child, skipping on her toes in place of walking. Her gran had only laughed at her, always letting her run ahead once they got close enough to the village center. There had been nothing like the joy of racing toward the festival, dust kicking up behind her feet and her hair flying.

Now her heart tripped for a different reason. Soon, she and Iris would sneak away and finally break through the stone wall in the tavern's cellar. She would finally retrieve what she'd left behind, what she'd come home to find.

"There you are," Sass said as she bustled up to her.

In honor of the occasion, Sass had wrapped her braid into a coil on top of her head. Her usual work dress had been replaced by a teal blouse made from a fine fabric with sheen and a smoke gray skirt that was gathered high on one side.

"You look nice," Lira said as Sass took the trays from her.

"Don't sound so surprised. I can clean up when the need arises." She gave Lira a cursory glance. "I hope you don't plan to come to the Night Faire covered in flour."

Lira realized that she still wore her apron, even though she'd finished all her baking. "I guess I should change."

She untied the apron from her waist, stepping away from Sass before shaking it. "How's it looking?"

Sass held the two trays over her head. "I have to say, for an above-ground celebration, it's not bad."

"I take it dwarf parties are better?"

"There's nothing like a celebration in an underground city with a thousand lights and the sound of drums echoing off the stone." Sass sighed wistfully. "But this isn't half bad."

Laughter erupted from somewhere in the village center, followed by clapping.

"That must be the folks from Elmshire." Sass glanced over her shoulder. "Word must have spread fast, either that or Pip and Fenni sent messages, because quite a few halflings are here, and one is an impressivly good juggler."

"I can't wait to see." Lira took a moment to hang her apron on one of the coat hooks inside the front door of the tavern and then smoothed down the front of her burgundy dress. It wasn't as fancy as what Sass was wearing, but it would have to suffice.

Sass handed her back the platter of apple dumplings as they walked toward the village center. As they got closer, the music grew louder, and more villagers crowded the main road. She spotted the halflings Sass had mentioned, as well as a few groups of gnomes, a handful of orcs, and the pair of ogres who'd delivered the chairs. Not to mention, a sizable number of humans and at least one satyr.

As expected, Pip had set out a table in front of his store, and the smell emanating from the trays and stands arranged on it almost made Lira's knees wobble.

"Those aren't lemon sweet rolls," she said reverently, detecting an entirely different flavor profile.

"They're not." Pip stood behind his table, still wearing his apron, a prodigious amount of flour in his hair, and a smudge of something dark on one cheek. "They're called doughnuts."

Lira eyed the rings of dough that were stacked high. One stack was glazed in something dark and glossy while another shone like glass. Yet another was covered in so much glittering sugar that her teeth ached looking at it. The warm, yeasty aroma pulled a moan from her lips. "Why doughnuts? Why not dough rings?"

Pip lifted one small shoulder. "Don't ask me. It's a gnomish delicacy all the way from the Skittering Islands."

A child rushed up and handed Pip a copper bit. "One of the dark ones, please."

"One chocolate doughnut." Pip beamed as he used a translucent square of paper to pluck one of the darkly glazed treats from the top of its pile and hand it to the child.

"Chocolate," Lira murmured. She'd heard of chocolate. It was rare and, like Pip said, hailed from the Skittering Islands.

"Try one." Pip used another paper square to take a doughnut from the pile and hand it to Lira.

Lira patted her pockets, realizing she didn't have a coin on her. "I don't..."

The halfling flapped his free hand at her. "On the house." Then he gave her a mischievous wink. "As long as you set one of those apple pastries aside for me."

Lira bit into the doughnut, groaning with pleasure at the rich flavor of the chocolate and yeasty soft dough as she chewed. "Consider it done."

Pip bounced on his heels and gave her a wave as she took sugar-stunned steps to follow Sass. Fenni was deep in conversation with a halfling couple debating the merits of a soft versus hard cheese with whipped honey from Elmshire. Instead of a table displaying his wares, Tin had created a stall filled with long ribbon wands for people to wave. Lira already spotted several children running with the colorful ribbons trailing behind them like dragon tails.

Then she reached Sass, who had all the baked goods from the tavern displayed on a table in front of the apothecary shop. Iris stood behind it, her smile tentative.

"No one wants to buy a poultice or talk about their maladies during the Night Faire," Sass said by way of explanation.

"Oh, I'm sure they do, pet," Iris corrected. "I just don't wish to hear about it tonight." She gave Lira a pointed look. "I have other things to do."

Lira pivoted to peer at the people laughing and gathering around the stone monument in the village center and spilling into the illuminated market. A juggling halfling walked past with several children following him, and Lira spotted a lute player busking in the corner outside the potter's shop.

Cali sauntered up chewing one of Pip's doughnuts, this one with clear glaze. "That baker outdid himself." Then she sniffed the air and followed the scent to the tray of apple dumplings that Sass was arranging on the table. "I guess both bakers did."

"Thanks, Cal." Lira looked over the pantheri's shoulder. "Where's Vaskel?"

"He's not charming the ladies, if that's what you're thinking," Sass said.

That had been what Lira had been thinking. She scoured the crowds, looking for the hellkin's distinctive skin. His task was to keep the wyvern occupied, but Vaskel had been known to get distracted before. Lira recalled one quest when he'd done such a good job of keeping the lady of the manor distracted that he'd ended up in her bed. At least the guards had been too busy chasing him to notice Lira slinking from the vault with pockets filled with jewels.

Finally, Lira spotted the hellkin on the outskirts of the crowd with Rygor dogging his steps. How had he managed to get the wyvern to follow *him*?

"Your hellkin friend is as clever as he is smoldering." Iris said, taking a copper bit from a pink-haired gnome in exchange for an apple dumpling. "He stuffed his pockets with gold to keep the wyvern's attention on him."

Lira took a final bite of the doughnut. "And Durn?"

Sass extended a finger to where the tavernkeep was walking next to Penny, bending down to laugh at something she'd said. "Both of them received lovely notes inviting the other to meet at the town square."

Cali crossed a hand at her waist and bowed. "I outdid myself, if I do say so."

Lira licked her sticky fingers and surveyed the crowd, the butterflies awakening in her belly. "It's all going according to plan."

LIRA HAD VISITED every stall at the faire and eaten far too many of Pip's doughnuts, not to mention indulging in one of Fenni's cheese and honey pairings that had been the perfect contrast of savory and sweet. But wherever she walked, Vaskel always kept Rygor on the opposite side of the faire.

The one person she hadn't seen yet was Korl, but she told herself that he must be on duty at the castle. He could be hidden within the crowd, but he was too big to go unnoticed for so long. Still, she couldn't let it bother her since Durn was occupied with the chandler and Rygor was following Vaskel's pockets filled with gold like a child trailing after a piper.

"It's time."

She hadn't heard Iris walk up behind her because of the din of the crowd and a fiddler who'd joined the lute, but she'd been expecting her. The faire was getting close to its peak, and they'd both put in enough of an appearance that they wouldn't be missed.

Without another word, the pair made their way to the tavern, smiling and greeting people as they went. When they reached the door, Iris did a full rotation.

"Cali should be here. I sent her ahead a few minutes ago."

Lira frowned. "I watched her walk this way."

Iris rubbed her arms, even though they were covered by her nubby, green sweater. "Maybe she stepped inside to wait for us."

Lira's pulse spiked, but it wasn't because she sensed she was being watched. Her instincts told her something was off. Cali was nothing if not reliable. If she'd said she would be outside the tavern, that's where she would be. Unless...

Lira wished she had one of her blades, but she hadn't taken the time to grab them before going to the faire, and she didn't want anyone to see her wearing them. She slid her gaze to Iris, whose hand was already going into one of the pockets in her voluminous skirt. At least the apothecary had tools that could be used as weapons.

Iris produced a chisel from one pocket and an iron hammer from the other. She handed the chisel to Lira and gave her a solemn nod.

Lira held her breath as she opened the tavern door. It was quiet and empty inside, which was an unusual sight now that they'd built up a bustling business. But since they were closed for the Night Faire, no one was in the tavern and no fire was lit. Iris kept close behind her as they moved on silent feet toward the cellar door.

Despite the empty great room and the silence that hung over the tavern, Lira's neck had started to prickle again. When they reached the cellar door, it stood slightly ajar.

Lira went still. That door was never left open. Not by her, not by Sass, not by Durn.

She hesitated, straining to hear voices. There were none, but there were footsteps. Iris put a hand on her arm, as if to pull her back, but the steps weren't coming toward them. Lira was sure someone was pacing.

She considered going upstairs for her blades, or even going back to the village and getting help. Vaskel would come to her aide without question, but that would alert Rygor. Besides, she still didn't know where Cali was, and she had a bad feeling that someone was using the cover of the Night Faire to make another attempt at the wall.

Her mind raced as she motioned for Iris to follow her, and the two walked gingerly down the stairs, the only light coming from the far corner.

Lira was right. Someone was there, and she would bet coin that it was the same person who'd tried to break through the wall before. As she crept on her toes around the corner, she raised the hammer and prepared to strike.

The light from the lantern on the dirt floor only extended a few feet in each direction, but it was enough to illuminate Cali, who lay sprawled unconscious on the ground. Lira pressed her lips together to keep from calling her name, but she couldn't stay silent when she saw who whirled to face her from where he crouched by the stone wall.

*"Malek?"*

# Fifty-Two

LIRA SHOOK HER HEAD, unable to believe what she was seeing. Malek's black hair had grown long, and it matched the dark veins that were visible beneath his chalky skin. His face was gaunt, and his eyes were entirely black and hollowed out. The spell caster looked worse for wear, but he also looked very much alive.

"Lira," he purred, a smile twitching across his lips before vanishing. "I thought I might see you here." He gestured to Cali. "Looks like we're getting the crew back together."

Iris rushed forward and put a finger to the pantheri's neck. "She's alive."

Malek's face contorted. "Did you think I would kill dear Cali?"

Lira didn't take her gaze off the man. "What are you doing here, Malek?"

He raised a pale hand and flicked his bony fingers at the wall. "I've come for this, of course."

Lira suppressed a shudder, certain that the cellar was even colder than usual with Malek there. The mage might not be dead, but she wasn't entirely sure he was living either.

"What is *this*?" Lira asked. She wasn't going to give him an inch. She knew Malek too well, knew that he was skilled at extracting information.

"The book with the moonstone on the cover, of course. And the gold. I won't lie and say I won't enjoy the gold."

Despite Lira's talent at deception, she couldn't stop her mouth from falling open. How did he know about the book?

Malek appeared bored as he released a sigh. "You only ever talked about a few things in your sleep, you know, and one of them was your gran's recipe book with the moonstone on the cover." He gave her a silky smile that almost seemed real. "Of course, you believed it to be a simple book of recipes, didn't you? I don't think you had any idea that books of that description were only created by the old magical guilds and only bestowed on mages."

For the hundredth time since she'd discovered the truth, she'd wished her gran had told her all this. She wished she wasn't learning this from Malek, of all people.

Instead of talking about the book, Lira locked eyes with him. "What happened to you, Malek? I thought you were dead. We *all* thought you were dead."

Instead of answering, Malek shook his head, and limp strands of ebony hair swung across his face. "You were all so scared of me doing dark magic. You were sure it would ruin everything, but it didn't. Don't you see?"

All Lira could see was that he'd wasted away as the dark magic had twisted him from within.

His head snapped up and the black beads of his eyes pinned her. "It was dark magic that saved me, dark magic that kept me alive in the sea, dark magic that revived me when my friends abandoned me."

"We didn't abandon you." Lira's voice cracked as she remembered that night on the cliff. "I tried to save you. Don't you remember?"

His dead eyes bore into her. "All I remember is pain, and when I finally emerged from it, I was alone."

Her heart constricted, the loneliness in his words palpable. "If we'd known—"

"You were never truly my friends, were you? You only used me for my talents and tossed me aside."

"That's not true." Lira was vaguely aware of Iris rousing Cali on the floor nearby.

A faraway look danced across Malek's contorted face. "You know, Pirrin said the same thing."

Icy talons of fear pierced Lira's heart. Malek had killed Pirrin. Regret stabbed through Lira as she thought of her ranger friend dying at the hands of someone they'd all trusted. If she knew Pirrin, he'd believed in Malek until the end.

"It doesn't matter. None of it matters anymore." Malek slid his gaze from her as if he found her presence tiresome. "Once I have a proper spell book, I won't have to hunt for spells like a beggar looking for scraps."

The thought of Malek using her gran's book curdled her stomach. "My gran's book won't have dark magic. She wasn't that kind of mage."

"You don't know what she was."

Each word that Malek spat out hit Lira like a blow to the body. He was right. She didn't know what kind of magic her gran had practiced or what was in her book, but she knew her gran had never been like this, had never used magic for evil. She couldn't let a mage twisted by dark magic get his hands on her book.

"The book doesn't belong to you, Malek."

He raised an amused brow at her. "What are you going to do, Lira? I know you don't have any elven powers."

"But I'm not alone like you are."

Malek looked from her to Iris and Cali on the ground. "Well, our archer friend is indisposed, and I doubt the old lady will be much help."

"But we might be."

Lira swallowed a grateful sob as Korl and Vaskel stepped into the light. Sass was only a step behind them with Crumpet riding on her shoulder.

Malek's lips curled briefly at the sight of Vaskel, but then his placid mask snapped back into place. "This is quite the assemblage."

Lira knew his remark was meant to be cutting, but she didn't care.

Vaskel withdrew a pair of blades and assumed a crouch, fire dancing behind his ice-blue eyes. "You should have stayed dead, spell-caster."

Malek sighed. "I should have killed you before you got here. No matter." He flicked his hand, sending a beam of blue light toward Vaskel.

The hellkin pushed Korl out of the way and dove forward, but Malek recovered quickly, flicking his hand again, blasting Vaskel back into a wall of shelves.

With a roar Lira had never heard, Korl lunged for the mage, knocking him on his back. Before Lira could scream a warning, Malek raised his hands from where he lay sprawled on the ground.

As if her hands were moving of their own volition, Lira thrust them toward Malek, sending a blast of energy across the room and killing whatever spell he'd tried to cast. His head swung to her, his eyes wide.

"I knew it!" Sass cried, producing a menacing curved blade from her waist and grinning at Lira.

Lira stared at her own hands in disbelief for a beat then she looked up as Malek pushed himself to his feet. He swung one arm wide, aiming for her, but Korl caught his elbow mid-swing. Malek used his other hand to blast Korl back, and the orc flew beyond the pool of light, slamming into something hard in the dark.

Sass surged forward with her dagger high, but Malek flung her aside with a twitch of his wrist.

Then he turned on Lira again and smiled. "Look who's alone again."

Before Lira could attempt to use powers she hadn't known she possessed, a blur of white flew at Malek, attaching itself to his neck.

The mage shrieked as Crumpet bit his throat, his claws tearing at the papery flesh. Black blood dripped down Malek's neck as he attempted to pull off the flutterstoat. When he finally succeeded, Crumpet hit the floor with a thud and lay still.

Lira didn't think. She hurled all her rage, all her hurt, all her fear directly at Malek. Searing white light poured from her hands and the mage went rigid, his feet lifting off the floor and his mouth opening as if he was attempting to scream. Then he went limp, still suspended in her blinding beam of light.

Lira didn't realize she was screaming until Korl put a hand on her shoulder. "You can stop."

When Lira did, she collapsed into his arms.

## Fifty-Three

"I DON'T THINK apple dumplings have healing properties," Sass said as they gathered in the great room and Lira fed a revived Crumpet bits of a dumpling that hadn't made the cut to be sold at the faire.

"That's what you think," Lira said without taking her eyes off the flutterstoat. "All pastry has healing properties."

"I agree with that." Korl's voice was low and even as he sat next to Lira on the long bench.

Lira looked away from Crumpet to smile at him. "Thanks."

He nodded, knowing that the thanks was for more than just sticking up for her pastry. After all, he'd been the one to tie up Malek and drag him to the dungeon at Greyhelm Castle.

"If that's the case, can I get an apple dumpling here?" Cali sat in one of the overstuffed chairs with a healing poultice on her head.

"Your head needs more than some apple wrapped in pastry," Iris said, but her tone wasn't unkind. She'd been more worried than she'd let on when she'd been trying to revive Cali, and she'd given the pantheri strict instructions not to confront any more dark mages on her own.

"Rude," Cali said in a stage whisper and then winked at Lira.

The two women laughed, even as Cali complained through the giggles that laughing made her headache worse. They hadn't talked about everything that had happened in the cellar, but Cali knew that Malek had killed Pirrin and would have been willing to kill every one of them.

At least it explained why they'd all had the feeling they were being watched. Malek had kept his eyes on all of them, waiting for his chance to pay them back for what he perceived as their abandonment. But his ultimate goal had been the same as Lira's—the book.

"That took some effort," Vaskel said as he emerged from the cellar covered in a fine layer of dust. "But here it is."

He strode to them and heaved a sizable iron box onto the table with a thud that shuddered the wood. "You didn't tell me the book was so heavy."

Sass stood up to assess the box. "Or that it was encased in iron."

Lira left Crumpet happily devouring the apple dumpling and walked to the box, touching a hand to the cool exterior that carried traces of the red clay it had been encased in for so long. She unhooked a small pouch on her belt and produced a key, sliding it into the lock.

Everyone held their breath as the mechanism clicked. Lira lifted the lid, reaching for the cloth-wrapped book as the gold coins slid from the top and fell back into the box. Setting it on the table, she placed a hand on the linen wrapping, feeling a pulse warming her fingers.

Lira didn't know if she was sensing the magic within the pages of the book or if it was her newly awakened elvish powers. She slipped the book from the fabric covering, smiling at the familiar leather cover and the moonstone that still glowed milky-white, although considerably fainter than she remembered.

"So that's a moonstone?" Sass wrinkled her nose, not impressed.

"It hasn't been exposed to moonlight for a long time," Lira explained. "That's why it isn't bright."

Cali leaned forward from the overstuffed chair and eyed the leather-bound book from a distance. "*This* is the book you thought just contained recipes?"

Lira laughed. "I was much younger then, and I only remember catching a few glimpses of the cover before my gran would tuck it away. And she told me that the stone had lost any powers long ago."

"Your gran planned to tell you everything," Iris said, smiling wistfully at her friend's spell book. "When you were older."

Lira was no longer upset about the secrets. She understood that her gran had only wanted to protect her. After seeing the lengths Malek went to in order to obtain the book, she understood why her gran had lived in such secrecy.

"At least spell books aren't outlawed. If that book wasn't destroyed when all the others were rounded up, it's yours to keep." Vaskel grinned at Lira, his grin wicked. "Imagine what a crew could do with that and your powers."

Lira shook her head at him. "No, thank you. My adventuring days are in the past."

"You're sure about that?" Cali asked.

Lira looked around the great room. Almost all the people she cared about were there, and most of them belonged right there in Wayside. Then she let her gaze linger on Korl. "I've never been surer about anything."

"Sometimes the bravest thing an adventurer can do is plant roots instead of pulling up stakes," Iris said.

Sass sniffed. "That sounds like something my mum would say."

"It's what Lira's gran said to convince me to come with her to a tiny village and settle down." Iris's eyes shone. "And I've never regretted it for a minute."

Vaskel muttered something about what he could do with Lira's powers, but Lira was too busy opening the book. She flipped through a few heavy pages until she landed on the one she wanted.

"Did you find a good spell?" Sass asked. "Maybe one that can enchant the brooms and make them sweep the floors themselves?"

Lira shook her head. "Better. I found my gran's recipe for teacakes."

"Cinders and dragon dung," Sass grumbled.

# Fifty-Four

LIRA HELD the closed spell book on her lap as she sat on the thatched roof, with her cloak wrapped around her to fight off the chill. The moonstone glowed brighter, seeming to pulse with life, as it soaked up the light from the moon.

After all this time, she'd finally gotten what she came for. It had been a more circuitous route than she ever could have imagined, but she'd done it. She ran her fingers across the buttery-soft leather cover, the gilded symbols glittering, and released a satisfied breath.

It was an odd thing, though. She'd come to retrieve the book, and she'd ended up finding so much more than she'd expected. She'd left

Wayside to see the world and find herself, but it wasn't until she'd come back home that she'd found what she'd been missing.

"Was this your plan?" she whispered to the book and hoped the spirit of her gran was listening. She wouldn't have put it past the old woman to know what Lira would need long before she figured it out herself. Whether it was because she was a mage or because she was a gran, the woman had always been a few steps ahead.

Lira's vision blurred as she thought of her gran's wrinkled hands touching the same book cover and reading the same recipes. She might not be with Lira anymore, but the book, and all the happy memories tied to it, tethered them together still.

Lira thought of the shock of finding her hiding spot walled over, her clever plan to stay close to the book by offering to revive the tavern and pulling a wannabe dwarf burglar into her plan, the villagers who'd rallied around their efforts, and the friends who'd risked themselves to save her.

"I'm sure you didn't plan for all of this to happen, but it turned all right in the end." She touched a finger to the moonstone, surprised that the surface wasn't cool anymore. "Then again, maybe you did intend all this to happen. I might not have stayed here if I'd been able to retrieve the book that first night."

But ghosts couldn't erect stone walls, could they?

A shuffling in the windowsill behind her made Lira turn.

"I thought you might be here," Korl said as he stepped onto the thatched roof and lowered himself next to her.

Even without him touching her, Lira could feel the heat of his body. Instead of scooting away to give herself, or him, space, she leaned into him. "I'm glad you found me."

His usual stiffness drained from his body, as he curled an arm around her shoulders. "And I'm glad you didn't find your book and leave that first night."

She tipped her head up. "You heard that?"

Korl grunted in response.

"It's not that I didn't want to stay in Wayside, but at that point, I was so used to moving on, it was more of a habit than a plan."

"You don't need to move on anymore?"

She didn't need to think to answer that. "No. I'm home." She pulled away so she could look him square in the eyes. "But it's not only because this *was* my home. I want to stay because Wayside has become my *true* home because of you and your dads and Sass and Iris and Val and Pip and Fenni and Tin and everyone who's become a part of my life since I returned. I've learned firsthand that a tavern is nothing but a building without the people who fill it and the warmth that's shared. And Wayside would be just another speck on the map without all the amazing people who live here."

Korl nodded then cocked his head. "You won't miss the adventure?"

"Trust me, tonight was up there in regards to adventure, and it was a good reminder that I'm fine without it."

"Even now that you have powers?"

Lira glanced at her hands, unsure exactly what kind of powers she did possess. Had they been activated because she was so desperate to save her friends, because she was so livid with Malek, or had she finally grown into them? She shrugged. "I guess it's nice to know they're there, but they don't change what I want."

Korl was quiet for a moment. "And what do you want?"

Lira's pulse quickened. "I want to stay in Wayside and keep baking, keep making the tavern into something special."

He made a sound that was half hum and half growl.

"If we're sharing desires, what do you want?"

He was quiet for so long, Lira wondered if he'd heard the question, although there was no chance he hadn't.

"I think I want you to have another reason to stay," he finally blurted, the words tripping over themselves. "I want to give you another reason to stay."

Lira turned to meet his gaze, her heart stuttering at the heat in his dark eyes.

"It's not easy for me to talk to people, but I can talk to you. I *want* to talk to you. You make me feel safe, and only my dads and Val have ever made me feel that way before." He took a breath. "I want to make you feel safe. I want to keep you safe."

The intensity of his words made Lira's breath catch in her throat. She pressed a hand to his chest, feeling the beat of his heart fluttering like a trapped bird. "You do make me feel safe. You came after me tonight. You risked your own life to save me."

He nodded, his gaze going to her lips. He cupped her face in one hand and brushed his thumb across her bottom lip. "I will always come after you."

"Then that's definitely another reason for me to stay," Lira whispered.

"I'd like to spend the rest of my days giving you more reasons," he husked, as he lowered his mouth to hers.

As Korl's lips brushed across hers, Lira's body hummed with pleasure, her skin tingling and her hands sparking with heat.

She'd never expected the orc to be so gentle, or that his touch could set her body on fire like it did. When he pulled away, she curled one hand around the back of his neck and tugged his lips back to hers.

The handsome orc was the right blend of warmth, spice, and sweetness. Just like the perfect cup of chai.

# Fifty-Five

IT HAD BEEN impossible to keep word of what had happened in the tavern cellar secret, especially when a dark mage was dragged out and carried to the castle dungeons in the middle of the Night Faire. But only those who'd been in the cellar knew about the book or that Lira had elvish powers, and they'd all sworn to take those secrets to their graves.

Lira hadn't tried to use her powers again, but she'd noticed that her hands now fizzed with faint sparks when Korl touched her or even when she was humming with happiness in the kitchen.

The dramatic events had done nothing to dampen enthusiasm for the tavern, and some might have said having a dark mage cross its threshold had increased its appeal. Whatever the reason, The Tusk & Tail was busier than it had ever been in the days following.

"Tell me the truth," Lira said as she held out one of the puffy, pale teacakes to Korl. "Do they need more sugar?"

Crumpet sat on the worktable next to Lira and nibbled on his own cookie, chittering at her.

Lira waved her wooden spoon at him. "I know what you think already, sir."

Korl took the warm cookie. "Is that a trick question? Doesn't everything always taste better with more sugar?"

Crumpet made excited sounds of agreement, and Lira could have sworn that the flutterstoat was laughing.

She shook her head at him then turned to Korl. "I had no idea that orcs had such a sweet tooth."

Korl snaked an arm around her waist and pulled her close. "What else can I teach you about orcs?"

"Grognick's beard," Sass groaned as she entered the kitchen and spotted the pair. "Let's not scar Crumpet for life."

"This is perfectly wholesome," Lira assured her as Korl reluctantly loosened his grip on her waist. "They're testing the teacakes."

Sass lifted a brow as she looked at the rows of cookies. "They don't look like cakes."

"That's just what they're called. Don't ask me why. They're actually cookies."

Sass plucked one from the tray and popped it into her mouth, chewing thoughtfully for a few seconds before swallowing. "I was going to say that they're too simple, especially compared to your scones or apple cider cake, but that's their appeal, isn't it?" She snatched another cookie and took a bite. "I could eat a dozen of these."

"I think you have your answer," Korl said.

"You mind if I take some out to our friends?" Sass started stacking the teacakes onto a tray.

"Who's here?" Lira asked, since they'd made quite a few friends in Wayside and Lira had brought in a few from her past life.

She'd expected Cali and Vaskel to move along once Malek was handled, but neither had shown any signs of leaving Wayside, and Lira was in no hurry to see the backs of them. She figured they needed a warm, welcoming place like Wayside as much as she did.

"Korl's dads are here for supper, Vaskel and Val are debating the best defenses when sword fighting," Sass said with a sigh that told Lira this wasn't the first time she'd heard this discussion. "And Iris and Cali are talking about the latest pirate romance Cali read."

"Take your dads some teacakes," Lira said to Korl.

He scooped several into his hands and kissed her cheek. "I should also talk to Vaskel. He's interested in a custom blade, and I know just the right hilt for him."

Lira would have put the cookies on a plate for him, but he seemed content to hold them in his massive hands.

"I'm glad you two are friends," she said.

"We're only friends now because I challenged him to a fight for your heart at the Night Faire, and the hellkin almost keeled over with laughter." Korl did not look pleased to recount this memory.

"You didn't tell me this." Lira frowned, not sure if she should be offended or not. The truth was, she'd rejected Vaskel long ago, and to his credit, he'd never seriously pressed his luck again. The two had become tight friends with not a hint of something more.

"I never told you that I saw you walking with him to the inn that night I bumped into you." Korl didn't meet her eyes. "I was sure there was something between you."

"So, you challenged a hellkin to a duel?" Sass hitched a thumb at Lira. "Over her?"

Lira shot the dwarf a withering look, which Sass ignored.

"He told me that there were many claims to be made about him, but that he would never risk his friendship with you. It was something he seemed proud of."

"For a hellkin, that's probably saying something," Sass said. "So, you didn't fight?"

"We didn't fight. But we did follow the wyvern to the tavern and prevent him from entering."

"I'd almost forgotten about Rygor." Lira picked up a warm teacake and bit into it. "Is that why he hasn't been around?"

"Vaskel and I might have knocked him out and tied him up to keep him from following us into the tavern."

Sass nearly bobbled the tray of teacakes. "You did what?"

Korl shrugged. "He was gone when we finally came back out. Vaskel thinks he might have been helping Malek, or Malek might have been using him for information, which is why he left town after Malek was taken."

Lira didn't like the idea of the wyvern out there somewhere, but she hoped he was smart enough to steer clear of Wayside.

"Good riddance," Sass said under her breath, as she backed out of the kitchen with the tray of teacakes.

"I'm glad you and Vaskel are becoming friends," Lira told Korl as they followed Sass from the kitchen. "He's as loyal as they come."

Korl grunted. "Val likes him well enough too."

Lira knew that Val's opinion carried a lot of weight, and she was glad that Val had befriended the hellkin. And despite her initial comment about how attractive he was, Lira was sure that Val would never fall for Vaskel.

Korl gave her waist a squeeze, before heading across the great room to give his dads some teacakes. Lira spotted Cali and Iris at the round table in the far nook with their heads bent in conversation. She crossed her arms over her chest as she surveyed the inviting tavern that was a world away from the place she'd stepped into that rainy night.

"Just the person I need to see."

Lira turned to see Durn standing at the end of the bar, and for once, he wasn't polishing a glass with a grimy rag.

She braced herself for complaints, even though she didn't see Silas slumped at the far end of the bar. The grumbling old man had shown up less and less as the tavern had improved, and Lira wondered if he'd only been happy when there was so much to complain about.

"Everything okay?" Lira asked, forcing a smile.

"I expect it is." Durn rocked back on his heels. "I never thought it would happen, but I got an offer on the tavern."

Lira's blood went cold. He was selling The Tusk & Tail, after everything she and Sass had done to save it? She opened her mouth to argue, but he held up a hand to stop her.

"Before you get yourself into a twist, nothing is changing." His face contorted. "Well, I'm moving on, but that's for the best. You've done an impressive job bringing this place back, but it only reminds me that this tavern was never my passion. Selling this place means buying a proper home for Penny after we're married." His cheeks reddened. "She asked me to the Night Faire, and I asked her to marry me."

Lira's plan to get them to the Night Faire had worked even better than she'd hoped, and apparently Cali's forgery had brought about an engagement. "I'm happy for you. Truly."

He nodded gruffly. "This doesn't mean you and the dwarf have to leave though."

Lira blinked at him. "I don't understand."

"The Tusk & Tail is in your names now." He held out a meaty hand. "That was the deal. I move on and you two keep the tavern."

Lira shook her head, not sure what she was hearing. "Someone bought the tavern *for* us?"

Sass walked up, her eyes wide. "What did you say?"

Durn blew out a breath. "I was saying that the tavern is yours now. I sold it. But it's in your names." He pointed to Lira and Sass. "Both of you."

Sass's jaw dropped, which about summed up Lira's feelings. She leveled a stubby finger at Lira. "Did you use your gold?"

Lira shook her head. To be honest, she'd thought about it but hadn't gotten around to bringing it up to Durn. She glanced at the apothecary at the back table, who was the only person she could think of who would do such a thing. "Was it Iris?"

Durn shook his head. "I don't know the fella, but he paid extra to keep his name out of it."

Sass threw her arms around Lira as she simultaneously jumped up and down. "The tavern is ours!"

Lira joined her in jumping, even though the shock and joy of being the new owners of The Tusk & Tail was surreal.

The tavernkeep snapped his fingers as he turned away, muttering so that Lira could barely make out the words. "I do know the fella who paid for this place was an elf."

LIRA TOSSED her apron at Sass and it landed on the dwarf's head, covering her face.

"What in the moldy ogre's—?" Sass spluttered as she pawed at the apron, flour dust sifting to her shoulders and the floor.

"Sorry, Sass." Lira was already hurrying toward the tavern door. "It's time."

"Time?" Sass succeeded in removing the apron and held it in her hands as she watched Lira hurry across the great room. "Already?"

Lira grinned over her shoulder and nodded. "Wish me luck!"

"Good luck!" Tin waved wildly as he joined Sass in watching Lira run from the tavern, her cheeks pink with excitement.

Lira slowed her pace once she'd dashed outside, smoothing her hands down the front of her favorite green dress and steadying her breath as she walked to the bridge to meet Korl. The orc was in the middle, leaning his forearms on the low wall and watching the water burble its way over smooth stones.

He straightened and smiled when he saw Lira. It had been a month since they'd shared their first kiss on the rooftop, and plenty had changed. Durn and Penny had married in a simple ceremony with a reception at the tavern, Cali and Vaskel had decided to stay in Wayside even longer, the Night Faires had become a regular happenings again, and no one had seen even a hint of Rygor. But Lira still got butterflies in her stomach every time she saw the orc.

"I hope I'm not late. I was pulling a batch of scones from the oven and then Crumpet wanted a bite and—"

Korl took her hand in his. "You aren't late. You're the one who asked me to meet here anyway."

"Right." Lira let out a nervous giggle. "I almost forgot that part."

Korl squeezed her hand, the warmth sending a calming pulse through her. "Did you want to take a walk or maybe visit the bakery?"

Lira guessed her obsession with Pip's baked goods wasn't much of a secret, but she pulled him forward. "Let's walk through town, but maybe not the bakery right away."

Korl shrugged. "I don't mind where we walk as long as we're together."

Lira's pulse quickened as they walked toward the village. She didn't know if she was more nervous or more excited, but she was grateful for Korl's firm grip on her hand that served to ground her. The sun was high in the sky but behind a haze of clouds, and luckily, there was a breeze to keep her from sweating.

She matched Korl's relaxed pace as they passed the first few shops, and she drew him closer to the side of the road with the chandler's storefront. A quick peek through the glass told her that Penny and Durn were chatting companionably behind the counter, as the pretty gnome handed him candles to stock on high shelves. Today wasn't a day to stop in and visit the newlyweds, though.

Lira slowed as they walked in front of the tinker's shop with the ever-present closed sign dangling at an angle on the front door. Ignoring the sign, she turned the knob and stepped inside.

Korl hesitated, but she beckoned him to follow her. "It's okay. Come on in."

"Is the shop finally open?" he asked.

"Not yet, but it will be when the new tinker moves in." She swept an arm wide at the dusty shelves filled with iron contraptions and rusty tools. "What do you think?"

Korl breathed in the stale air. "There's a new tinker?"

Lira bounced on her toes. "If you want the job, that is."

Korl blinked at her. "Me?"

"The old tinker wanted to sell, so I decided to use some of the gold I'd saved to buy it. I know the place needs a bit of work, but after fixing up the tavern, how hard could it be? But if you don't—"

"You got me a tinker shop?" Korl's voice was a low rumble.

Uncertainly filled Lira, and suddenly her marvelous idea didn't seem so great. "I did, but if you hate the idea—"

She didn't get to finish her sentence because Korl swept her into his arms, his lips silencing hers with a kiss. She threw her arms around his neck, sinking into his embrace.

When he pulled away, she noticed faint sparks of gold escaping from beneath her hands. "So you like it?"

"If I'm a tinker, I don't have to be a guard anymore." His voice cracked. "It's the nicest thing anyone's ever done for me."

"Nicer than the spice cake I made for you?"

He chuckled. "Even nicer than that."

Korl peered around the dimly-lit shop. "It's really mine?"

"Really, really. And there's an apartment above the shop, so I thought maybe we could..."

His eyes darkened. "You're sure?"

"I'm sure I don't want to share a room with Sass forever. The dwarf can snore loud enough to wake the dead."

"What if I snore?" he teased.

She pressed a hand to his muscular chest. "That's a risk I'm willing to take."

Korl nodded then reached into his pants pocket, producing a glittering silver ring. "Then I suppose Sass was right that it's a good time to give you this."

Lira's mouth opened and closed like a hungry fish. "Sass? But she helped me plan this! That double-crosser!"

Korl shrugged. "She didn't tell me why today was a good day, but she said I'd know when the time was right. Usually, I don't know those things, but today I do."

Lira lost the ability to speak as the orc dropped to one knee and took both her hands in one of his.

"Lira, I've loved you since the day you walked into me in front of TinPin's shop, and every moment I've spent with you since I've loved you more and more. Will you marry me?"

Lira's eyes swam with tears as she managed to bob her head, her hand shaking as Korl slid the delicate ring onto her finger. There might still be some uncertainties in her life—where Rygor had gone, who had bought the tavern for her and Sass—but her feelings for Korl was not one of them.

Then the orc stood, picking her up as he kissed her again, this one soft and tender. When he broke the kiss, he gave her a wicked grin. "Why don't you show me our new apartment?"

So she did.

# Epilogue

SASS SWEPT a curl from her face, as she leaned one elbow against the end of the bar and caught her breath from the evening rush. The fire was roaring and the tables were filled with customers, both old and new. A gnome couple sat at the nook table enjoying supper, and the long tables were filled with those eating and those who'd only stopped by for a pint.

Val and Korl occupied their usual chairs by the fire—all the regulars knew that those were to be left for them—and Val had started on a new scarf, the ball of lavender yarn balancing on one knee as she knit. Korl kept one eye on the kitchen, like he always did, waiting for when

Lira would finish her work and come join him, sitting on his lap with her arms wrapped around his neck.

She cut her gaze to the bar where Vaskel was sliding a tankard of ale to a new patron and grinned. Although the hellkin had grumbled when she'd begged him to step in after Durn had left, he was a natural behind the bar. She doubted he'd stay forever, but they didn't need forever.

She was as shocked as anyone that *she'd* stayed so long. If you'd have asked her the night she'd tried to rob the till, she never would have guessed that she'd still be in Wayside running the tavern instead of stealing from it.

Sass shook her head. A lot had changed since she'd stumbled into Lira that night, and she would never regret any of it.

Her chest swelled as she surveyed the bustling tavern and all the folks she now called friends. No, her only regret was not telling Lira why she'd been so desperate that night, why she'd been on the run.

In her defense, she hadn't known whether she could trust the elf—correction, half-elf—or if Lira had been serious about reviving the tavern. She'd just been relieved to have a place to bed down and food in her belly.

Pressing her lips together, Sass's pulse jangled. She'd been lucky so far. No one knew where she was, and no one from her past would imagine that she could be working at a tavern in a tiny village. But how long until her past caught up with her?

She glanced at the kitchen doors, telling herself for the hundredth time that she should just tell Lira. Lira would understand. But every time, she thought better of it. Then Val caught her eye from across the room and smiled, giving her a slow wink that made heat blossom in the dwarf's chest.

"Tomorrow," she said under her breath with a determined nod. "I'll worry about all that tomorrow."

Then she picked up a plate of meat hand pies from the bar and made a beeline for the hearth, too distracted by the blonde smiling at her to notice that someone from her past had just slipped through the front door.

* * *

Thank you for reading *Tusks, Tails & Teacakes*!
Want to read the scene from the Night Faire where Vaskel meets Korl—and they both take on Rygor? Get the bonus scene here>
https://BookHip.com/JCRCALJ

* * *

Ready to find out what Sass is hiding? Don't miss the next book in the series, *Sorcery, Swords & Scones!*

*"Stone's writing is like a warm cup of chai. It's perfect for when you are craving something cozy, sweet, and comforting. So, grab your copy, a cozy blanket, and your favorite warm drink (bonus points if it's chai) and enter the magical world of Wayside. I promise you'll be glad you did."- Amazon Reviewer*

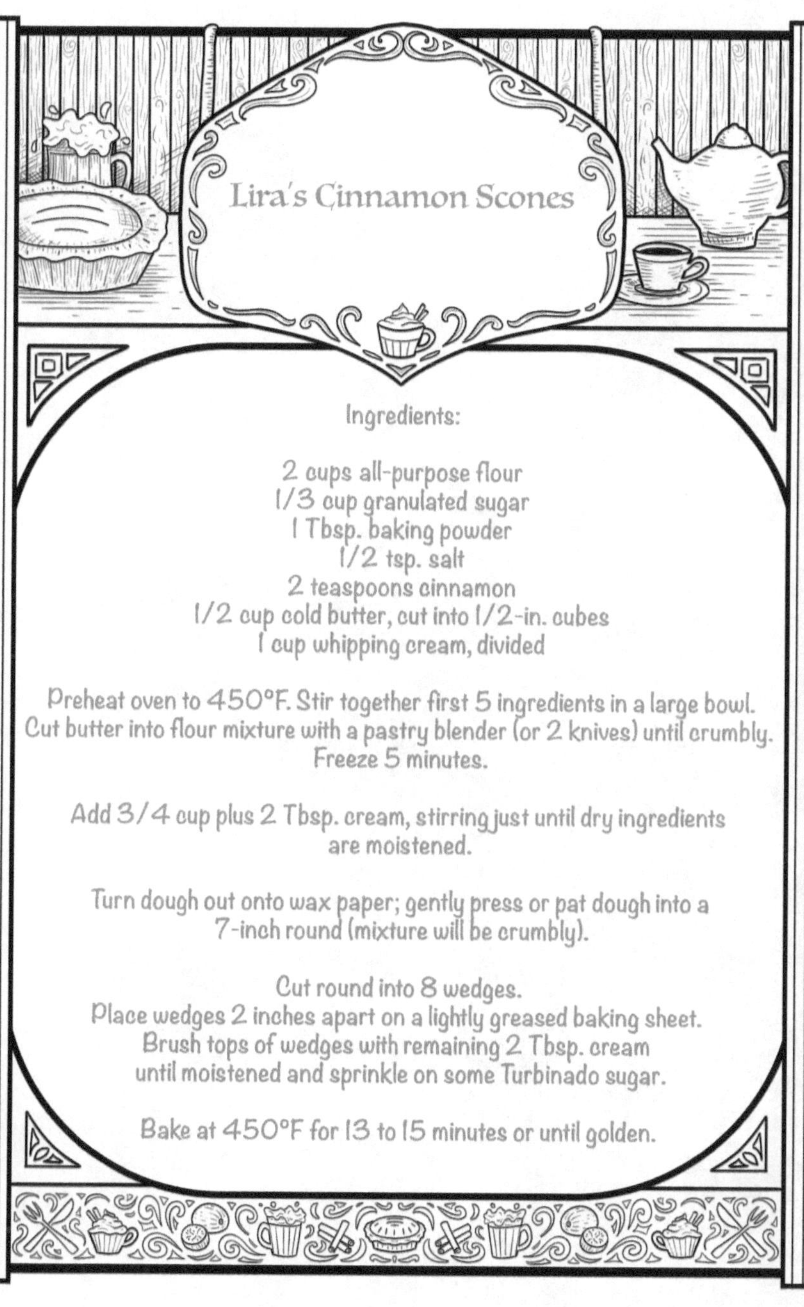

Lira's Cinnamon Scones

Ingredients:

2 cups all-purpose flour
1/3 cup granulated sugar
1 Tbsp. baking powder
1/2 tsp. salt
2 teaspoons cinnamon
1/2 cup cold butter, cut into 1/2-in. cubes
1 cup whipping cream, divided

Preheat oven to 450°F. Stir together first 5 ingredients in a large bowl.
Cut butter into flour mixture with a pastry blender (or 2 knives) until crumbly.
Freeze 5 minutes.

Add 3/4 cup plus 2 Tbsp. cream, stirring just until dry ingredients
are moistened.

Turn dough out onto wax paper; gently press or pat dough into a
7-inch round (mixture will be crumbly).

Cut round into 8 wedges.
Place wedges 2 inches apart on a lightly greased baking sheet.
Brush tops of wedges with remaining 2 Tbsp. cream
until moistened and sprinkle on some Turbinado sugar.

Bake at 450°F for 13 to 15 minutes or until golden.

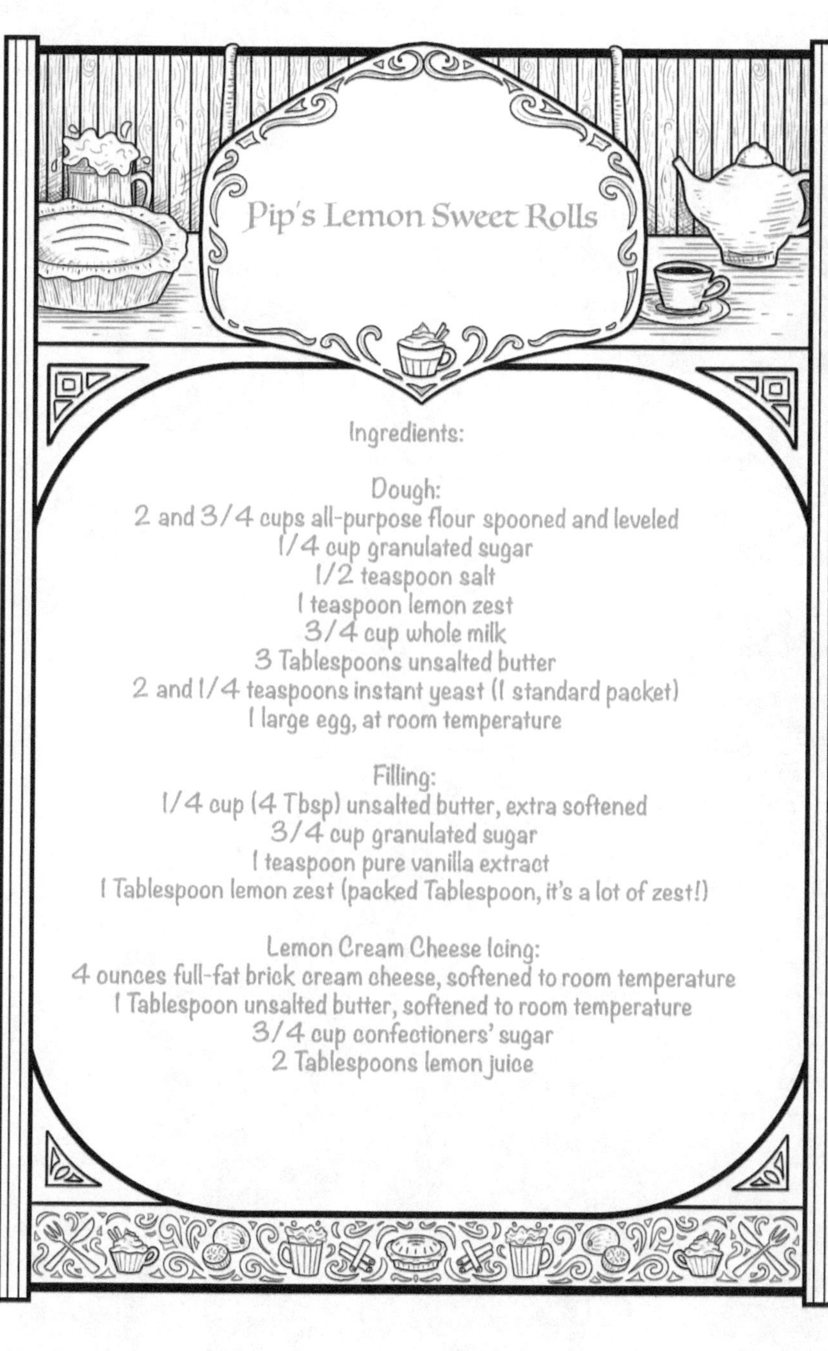

# Pip's Lemon Sweet Rolls

Ingredients:

Dough:
2 and 3/4 cups all-purpose flour spooned and leveled
1/4 cup granulated sugar
1/2 teaspoon salt
1 teaspoon lemon zest
3/4 cup whole milk
3 Tablespoons unsalted butter
2 and 1/4 teaspoons instant yeast (1 standard packet)
1 large egg, at room temperature

Filling:
1/4 cup (4 Tbsp) unsalted butter, extra softened
3/4 cup granulated sugar
1 teaspoon pure vanilla extract
1 Tablespoon lemon zest (packed Tablespoon, it's a lot of zest!)

Lemon Cream Cheese Icing:
4 ounces full-fat brick cream cheese, softened to room temperature
1 Tablespoon unsalted butter, softened to room temperature
3/4 cup confectioners' sugar
2 Tablespoons lemon juice

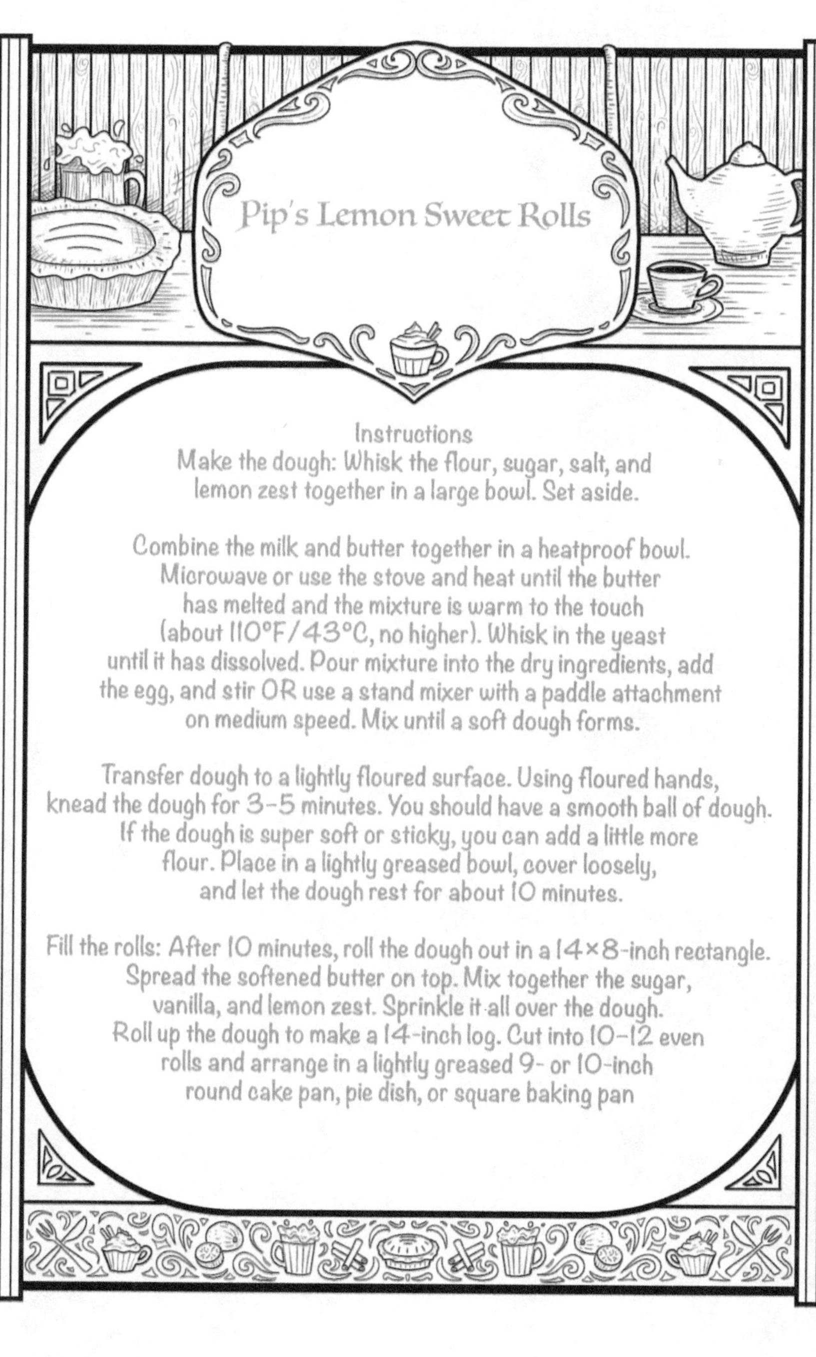

# Pip's Lemon Sweet Rolls

## Instructions

Make the dough: Whisk the flour, sugar, salt, and lemon zest together in a large bowl. Set aside.

Combine the milk and butter together in a heatproof bowl. Microwave or use the stove and heat until the butter has melted and the mixture is warm to the touch (about 110°F/43°C, no higher). Whisk in the yeast until it has dissolved. Pour mixture into the dry ingredients, add the egg, and stir OR use a stand mixer with a paddle attachment on medium speed. Mix until a soft dough forms.

Transfer dough to a lightly floured surface. Using floured hands, knead the dough for 3–5 minutes. You should have a smooth ball of dough. If the dough is super soft or sticky, you can add a little more flour. Place in a lightly greased bowl, cover loosely, and let the dough rest for about 10 minutes.

Fill the rolls: After 10 minutes, roll the dough out in a 14×8-inch rectangle. Spread the softened butter on top. Mix together the sugar, vanilla, and lemon zest. Sprinkle it all over the dough. Roll up the dough to make a 14-inch log. Cut into 10–12 even rolls and arrange in a lightly greased 9- or 10-inch round cake pan, pie dish, or square baking pan

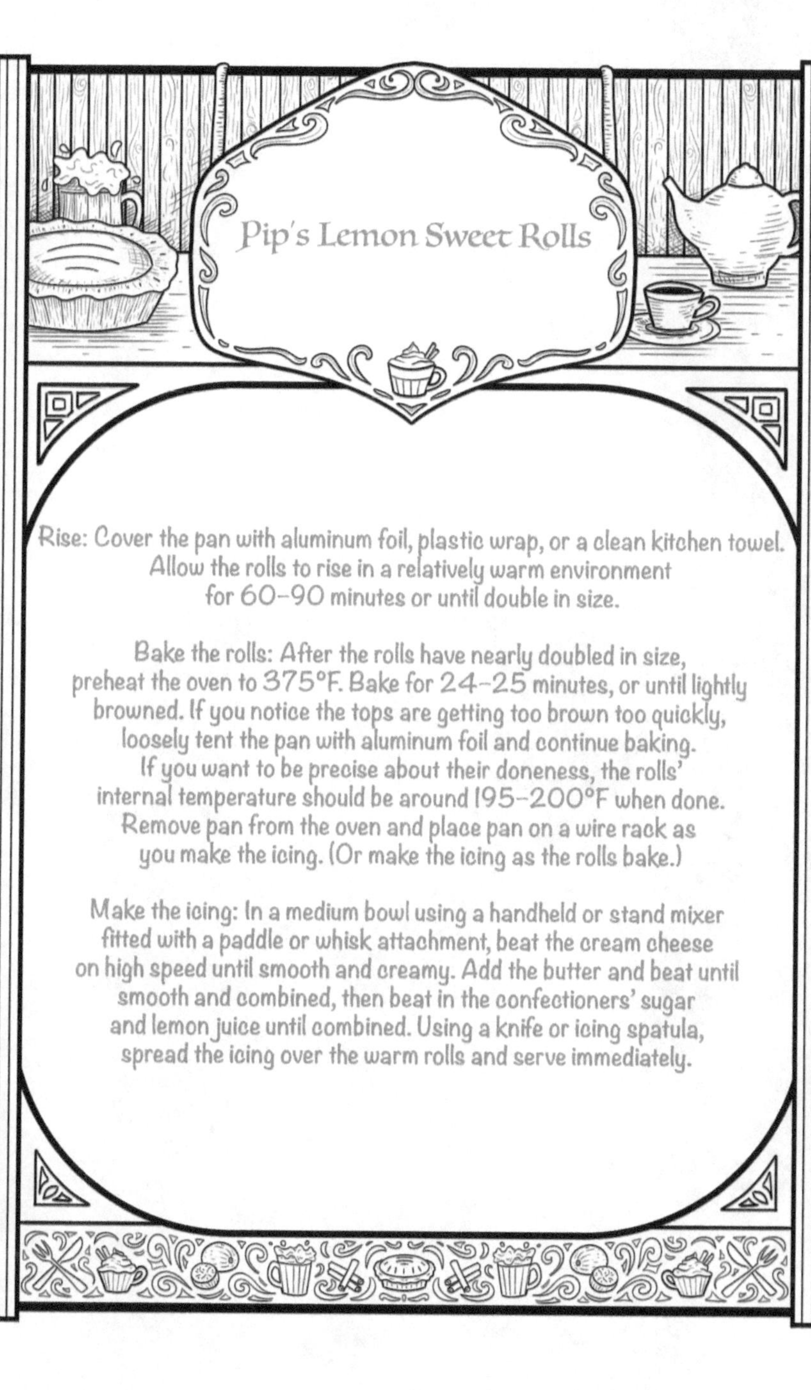

Pip's Lemon Sweet Rolls

Rise: Cover the pan with aluminum foil, plastic wrap, or a clean kitchen towel. Allow the rolls to rise in a relatively warm environment for 60-90 minutes or until double in size.

Bake the rolls: After the rolls have nearly doubled in size, preheat the oven to 375°F. Bake for 24-25 minutes, or until lightly browned. If you notice the tops are getting too brown too quickly, loosely tent the pan with aluminum foil and continue baking. If you want to be precise about their doneness, the rolls' internal temperature should be around 195-200°F when done. Remove pan from the oven and place pan on a wire rack as you make the icing. (Or make the icing as the rolls bake.)

Make the icing: In a medium bowl using a handheld or stand mixer fitted with a paddle or whisk attachment, beat the cream cheese on high speed until smooth and creamy. Add the butter and beat until smooth and combined, then beat in the confectioners' sugar and lemon juice until combined. Using a knife or icing spatula, spread the icing over the warm rolls and serve immediately.

Tusks, Tails & Teacakes

Sorcery, Swords & Scones

Solstice, Spice & Everything Nice ( A Tiny Tale from the Tavern)

Cauldrons, Charms & Chai

Potions, Pirates & Pie

# Acknowledgments

I owe a debt of gratitude to so many people who have helped me create this book: Cristina, Sav, and Len for being brilliant and on top of all the things I wasn't. Talina at Bookin It Designs for the fabulous cover art, Illustrated Page Book Design for the fantasy world map, Emma for beta reading, Gloria for proofing, and my many author friends who have cheered me on. Kisses to my lovely husband for helping design the recipe cards and printed swag. Thanks to all the cozy fantasy authors who have inspired me, notably Travis Baldree, Sarah Beth Durst, and Rebecca Thorne. A special shout-out to the real-life Crumpet and to my dear friend Kate for generously sharing her adorable dog's name with me.

Special thanks to the amazing members of my Cozy Crew, who have helped share the word about my debut cozy fantasy novel. You are the BEST! Thank you Wendy, Jen Miller, brynna.reads, Jenn Adams, Rozanne Visagie, Sadie Young, Annie, Ashley, Taylor Parker, Andrea Wooten, Melinda Trimble, Sammy Taylor, Bianca, Katherine Ramos-Thompson, Cambria, Steph Barker, Jessica Rose, Kate Kempster, Layne, Melissa Ehrlich, Simon Howard, Nicole Parsons, Danielle Gant, Melissa Wilson, Jacklyn Furlong, Velishia, Tiffany S., Kate Brasington, Stephanie Lewis, Mindy Woolf, Kallie Street, Sabrina Kaeder, CinnamonBunReads, Madison Schroeder, Ericka Guernsey, Sarah Donaldson, Sabie, Marisela Lopez, Harley Grenier, Jessica Booth, Teah, Madeeha Idrees, CJ Jones, Jamie, Jada La Belle, Ashlie Hakes, Emily Buchanan, Leora Gulkarov, Jess Moran, Kayla Sibley, Dianne Lebold, Chelsea Pawer, Tarasbookrecs, Brie Starkovski, Maggie Jatzlau, Heather Close, Mott Foxdene, Jessica Steed, Emma M Castiglione, kimthebookishbaker, Amber Spiewak, Annette Palma, Hollie Lake,

Jaime Katz, Kelsey Warren, Jamie Brandenburg, Nash Wood, @bisexual.book.lover, Shannon LeBoeuf, Kaitlyn Rautine, Danielle Hardie, Sarah Robinson, Gilli, Trisha Thompson, Kendra Hart, Ivy (@readwivy), Emily Denton, Hannah, Amy Hausey, Madi Johnson, Maddie Rice, Genna Godley, Nicole Garcia, Cecilia de Alvarado, Kaitlyn Cohen, Erin Sherman, Holly Mayes, Jessica White, Shelby Martin, GinnyB, Morgan Crum, Steph Serrano, Susan (@Ravenbooklover), Cali Kavanagh, Sara Allison, Amber Mars, AmyzBookNook, Liz Stathakos, Molly Palmer Masood, Erin Shea, Tanvi, Nadia Gardner, Maggie Haley, and Veronique Lessard.

T.L. Stone is a cozy fantasy author who loves writing and reading about friends who become family, fantastical realms, and cozy moments where everything is right with the world. She likes her books and sweaters thick, her drinks sweet and hot, and her pastries buttery.

She's on a quest to make the perfect brownie, and her almond pound cake is swoonworthy. When she's not writing, you can find her cozied up to a crackling fire with a good book or planning her next travel adventure.